EXECUTION OF ANGUISH

The Shadows of Wildberry Lane

M. SINCLAIR

Lost & Bound Publishing

Execution of Anguish

The Shadows of Wildberry Lane - Book Two

Editorial Team
Refined Voice Editing & Proofreading

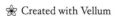 Created with Vellum

The Union of Love & Madness

DESCRIPTION

An underworld empire put at risk for one woman -
Dahlia Aldridge.

My love for the men of Wildberry Lane had never been in question. But now that I was aware of the true darkness that had always surrounded me protectively? I craved to know more. I wanted the curtain drawn back fully on just how dangerous they were. More than anything? I found myself wanting to be a part of those shadows - branded by their darkness.

Kingston & Dermot Ross. Stratton Lee. Yates Carter. Lincoln & Sterling Gates.

I was no longer scared of how strongly I felt for them. I just hoped they understood the lengths I would go to protect them. Protect the family that I valued above anything else.

The Brooks had been a problem from the start, but now that they were possibly threatening Wildberry Lane? Causing problems for both my men and my family? That changed everything. An inner strength I never expected was growing inside of me and it was one I refused to shy away from.

I would be strong for my family. For my men. But I knew in order to do that, I would need to kill my own demons.

I would need to execute the anguish that had been devouring me whole.

Wildberry Lane - Home to the extremely wealthy and powerful Southern elite.

Execution of Anguish, book 2 in The Shadows of Wildberry Lane trilogy, is M. Sinclair's debut contemporary reverse harem series. This work features a naive female character hiding a dark secret of her own, the men in her life that will do anything to keep her safe, and a scandal that stretches far beyond the safety of Wildberry Lane's gate.

Warning: This book does contain sexual content for +18, swearing, violence, and triggers including, but not limited to, eating disorders and bullying. Important to note, the bullying is NOT done by the harem, but rather by outside sources. This is a slow to medium burn series. This novel does end on a cliffhanger.

PROLOGUE

Dahlia Aldridge - Sophomore Year

I officially hated someone.

It was the first time in my life that I could definitively state that without a doubt in my mind.

I *hated* Selena. I hadn't thought it was possible for my heart to actually contain this much frustration, sadness, and jealousy all at once. I had disliked people before. I had found them irritating. But this was actual hatred, and I hadn't thought I would ever feel that way towards someone. It seemed I had been extremely incorrect on that front. I tried to swallow down the panic and uncomfortable gut reaction I was having to her assigned partner for our biology lab that day.

He hadn't had an option. I couldn't be mad at him. In fact, he looked rather uncomfortable and annoyed.

But I could be mad at her. Mostly because her hand, the one that I was trying hard not to glare at, was wrapped around Stratton's bicep.

I should have looked away, I knew that. Stratton hadn't talked to me most of freshman year, and during the summer he'd been notably absent from anything we hosted. It wasn't just me he seemed to be ignoring, either—the three men at my table had been equally dismissed.

Although they seemed to be handling it far better than myself, and they also were obviously not bothered by Selena touching Stratton. No, that particular affliction was completely my own.

"Princess," King said, his voice soft and concerned as his hand wrapped around my wrist in a gentle hold. He sat at the lab table next to me, his thumb rubbing over my pulse. I tried to pull my eyes away from Stratton and managed to do so briefly, finding both Lincoln and Sterling staring at me from across the table with worry in their eyes.

Crap. How obvious could I manage to be? At least Yates wasn't in this class with us. He would have found a way to make fun of me for this, and right now my emotions were a bit too raw for our normal back and forth.

"I'm fine," I mumbled and looked back at where Stratton was leaning away from Selena, her eyes glued to his expression instead of the lab work in front of them. He didn't seem to like her touch. I hadn't heard they were dating or anything... So why were they acting like this? Why did she think she could touch him so openly?

For the record, if anyone deserved to be touching his biceps, it was me. *Just saying.*

The most surprising element to all of this was my temper, which was normally non-existent. Yet I found myself angry. Really, *really* angry. It just felt unfair. I had lost one of my best friends, received no explanation for it, continued to be rejected when I tried to reach out... and she was practically clinging onto him as she laughed about something he said. I tightened my jaw and looked away moments before I felt his eyes on me from across the aisle.

Something I felt more often than not, only adding to the complexity of this problem. His eyes were always on me, and it made it impossible to ignore him. Made it impossible to not notice the subtle changes in his mood, from his temper to the almost numbness that would infiltrate his gaze. Sometimes I felt like Stratton was unbearably sad, as if there was a massive weight on his shoulders that I didn't know the origin of. Then there were times when I think he even considered coming over to us, but something always stopped him, and no one had any idea of what. I shook my head and tried to focus on the piece of paper in front of me, the words blurring slightly.

Looking down at the skirt I wore, the cream and pink pleats matching the soft pink sweater I picked for the slightly chilled October day, I pretended to pick off lint that didn't exist. I schooled my emotions, or attempted to, before offering King a smile. He frowned, his eyes searching my expression, before darting over my shoulder, a tick forming on his jaw.

"We should try to finish the lab now—" I began, my voice shaky.

"Stratton." Selena's voice was almost sultry in tone and easily eclipsed mine. I was jealous of it. In fact, everything about Selena was the exact opposite of me. Where I was a bit more lanky and awkward-looking at sixteen, my curves unfortunately not making a full appearance yet, she had completely filled out. Something that even I couldn't ignore because I had to admit the woman was gorgeous, and it made all of this so much worse. Who *wouldn't* want to be with someone like Selena?

My eyes darted over to find her leaning into him, her massive boobs practically pressing against him, and I let out a small hiss of frustration.

Okay. I wasn't positive I could sit through this. I legitimately considered getting up, but I was suddenly transfixed by the conversation taking place.

"No," Stratton said, his voice almost cold, if not indifferent, while removing her hand from his bicep.

"I don't understand," she pouted. "Everyone is going to the dance."

Her friends across the table nodded in agreement. Then her words hit me. *Homecoming*. She wanted to go to Homecoming with Stratton. Bile rose in my throat as I blinked back emotion that threatened to expose my attempt at indifference.

Stratton's eyes darted over to me, and his gaze almost softened for a moment before he spoke. "I'm not really interested in going with you, Selena."

I blinked, surprised at his bluntness, feeling like his gaze was trying to tell me something before he looked back to the woman in question. I felt more confused than ever, and then a tiny bit amused at the shock that filled her face as she snapped her hand away, a sneer covering her expression. I didn't want to take pleasure in her rejection, but it wasn't like she was the nicest person to begin with.

"Fine. Fuck you then," she growled, straightening herself. Her eyes darted over to me, her gaze growing cold as I realized that she now knew I had been an audience to her humiliation.

That wasn't good. Especially since the woman was a known bully.

"Dahlia," she purred, leaning forward, "are you going to Homecoming?"

I had a feeling this question was a trap to get me back for witnessing the moment between her and Stratton, so I was hesitant to answer. After a small sigh, I conceded. "Yes, we are going as a group, like always."

She knew that. Everyone knew that.

Her head tilted as she put a hand to her jaw and rested it there. "Are you sure you don't want me to set you up with one of my friends? I mean, at least then you will be going with someone that likes you, you know, *like that*."

There it was. Was it obvious how into my best friends I was? Most likely.

I kept a polite smile and offered her my best answer. "I'm good. I am pretty stressed this semester as it is, so adding someone—"

"Too good for them?" she sneered. "Too good for any of us?"

I hadn't realized how quiet my friends had grown until King let out a chuckle that was decidedly not friendly.

"Correct on both accounts," King said, watching her with narrowed eyes. "Dahlia is going with us. She doesn't need a date."

His words both made me happy and bummed out because they so clearly didn't view it as a date in any way, shape, or form. I nearly sighed over that, but I was a bit too fascinated with the way Selena gave King a cautious look before offering a dismissive wave and pulling out her phone, clearly over the conversation. Honestly, it didn't surprise me all that much. Usually when King got involved, people went quiet. You didn't really want him as an enemy.

My eyes moved to Stratton, who was watching me with that look again. The profoundly sad one. I wanted him to come with us to Homecoming. It would never happen, but it didn't stop me from wanting it. Offering him a somewhat sad smile, I looked down at my biology packet and shook my head.

When had things gotten so complicated?

I knew the answer though. Things had gotten complicated when I realized that my feelings towards my friends were anything but just friendly.

Too bad that would have to stay my secret... forever.

Chapter One

DAHLIA ALDRIDGE

My heavy eyelids struggled to open, a light, cold sweat breaking out across my body and causing a tremble to work its way through me until I was gripping the blanket so tightly my fists hurt. My body was sore. My throat especially, and I knew it was from yesterday. I felt dehydrated, and my stomach churned, clearly far too empty despite the pasta I'd had hours ago. I felt like total crap.

A shaky exhale broke from my lips as I forced my eyelids to open completely, my gaze focusing on the slowly encroaching dawn light that was illuminating the dark floors of my bedroom inch by inch.

It was going to be a sunny day.

Something about that felt extremely out of place. The past twenty-four hours had been anything *but* sunny, so the concept almost felt mocking. Muttering a small curse under my breath, I tried to shake myself from the moment. I was normally decent at staying positive, but that was clearly not on the agenda today.

No. I couldn't think that way.

I could be positive! I had to be. Or at least try.

Maybe the blue skies and sunny weather would make today easier. After all, while it felt like my entire world had been flipped upside down in a matter of twenty-four hours, to the rest of the world, it was a normal Wednesday morning in late August. Not one filled with confusion and a contrasting sense of relief that most of the secrets between my boys and I had been laid bare.

I still didn't understand everything, but I also knew now that if I wanted to know something, all I had to do was ask and the information would be at my fingertips. It was that easy and that complicated. One, because I would have to actually decide what I wanted to ask first, and considering the ridiculous amount of questions popping through my brain, that was challenging. But secondly, I had to be prepared for whatever answer I may receive.

My boys may not have told me everything, but they wouldn't lie to me. That much was clear.

I swallowed, thinking just how clear King had been about his feelings towards me. My skin flushed as I squeezed my eyes shut and tried to get my body to behave, knowing now was not the time to be getting turned on.

Despite the hell that the last twenty-four hours had brought between the social media attack and the realization that the Brooks family was possibly putting my boys in danger, I was finding that there was a small reason to be positive. A ray of light that was successfully breaking through all of that, removing years of doubt that had accumulated on my soul.

My guys loved me like I loved them.

Not in a friendly way—although they were very much my friends—but in a much more complicated way that was tinged with a darkness that I hadn't expected. While only King and Sterling had told me directly, I was starting to see clearly how all their actions had reflected that truth. I honestly felt a bit dumb, because they had made it very obvious this entire time how they felt, and I had been so caught up on being insecure that I had never realized it.

Biting down on my lip, I considered the only part of the equation King hadn't included. *His cousin.*

There was a very large chance that I was going to fall down that rabbit hole of emotions regarding Dermot much faster than he did, if he did at all. I'd made it clear how I felt about him, and while I knew he liked me, there was a level of insecurity that paired with not having as close of a relationship with him. Even Stratton was easier to be sure about than Dermot, mostly because I had been right about Stratton. I had been right to never give up, despite him pushing me away time and time again.

Never again.

Suddenly, a heavy arm shifting around my center pulled me from my thoughts as it tugged me against its owner possessively. My toes curled as a large hand slipped underneath my sleep shirt and splayed across my stomach, an exhale against my neck causing a heated shiver to roll through my frame. My skin prickled, and their nose brushed against the sensitive skin there, making my attempt to not get turned on a complete and utter failure. Something that I had no doubt the man in question would love and goad me about endlessly.

Yates Carter.

The cocky, blunt, oddly possessive, brilliant man had left me reeling in the past twenty-four hours. I thought I had known everything about Yates, and maybe I had always known this side of him existed, but if you had told me before this past weekend that I would be waking up with his arm around me, I would have laughed. Not because I wouldn't have wanted that. No, I think I had come to terms with my not so little crush. More because I didn't think either of us would be able to stop arguing for long enough to fall asleep like this.

Then again, the Yates I experienced last night in the midst of the crisis was a far stretch from the man I enjoyed poking at and teasing. No, this man had been controlled, eerily calm, and left me nearly melted with desire at the way he took charge of the situation and, more importantly, me. I was positive there was a problem somewhere in how much that concept appealed to me.

So while it should have been surprising, it felt right that he had me currently wrapped up in a tight, possessive, cocoon-like hold that surrounded me with his warm, familiar scent. My lips pulled up happily as I curled further into my soft, luxurious bed, wondering how long the two of us could stay like this until he decided to wake up.

From what I knew about King and Yates, both of them were morning people, and while I didn't know what time it was besides ungodly early, I figured his internal alarm would be ringing in no time. Then again, last night had been a late one, and I had fallen asleep on his lap in my father's office before they had even finished working, so I had no idea when he actually fell asleep.

My guys had spent several hours sorting through boxes of information, along with files from a few laptops I had never seen before. Everything had been extremely organized, impressively so, and stored in not only paper format but electronic as well. I wasn't one to normally find organization sexy, but somehow Yates had made it exactly that, which was absolutely dangerous.

No one needed to have so much sex appeal that they could make file folders sexy. *Just saying*.

Unfortunately, now that it was morning and my adrenaline from last night was gone, I found myself frustrated that I hadn't asked more questions. I had simply laid there, curled up against Yates, watching my boys with a sense of numbness that blocked out the anxiety. I had finally felt safe enough to do so, after months of secrets and living with the fear of never wanting to look at my phone, so when I had the opportunity to finally relax, my body completely jumped on board.

Now though, I needed answers. Starting with what all of those boxes had contained. Were they the boxes and files that made up the dossier of everyone in Camellia? And why did all of the guys seem to offer Yates a series of odd looks after returning from his house? What was in that fourth-floor room? Because I had one hundred percent not missed the tone of voice King had used when asking Yates if he was sure about him going in there.

Had I ever even been to that floor of Yates's house? I frowned, realizing that I hadn't because his bedroom was on the third floor. *Well*... that would clearly need to change.

I know, curiosity killed the cat... and I would no doubt end up in the same situation... but it was a wonderful distraction from the other, more daunting questions running through my head.

Like, why had the FBI decided to work with them? Why not contact our parents? What did that say about the influence that my boys had, and why did I feel like it was far more than I realized? Also, how did the Brooks family play into all of this?

Was it possible that Abby's father was truly responsible for causing all of these problems in town? Was he working for an escaped drug felon and spreading products throughout town to continue his business in the state of Alabama? And what did that mean for the way that Abby had been bullying me? Was that coincidental, or targeted? After all, it wasn't exactly a secret that Wildberry Lane held a large amount, if not all, of the true power in the town that her father was possibly selling in.

I knew it seemed not nearly as important now, but I was even curious if it was possible to confirm that she was, in fact, the one sending all those messages. Had my instincts been correct? My head pulsed thinking about how much more my boys were going to want to know about my theory regarding her. Well, her and her brother, considering he had somehow known the guys had been keeping secrets.

They hadn't been the only ones.

What would I say to my parents once they called about the disaster that had been yesterday? What would we say to the national media? My breathing went tight as anxiety began to poke through that numb barrier I had resurrected to deal with all of this.

Christ. Today was going to be a very long day.

So much for being positive, Dahlia.

"Bunny." Yates's sexy voice vibrated against my neck and caused me to still. I considered turning into him but let out a small squeak as he tightened his hold on me and nipped my shoulder, causing me to squirm against him in order to break free. Not that I really wanted that, but the idea of pushing Yates a bit was honestly sorta hot. I knew he wouldn't like me trying to get away from him.

Proving my point, he bit down harder and let out a disapproving noise as his cock pressed against my butt and caused me to let out a soft moan. I attempted to hide my reaction, but his chuckle had me knowing I failed. I looked back at him, scowling, despite the blush lighting up my face and the way my entire body was broken into shivers. It was hardly fair that he affected me so much.

"What?" I asked, trying to sound indignant at his rough treatment of me but failing as his lips brushed along my neck, causing me to tilt it and expose myself further to his touch. I may have been honest with myself, admitting that I loved the way he handled me, but I would be damned if he knew the extent.

Which was why I had to find a way to get what I needed from him without directly asking. That 'pushing' concept didn't seem far off... it hadn't seemed to take a lot at his father's office before he'd broken, so maybe the same principle could apply here? I wanted to ask him to kiss me more, to bite me more, literally just to touch me more, but I didn't want to sound needy. Although, at least now I knew that my neediness for all of these men wasn't bad or wrong, at least in their eyes.

How had I been the only one not aware of the fact that we had been essentially dating this entire time? *Freakin' boys.* I swear. How I could be that oblivious was both embarrassing and infuriating, considering they had been completely on board.

My brow dipped as I once again went back to worrying about how I was going to explain this to my parents. I felt like stating that the guys and I were 'dating' was a gross misrepresentation of this situation and would probably confuse the heck out of them.

"I can hear you overthinking everything. Talk to me," Yates murmured, a soft demand. His voice took on a gentler tone than normal, one that only existed in reference to me.

I turned into him, his grip loosening momentarily enough to allow me that, so I could curl against his chest and look up into his nearly metallic silver eyes. My leg rubbed against his as he brushed his nose against mine and let out a soft almost-hum from his throat. I felt dizzy at the action, the softness paired with the intensity between us making me wonder how we'd gone so long without kissing. I tilted my head back, offering my lips as he let out a soft groan and kissed me lightly.

It was teasing and light enough that I was clutching him

to get closer. He smiled against me, locking me in place as the kiss turned a bit harder and more demanding. I whimpered as he pulled back, the searing action making me feel off balance as he flashed me that cocky smile I should have hated. Unfortunately, I did not.

How had I ever thought we could stay enemies? That was a horrible idea.

"Dahlia," he said, his voice rough, "as much as I love kissing you, I need to know where your head is right now."

"There is just so much I don't understand," I admitted. "I have a lot of questions."

His hand slid up my jaw and into my hair as he offered a sexy, knowing smile. "You? Having questions? Shocking."

I huffed, offering him a narrow-eyed look before sitting up and stretching my arms above my head. Yates let out a low, throaty sound, my gaze snapping to find his eyes tracing over the oversized shirt I slept in, the material nearly at my hips and my breasts pressed against the front, making it all too obvious how turned on I was. I felt my toes curl as his eyes darkened to nearly charcoal and his hand darted out to no doubt grab me. His attempt failed, much to his frustration, as I flashed him a smile and slipped from bed before he could catch me.

"Bunny." His growl was low and dangerous as he sat up, the comforter falling to reveal his golden, muscular chest that was shown off by his unbuttoned dress shirt. It was a messier, sexier look than normal, and his platinum hair was unstyled and created an urge inside me to run my hands through it.

I stepped back from the bed and offered him a coy smile, trying to stop myself from giving into the desire to touch him, knowing I would never get answers if I did that.

"Shower," I explained in a light voice.

Yates offered me a narrowed gaze before falling back on

the bed, muttering something under his breath. He ran a hand over his face. "Fine. Back to bed after."

"Bossy," I sang, his lips twitching up in a smile as he offered me a look I didn't fully understand. As if what I was saying was more accurate than I had intended it. I saved that thought for later, along with the fantasy of how else he could be bossy... specifically in the bed he was laying in.

Goodness, I really needed a cold shower.

Before I could turn for the en suite, my gaze fell on the rest of my room, the two-story tall space filling with light. It highlighted the cream walls, dark wood floors, and large arching windows, showcasing it in its best light, in my opinion. The plants that filled the space brought an earthy scent to the room that, paired with the humidity that came through the windows, left me with the feeling of *home*. That was what this room, this space, felt like. Home. It was a sanctuary from everything else outside of Wildberry Lane.

While I knew my six-estate community had its shadows, it was more comforting and safer than the exposed, raw ugliness that lived outside of our gates. Something that I was discovering more and more each day. I had never been so thankful for the privacy our lifestyle afforded us following such a large-scale social media attack. Unfortunately, I had no doubt that the national media would find out where we lived, but getting through the gates was a different story.

I was safe in Wildberry's shadows, that I knew.

My heart squeezed tighter as a small surge of happiness and excitement ran through me, feeling almost alien after such a hard day. I couldn't help it though. I hadn't realized we weren't alone in bed, and seeing the twins sleeping peacefully on the other side of Yates left me with a feeling of contentment and a sense of this situation being *right*. This was how it was supposed to be.

Lincoln's dark-rimmed glasses were tossed aside in the

space between Yates and him, a pillow tucked underneath his handsome, tan face. I frowned, suddenly wishing that I was the one he was wrapped around instead, that I was underneath him... and *I was jealous of a pillow.* That was an accurate and absurd truth that I blinked away as I refocused on the way his white-blonde hair seemed to glow with strawberry undertones because of the light falling across him and his twin.

Holy moly. These boys were far too attractive. It was nearly unfair.

Scratch that. Not 'nearly.' It was.

It was unfair because I had questions this morning and my body was betraying me, trying to convince me to go over there and kiss him awake. Or to crawl between Sterling and him until they were both looking at me with their bright, azure blue eyes.

Sterling, on his right, was fully stretched out on his back, his large semi-pro-rugby-worthy muscular arm bent underneath his mess of rich cinnamon-colored hair. His brow was tightened with a scowl that permeated his features as if he was having a bad dream. Something that had me wanting to cross the room to wake him up.

Yes, because that wouldn't be weird Dahlia.

What would I even say if he woke up?

Hey handsome, just wanted to make sure you were okay... you know, because you were frowning in your sleep and I was worried you were having a bad dream. Yes. I was staring at you while you slept. Why? Is that weird? Surely not.

Then again, it wasn't as if they had ever minded me staring at them, and I was nearly positive that they caught me more often than not. Unfortunately for my pride, mind you. My eyes widened, thinking about all the times that I had been caught staring at these men or used the excuse of photography to do the same.

Oh my. Was I a bit of a creep? Sort of...

My smile grew realizing that they knew I was and were still in love with me.

Well, that did loads for my confidence.

I think it was in that moment that I decided I needed to stop overthinking this. I had spent my entire life with these men, except for Dermot, and I knew that I was only over-thinking any of this, any of their actions, because of my own insecurities. They knew who I was, and the recent revelation of what was going on with me wasn't going to change how they felt.

I just had to continue to repeat that. To believe that. They knew my faults and they still loved me. I had to believe that wasn't going to change because of what had happened yesterday.

"Dahlia." Yates's voice pulled me back from my thoughts as I met his gaze. "Everything okay?"

"Yes." I sighed before adding, "It's just been a very odd twenty-four hours."

Yates examined my expression before nodding in under-standing, his gaze following me as I turned from the bed and made my way towards the en suite. Despite the change in tone, now knowing how they felt, it wasn't odd having these men in my room. It felt right. It should have been a bit awkward or even seem out of place, but I think because I'd been falling asleep at their houses from the time we were kids, it wasn't as jarring as you would assume. I'd woken up between the twins more times than I could count. I smiled as a memory from this past summer sparked through my thoughts.

"It's almost dawn," I pointed out as a small yawn broke from my lips. I ran a hand over my face, no doubt leaving a trail of wet paint on my

skin. Lincoln let out a grunt of agreement, his paint-splattered shirt tucked underneath his head where he laid out next to me on the futon Sterling kept upstairs in his studio. I tried to ignore how good Linc looked shirtless, but considering I was tired, I was near positive my eyes were wandering over his muscles. Muscles that had gone from lanky and toned to extremely built from training with his new rugby team.

If I wasn't so tired, I would have tried to walk home. Honest. I didn't trust my control right now. It was totally possible I was going to end up saying something really stupid or embarrassing.

"Is it?" Sterling's gaze snapped towards the massive window of his attic studio that was opened, allowing for slightly cooler morning air to drift into the space. It brought a slight shiver to my skin, but it felt pleasurable in comparison to the heat flashing across my body because of Lincoln's proximity.

It didn't surprise me that Sterling had lost track of time. When he was working, it was the case more often than not. Linc and I had started helping him yesterday afternoon, and I couldn't for the life of me tell you what was supposed to be on the canvas besides an array of stunning shades of green and pink that Sterling seemed to appreciate.

In my mind, that was all that really mattered. If he was happy with it, so was I.

I needed sleep though, and soon. I also needed a shower because my hands, arms, feet, and hair all were covered in pink and green. I wasn't convinced I could make it through a warm shower, though, and stay upright, frankly. Maybe I needed a cup of coffee...

"Lay down, sugar," Sterling insisted, his bright eyes alert and full of energy, unlike his brother and I. I looked down at the futon that Lincoln was so comfortably spread out on and knew that if I laid back, it would be an end game for me. I would fall asleep so fast it wasn't even funny.

I looked over Sterling and tried to not stare at his cut golden chest and abs as well. Was it possible they were this cut and large? Maybe I was imagining it. I felt like I needed a closer look... or touch. I mean,

I just wanted to make sure I was being accurate here! I really hadn't considered what their new training schedule would do to my twins, and honestly, you wouldn't hear a peep of complaint from me. I had always found the twins attractive, but this was just unreal.

"You need to sleep also," I pointed out.

"Leave him to his insanity." Lincoln tugged me backwards, his arms around my waist as I groaned, rolling onto my stomach and spreading myself half across his body. He cursed as I buried my nose against his throat, smiling.

What? He was the one who pulled me onto him!

I swallowed nervously at how hard he was, trying to not react because I knew it probably meant nothing. It was just a natural reaction to a woman laying on top of him in bed, obviously. So I would do my darn best to not be flattered by his attraction.

Letting out a sleepy, small sigh, my eyes closed as I finally resigned myself to taking that hot shower after a few hours of sleep. Plus, Lincoln was ridiculously comfortable—it would take a lot to get me off him.

Even better? When I had woken up a few hours later, I had found myself surrounded by two hard, muscular bodies, a twin sandwich in the truest sense. The early afternoon sun had been flooding the studio and heating it up, making me feel lazy and comfortable enough that I had laid there for nearly an hour before I finally decided to 'wake up.' At that point, I still hadn't left their arms because they hadn't acted as if it was a big deal and had continued to doze in and out of sleep until it was nearly night.

I wanted to smack myself in the head, feeling stupid for not seeing the obvious nature of our relationship this entire time. Talk about embarrassing.

Well, at least King had made it crystal clear how everyone felt. His method had been extremely effective. Subtle cues for several years? Constantly being a reliable source of affection and support? Possessive and protective tendencies? Nope! Pinning me up against the shower wall, making me come, and then telling me they all loved me? Yep. That had cleared up everything very quickly.

As I made my way into the bathroom, I considered telling them that was the best way to explain everything to me...

Somehow, I didn't think they would mind.

Chapter Two

DAHLIA ALDRIDGE

As I entered the white tiled bathroom, sunlight peeking through the large window that faced Stratton's house, I didn't bother locking the door, deciding instead to just close it. I mean, what was the worst that could happen? A sexier-than-sin man showing up and taking a shower with me? That sounded the opposite of horrible. All three of the men in my bedroom were more than welcome to join me any time they wanted.

I tilted my head briefly, wondering where Kingston, Stratton, and Dermot were. I suppose it was possible they went home, but somehow I didn't think that was the case. In fact, it was more likely that King was still up working on this situation however he saw fit, and as for the other two, the first was no doubt very worked up and the second was probably helping King like last night. The twins and Yates weren't exactly relaxed by any definition of the word, but Stratton was a chronic overthinker, King was extremely intense, and I was finding that Dermot was very determined when he wanted to be.

Especially when it came to easily and flawlessly working

his way into my heart. I had no idea how the man had done it, but something about his personality just clicked with mine. I felt like I had known him for years, and I was already fostering a sense of trust with him that should have taken years to form.

It made no sense, yet it was undeniably true.

Letting out a tired sigh, I stripped out of my sleep shirt and turned on the shower. A shiver ran over my skin as I watched the water begin to steam up the massive glass box, memories of my panic attack yesterday playing through my head.

No. I was not going to let that ruin my shower. I loved showers, especially burning hot ones, and now that King had taken one with me, even if briefly, I wanted that memory to cancel out the panic attack one. I felt like that was fair.

Letting out a soft, relieved groan, I stepped underneath the heavy shower stream, letting it massage the tension from my frame. Holy moly. Talk about a much needed moment of relaxation. I ran my fingers over my face, letting my neck hang down and stretch the tension out of my upper back and neck while water pounded down.

Today was a new day. Normally a positive phrase, but somehow I knew it wasn't that easy. It was a new day, but it was a different type of day than ever before.

Attempting to gather myself, I considered all of the questions I needed to ask and the possible answers I may receive. I tried to imagine the conversation I was going to have to have with my parents when they called and how I would need to be firm with them, because I had no doubt that they would want to come back almost immediately in order to be here for me. Something that, for the first time in my life, I didn't want. Not that I didn't want their support or to see them, but if my guys were right and there was a larger issue going on with the Brooks family, then I wanted to try to handle it. My parents had done so much for me in my life; I wasn't about to bring them into this nonsense unless it was absolutely necessary.

I just hoped that we wouldn't end up in over our heads.

I let out a slow, calming breath. We could handle this... Right? I mean, I was aware now more than ever that my boys had their shadows. Shadows that I was finding I loved... but the concept of the FBI? A drug ring? An escaped drug convict? It seemed almost unreal that we would be part of something like that. Or maybe I had been living in a box for too long, because my boys hadn't seemed nearly as surprised.

Speaking of boxes, maybe I could get down to the office after this and look through some of them. I just needed to pull myself out of this dazed state, which I could only partially blame on my lack of coffee. I'd been on such an emotional high over the past few days, and then my panic attack had hit, and hit hard. The low that followed the exhilaration and adrenaline that came with extreme emotions always resulted in this numbness. This mental distance that I know my brain provided for me to heal myself.

Too bad I couldn't afford that right now. Unlike when Sterling had found me in the school bathroom crying over the messages I'd been receiving, I didn't have a week to phase out. I didn't even have an hour. There were too many aspects we needed to consider.

Most importantly, my guys needed me, and I needed them. I didn't want to say I couldn't afford to be 'weak,' but that was really how it felt. In the face of learning about all of this, I didn't want to be viewed as a liability, and right now I feared that's what I was. My emotions were less controlled and my reactions raw. I found myself wanting to overreact, underreact, and not react at all to the things going on around me. If my boys had to worry about that, we wouldn't be able to focus on the situation at hand.

It didn't help that lately I felt like I'd been relying on them so heavily. I knew I had told Stratton that it wasn't a bad thing to rely on those that you love and those that loved you. And I should have told my boys what was going on, but now that they knew? I wanted to prove that I was more than that. I had strength in me, and while I knew they would never want me to feel like I had to prove anything, it didn't change the fact that I wanted to.

Attempting to distract myself, I grabbed a bottle of shampoo and squirted it into my hand. The smell of mint filled the steamy space as I began to scrub my messy tangle of dark hair. It was still stiff from yesterday when I had let it dry without brushing it, and as I closed my eyes, I felt them sting a bit, still a bit dry from all the crying I'd done. It felt good, the water, almost therapeutic, and when I was done I made sure to condition and wash every part of me. Cleansing. The process of showering after a panic attack felt cleansing.

I wanted to erase yesterday. Okay... not all of yesterday. I wouldn't mind reliving the part where Dermot and I were in bed.

A nervous tightening filled my stomach. How would things be between us today? Weird? Normal? Letting out a small, frustrated sound, I turned off the shower and wrapped myself in a comfortable robe.

Walking towards the large mirror that bounced light through the room from where it hung over the vanity, I examined just how exhausted I appeared. Lovely.

Leaning over the vanity, I traced the dark circles under my eyes with shaky fingers, wondering if I was imagining the slight dullness in my gaze. Maybe it was a good day to wear some makeup; I was looking a bit rough. I brushed my teeth while I weighed if it would actually make me feel better or not.

I had absolutely no idea who assumed or made up the

rumor that women wore makeup for men. Maybe that was the case for some women, but for me? If I wore makeup, it was because I felt better in it that day. It took a lot more time and effort than most men would ever realize, and that alone was a solid reason to never wear it for them. I mean, if they noticed, great, but to spend hours painting your face for someone that probably wouldn't appreciate it? No thank you.

Then again, maybe I was a bit spoiled, because my boys had been seeing me without makeup my entire life and had always told me they thought I was beautiful without it or with it...

And I was still wondering how the heck I hadn't caught onto their feelings.

Shaking my head, I began to brush out my dark hair and pulled it into a loose braid before applying some light concealer under my eyes and a bit of lip stain, noticing how pale I was looking. Afterwards I felt far better, and except for my throat being sore from throwing up yesterday, I felt considerably more myself.

Adjusting my robe, I muttered a curse under my breath, realizing I hadn't brought my clothes in here with me. I nibbled my lip and prepared to walk back into the bedroom somewhat undressed. Maybe they would still be sleeping? I mean, I had no reason to be embarrassed—they had all seen me in far less by the pool—but there was just something more intimate about it being in my bedroom and being naked under a robe.

Heat flashed over me, contrasting the embarrassment. *Well, that was a bit confusing.* Inhaling sharply, I tried to not consider how easily one of them could take off the robe and...

No! I needed answers. Answers first.

As I neared the door, I paused in front of the scale and examined the small silver device that had so quickly become a focal point in my life. I considered stepping onto it but made myself stop, pausing to consider how it would either improve or ruin my morning. Was I willing to take that chance? I knew without a doubt that if it showed I'd gained weight, I would feel ten times worse.

My throat pulsed with pain as it did after a particularly bad episode.

This. This was why I had been avoiding not only admitting my problem, but telling others. I couldn't ignore it anymore. I hadn't just avoided telling my boys about the bullying because I didn't want them involved. No, it was very clear that now I had to reckon with the notion that bullying had created and allowed a much larger and dangerous problem to grow in my life. One I couldn't avoid and one I had no idea how to approach successfully to fix.

Was there a fix?

I wasn't positive there was when you viewed food and eating the way I did. When it became everything, it was impossible to not consider it every time that you took a bite. Every time you ordered something on the menu.

I hadn't confirmed my eating issue to my boys, not fully, but they knew. I was almost positive.

The worst part? Unlike the bullying, it changed nothing. It was one of the reasons books and movies that dealt with anxiety, depression, and eating disorders drove me crazy, because there wasn't an easy fix. It wasn't like their love would suddenly resolve the much deeper issue that I had, the craving for control and a lack of love and confidence I had for myself. Sure, reassurance helped, a lot. But did it change the fact that not weighing myself made me feel out of control? Or that I would have a good or bad day based on the number on the scale?

No, it didn't.

Finding out the men I loved felt the same way was absolutely amazing. But the raw truth of the matter? I still had a problem. A problem that I felt ill-equipped to handle on my own. Where did I even begin?

"Princess?" Kingston's warm voice, filled with a darkness that had seemed to develop this past summer, had my gaze flicking up from the scale. I opened my lips to say something... maybe sorry? But for what? I wasn't doing anything wrong, but suddenly I felt guilty. It made no sense.

Maybe because I hadn't said the words to him? Admitted what was truly wrong with my broken psyche?

"Morning." I offered a small, hesitant smile, knowing he would see through it.

Sometimes I felt like the man could see into my very being, and that made me a nervous wreck. I also loved the idea of being that connected... it was very confusing.

The questioning look on his handsome, sculpted face told me that he was aware of what I had been doing, or had at least been watching me for a bit, making me wonder how I hadn't heard the door open. His eyes flashed down to the scale before looking back up at me again, his silence making me know that he was waiting for me to say something. Giving me some time to formulate how I wanted to handle this.

I didn't think for a second he would let it go.

When his large hand slid up my arm, cupping my shoulder and then moving across my collarbone to the hollow of my throat, my body trembled slightly. I let out a small, breathy sigh of relief as he stepped closer, his massive frame shadowing me in his warmth as his thumb ran over the pulse at the base of my throat, making my eyes feel heavy. The man had far too much influence over my body.

"Are you okay?" His voice rolled over my skin as my fingers ran up his chest and tightened on the fresh shirt he had changed into. Had he run home to change? Now that I was looking at him, he looked like he may have done just that and also gotten in a quick shower. He was dressed in a pair of dark gray suit pants and an untucked button-down that was rolled to his forearms, the material tailored to hit his chest perfectly. He looked far too handsome for this early in the morning, making me wonder how he managed that on little to no sleep.

Inhaling his cigar and vanilla scent, I looked all the way up to meet his gaze, forgetting his question because I was distracted by the way the morning light danced on his honey-blonde hair.

"Dahlia." His voice thickened with warning and heat as that darker side of King that I was learning to love to play with flashed across his face, making me want to talk about everything *but* the scale on the floor next to us.

I wanted to see that expression on his face far more often. It reminded me of the intoxicating way he had looked at me while pinning me to my bed, his fingers taunting my bare skin, before tasting just how much he affected me. Although, if he wanted to know now, all he had to do was slide his fingers between my legs. Or better yet, slide his large...

King's fingers tipped my chin up to where my gaze had been moving down his body. His expression was both amused and hot.

"Just gathering my thoughts." I bit down on my lip and his eyes sharpened on the action, his energy intensifying and nearly pulling me into the all-encompassing vortex that was this amazing man. That was how it always was with Kingston, though. He had an element to his personality that truly intoxicated me. I couldn't control it. It was past my ability to do so, and that was just how the two of us existed in the world when we were alone.

I swallowed a bit nervously, not knowing how to explain myself.

His expression changed, softening as he seemed to consider something. I saw when he decided to back down from the scale conversation, but I knew it was a temporary reprieve. One I was nonetheless thankful for.

"Coffee may help with that," he pointed out, his lips pressing into a sexy, relaxed smile. This King, the one I had spent most of my life with, I was a bit more comfortable with. I leaned into him easily, running my fingers over his chest as a happy sound left his throat, his arms tightening around me.

"That sounds wonderful," I murmured a bit sleepily and then smiled. "Have I ever told you that I love your ideas?"

And you.

"Is that all you love?" He chuckled softly, his fingers brushing up my jaw again to tilt my head back. His lips brushed mine in a gentle kiss as my body absolutely melted into his hard frame.

The man knew me far too well.

"Say it," he demanded softly, his eyes flashing down to my lips.

"I love you, King." I shivered at the heat there as he leaned forward and nipped my bottom lip, still sore from his treatment of it the other day.

"I love you more than you will probably ever realize, Dahlia."

Oh, I doubted that.

Before I could respond back with something probably embarrassing, a large figure stumbled past us, a tired groan breaking from their throat. I turned in King's arms, leaning against his chest, as I watched Sterling turn on the sink faucet. He began to scrub his face before pressing a dry rag to it and squeezing his eyes shut, seemingly in pain.

"You okay, man?" King asked, seeming half concerned and also amused.

"No," he muttered. "I feel asleep with my damn contacts in."

I couldn't help but smile, because I wasn't surprised. This happened often. Often enough that I was able to walk over to the fifth drawer on the right of the vanity and pull out one of the many spare, empty contact cases and solution kits I kept for exactly this reason. Sterling did a lot of amazing things, but one of those things was *not* being good at remembering to take out his contacts. He let out a sigh of relief and kissed the top of my head before leaning over to take them out.

Turning towards the door, I flashed King a smile and squeezed past him, his eyes tracking me with amusement and a string of happiness that I loved seeing. I had no idea how the man's emotions changed so easily. I mean... It was literally like a switch. Somewhat impressive, if we were being honest.

My memories returned to finding him covered in blood in Dermot's kitchen and the stark, almost empty expression that had filled his face. Was it wrong that I found his unpredictable emotional range sort of fascinating? My fingers twitched at the idea of capturing all of them on camera.

Yes, even the one when he was covered in blood.

Lord, there was something very wrong with me.

Shrugging off the concern, knowing I had much larger worries, I made my way over to my closet. Lincoln was standing near my balcony door, letting out a yawn and stretching. His muscular back distracted me enough that I had to look away before I slammed into something.

Lord, his sexiness that was so easy to gawk at. Who did he think he was?

Searching through my clothes, I pulled out a paisley pink and blue sundress that tightened at the waist, along with a matching blue pair of panties. I tilted my head, looking at the lace item and wondering if I should pick something sexier...

"I like that color blue on you." A heated voice brushed against my ear, causing me to jump and nearly throw my elbow back instinctively. The man behind me chuckled at my surprise. Luckily for him, his firm grip on my arms didn't allow for any drastic movements, so I didn't end up gut-punching him by accident. I winced, knowing I would have felt bad about that as I tilted my head up and scowled at an amused Lincoln. His bright blue eyes were filled with a happy light behind his glasses, and I found I couldn't be too upset, especially considering how much lighter and more relaxed he seemed than he was last night. I still wanted to kick his butt.

I turned into him and poked his chest. "You scared the mess out of me."

"Sorry," he mused at my admonishment, not looking apologetic in the least. In fact, the only thing he was thinking of doing seemed to be kissing me because of the way he was looking at my lips.

Clearly not an apology... but I would take it. I'm nice like that.

"Not very believable," I teased as he chuckled softly, the sound tinged with a dangerous edge, before he stepped back and lifted my finger from his chest, nipping the tip of it. I shuddered, and without another word, he walked out after winking at me. I swallowed as my heart skipped a beat, feeling the pulse from his bite through my core.

Did he even realize how much he affected me? Lord. I hoped not.

Grabbing my clothes and turning back towards the room, I found King and Sterling talking near the door that Lincoln passed through to go downstairs. Yates was still sleeping, spread out and looking perfectly comfortable.

They were everywhere.

I mean, seriously. These large, muscular, sexy men were all in my space, and if King was telling the truth, then I was for sure going to need to get used to it. Honestly though, it was nothing new. They had always been around, this just seemed more claiming. Before, they offered me the choice to have them leave, but now? I don't think I was going to get that option, especially since I told them I felt the same.

Which was good, because this was literally all I had been wanting. Them. In my space. Touching me. Kissing me. For sure more than that as well. Although I had a feeling I was going to need to step up my seduction game if that part was going to happen as soon as I would like.

Slipping into the bathroom, I quickly got dressed and then nodded at my reflection, already feeling far better about today. I imagined coffee would make me feel human, so that was next on the agenda. Hopefully the boys would be okay with sitting by the pool and drinking coffee? There was something to be said for keeping habits in times of crisis, and I had been doing this morning routine all summer.

Partly, and I could admit this now, in a bid to see Stratton, who was usually up early. He always tended to be in the back yard at some point in the morning, which I was realizing now may have been on purpose. That he may have wanted to see me as much as I wanted to see him. It didn't hurt, I guess, that I always had a bikini on. I wondered what exactly he had thought of that, because I could tell you exactly what I thought of how he looked shirtless as he worked.

Suddenly I frowned, doubting my earlier assumption about him having stayed overnight. I knew he didn't like to leave Ms. Lori for long. Was it too early to go over there and wake him up? He would probably be up, but I didn't want to ring the bell. Ms. Lori would be sleeping, so maybe I should call instead.

The smell of coffee wafting up from the kitchen urged me to get downstairs. I looked back at my closet, considering the stack of the boys' clothes that I kept, and wondered if I should bring any down. Or would everyone leave to go home and change? I didn't want to hand my collection over... I mean, it wasn't that far of a walk... but I also hated the idea of them leaving.

Honestly, I was a bit possessive over their clothes that they gave me. For the longest time, that was the closest I would get to having them in bed with me on a regular basis.

I know, that made it sound way better, right?

I tilted my head in thought. Maybe now I wouldn't have an issue giving them back since I had the real thing. Speaking of which, I walked over to the bed and sat down on the edge, wondering if I should wake Yates. He looked so peaceful.

Part of me wanted to wake him up just to see if he would be cranky, and then there was an equal part of me that wanted to cuddle. *Choices, choices.* My fingers reached out to brush a messy piece of hair from his face. The moment my fingertips brushed his skin, his eyes flashed open and... I was pinned underneath him on the bed.

How the heck had he done that?

I blinked rapidly, trying to process how fast he had grabbed my waist and rolled me onto the bed so that he was caging me from above. A small, confused noise left my throat, realizing that like this, he managed to cover my frame completely, encompassing me with his muscular form. My breathing turned faster and my face flushed, loving how easily he handled me.

A shiver broke over me as his metallic gaze went dark, turning from a cool, sleepy color to a deep, warm, melted silver tinted with charcoal. No one's eyes should be that expressive. His lips dipped to press to my collarbone as he seemed to wake up fully. Had he really been that deep asleep that he'd reacted so dangerously when I touched him?

I had never slept next to Yates before. Well I had, but he'd always been awake, so it surprised me that he moved so fast upon being woken up. It was a bit terrifying and a lot hot. It didn't help that there was a bit of adrenaline running through me at how large he was and how hard he felt pressed against me... And no, I wasn't just talking about his muscles.

My pulse jumped as he continued to run his lips over my body.

"Yates?" I breathed out a bit nervously as his teeth nipped my neck before he pulled back and examined my expression.

"Sorry, bunny," he breathed out. "I'm a bit more tired than I realized. I didn't mean to scare you."

Should I be more scared of Yates? Sometimes the man seemed more than a bit intense.

"Sleep more," I insisted. "I need some coffee though. There is no way I am getting back to sleep."

A familiar scowl formed on his face. "And what if I don't let you get up? You need sleep for sure, even if you don't think so. Both of us could use a few more hours."

I had a feeling that I may have to bargain in the future to get out of Yates's bed, and I loved that, but I think today he would probably understand my reasoning. I lifted a hand and ran it through his hair. "I have too many questions to sleep, but you should—"

"No," he growled and then groaned. "If you're up, I'm up. Your little ass is going to have a million questions, and I need to be up to make sure they are answered fully. We are taking a nap later, though. No arguments."

He sat up and released me, my eyes sliding down his muscular frame to how hard he was. My eyes widened as that surge of excitement brushed through me again.

"Who knew you would be such a cuddler," I teased, trying to not sound breathless.

It was possible I was maybe fishing a little bit to see if he had been a cuddler with anyone else ever... For the record, I had absolutely no knowledge of them ever dating anyone. Even Stratton. My brain sputtered at that. Was it possible...

no, there was no way. These men were not virgins, it wasn't possible.

As much as my little romantic heart would have loved to disagree, there was just no way that men like them, that confident and sexy, were virgins. I refused to believe it. My throat tightened at the concept of them being with anyone else, and then I immediately felt selfish. Here I was, wanting to be with six different men, and I was getting sad about the idea of them having possibly been with someone else. I had no proof of it and could probably ask them, but did I really want to know the answer?

Now, it was completely possible and more than likely that I was out of my league when it came to these men, especially Dermot. He was not only older, but had probably dated a bunch of stunning women from overseas. Why did that concept gut me so much?

I think it was fairly obvious 'why.'

"Dahlia, you bring out a lot of sides of me that I didn't realize existed." Yates's voice was almost dangerous as he offered me a searing look before tilting his head curiously. "What were you just thinking about?"

"Hm? I wasn't thinking." I offered a small smile. "But wait, what sides?"

Somehow I felt like that was a loaded question.

Yates examined my face. "Does that count as your question? I've decided that each question I answer today means you owe me a kiss, so better think them through, bunny."

"That seems like a surefire way to get absolutely nothing done," I mused.

His eyes danced with humor. "I'll give you a free question if you tell me what you were just thinking about."

I swallowed and decided that I may as well tell him. If anything, it would throw him off his game. I couldn't resist a chance to mess with Yates, even if this particular situation had the ability to gut me.

"I was thinking if... well, if anyone else had ever thought you were a good cuddler."

True confusion filled his face, his silver eyes peering into my soul as I waited for his answer. He moved forward again as I sank back onto the bed, his body back over mine as I tried to not love the way his fingers brushed through a few pieces of hair that had fallen from my braid.

"Are you asking if I have ever been with anyone else, bunny?" His tone was teasing, but his expression was anything but.

"Yes," I whispered nervously.

His eyes turned dark as he leaned in and brushed a kiss to my lips, making me let out a needy sound as I tried to deepen it. He locked my hips to the bed and spoke in a heated, husky tone. "How could I stomach being with anyone else when I spend every single day with the woman I love?"

His words had my eyes widening as he brushed another kiss to my lips and sat up, leaving me in a state of shock on the bed. I knew what King had said, but hearing the words of love from his mouth were completely different. And the fact that he'd been with no one else? Oh man. I could feel this Yates-and-Dahlia train speeding down the tracks, and I wasn't positive there was a way to derail it even if I wanted to.

Although, for the record, if the man ever needed a bop over the head for being a jerk, I would still do it.

The bathroom door closed as I blinked, trying to clear my thoughts and wondering how I was going to make it through a day with these men without completely detonating, both from desire and affection.

How had I gone so long without any of this? I mean, it had come at a time where the other side of the coin was that

I was having a personal crisis... but I wouldn't trade any of this. This was what I had wanted for so long.

I let out a small groan, staring at the ceiling. My entire body felt needy. My skin was hot and tight, and my center was drenched. I felt my nipples tighten against my lace bra as I considered touching myself again, wanting some level of relief from this insanity. But if King caught me... well, actually, that was probably exactly what I needed right now. King's form of punishment came with orgasms, and I was absolutely about it. My eyes closed as I imagined his hand around my neck and the firm grip he had been taking lately.

It wasn't too tight, but it was enough to know exactly how he felt.

When I heard Yates turn the shower on, I hopped out of bed and made my way towards the door, not trusting myself to not join him. My stomach fluttered, wondering how he would react. Something told me I would be way in over my head with Yates, no matter when I decided to make my move.

Shaking my head, I headed towards the door, knowing there was only one way to survive this morning. Coffee.

Sweet, delicious, caffeine-so-you-don't-attack-your-boyfriends coffee.

Chapter Three

DAHLIA ALDRIDGE

As I left my bedroom, jogging down the large marble steps that circled up five stories, a soft hum of appreciation left me because of how beautiful our house looked at this time of the day. The early morning sun and how it showcased the bright white marble left me in a state of awe despite having grown up in this house nearly my entire life. There was just something utterly magical about the place, and I found it hard to imagine living anywhere else.

Then again, the idea of another house, created to be a home for the guys and I, was extremely appealing. But if it meant leaving Wildberry Lane? It was something I would clearly have to reconcile with, despite hating the concept.

Before my thoughts could turn heavy, I slammed right into a very hard, shirtless chest. A sound of appreciation left my throat because, *sweet christ*, I knew exactly whose thick, muscular chest this was, and I had only seen it a few times. I swallowed before my eyes flicked up to meet a pair of bright green eyes, streaked with emerald, that were shining with an emotion that I didn't even know how to begin to process.

For the record, looking *up* was very much way up, up, and up... because Dermot Ross was around two inches taller than his cousin at 6'5", if not taller, and was so large that he seemed to literally command the entire space around him by just being there. There was no light and no oxygen. Just him and his sexy Irish accent. Our natural connection strummed between us, and any insecurities about how it would be between us after last night disappeared, reaffirming that whatever it was about how the two of us 'worked,' and there was absolutely no room for weirdness or awkwardness. Those elements should have existed, considering our lack of history, but they just didn't.

Some people were just connected like that. I didn't want to sound cheesy, but that was truly my opinion on the matter.

"Careful, baby girl," Dermot mused, his fingers sliding down my waist to my hips as my fingers brushed over his chest. Not to push him away, either. No, I was fighting the urge to dig my nails into him so I could leave small crescent moon-shaped marks. I wanted to mark the man... which was so incredibly not like me.

Unlike King, I could see a bit of sleepiness in his vibrant eyes, and his dark reddish-brown hair was damp as if he had just taken a shower. Had he showered here? If so, why the heck hadn't he invited me...

No. No, I was not making showers a *thing*. If I did that, I would never be able to look at a shower without getting turned on, and that was terribly inconvenient. Then again, could anyone really blame me considering the stunt King pulled just the other day?

"You," I began, feeling my throat go dry as my pulse picked up, "You are shirtless."

My body was betraying me, already deciding the answers I needed weren't nearly as important as feeling his shirtless body pressed against mine. Both of us, completely naked, skin to skin. My words and thoughts dried up as I continued to just stare at his chest, noticing that he had a tattoo over his right pectoral that I was almost damn positive was the Ross family crest. My fingers twitched to run over it with interest.

"That is correct." His voice was amused and thick with heat as he stepped further into me. "Is that okay with you, Dahlia?"

"Okay with me?" I questioned, a soft squeak escaping my throat as I nodded sharply. "Oh yes, totally okay. I mean, wait, that sounds weird. You know what? Whatever you're comfortable with—shirt, no shirt. Pants, no pants. Wait! Not no pants. Well, unless that's what you want—"

Dermot's lips suddenly seared to mine in a hungry kiss, pulling a surprised moan from my mouth. He just kissed the heck out of me, and when his hand wrapped around my braid, letting him position me how he wanted, he deepened and slowed the kiss. I didn't even try to stop myself from digging my nails into his hot chest, the groan that escaped his mouth making me realize that I'd left deeper marks than I'd originally intended. I started to apologize until I pulled back and met his nearly feral gaze, his now dark eyes moving from the markings to my lips, his breathing rough.

Nevermind, he *clearly* didn't mind, and I more than liked them.

Was that weird? Weird that I loved marking him?

A throat clearing had me jumping as Dermot's intensity disappeared almost instantly, an amused sound leaving his lips as my eyes moved to the doorway of the kitchen where King was leaning and staring at the two of us. I worried momentarily that he would be pissed or something, considering Dermot was his cousin and not one of the others, but instead he just looked pleased and entertained at my surprise.

"Need anything?" Dermot called to King, not taking his eyes off mine while running his rough fingers up the back of my neck and tightening on my braid once more. "I'm stopping over at the house to grab some shite."

"Nope," King answered as Dermot leaned down, kissing me hard again and leaving me breathless before offering a wink and striding past me. I looked over at King and found him staring at me with an intensity and a hot smirk that had me blushing.

"What?" I murmured, slowly approaching him and stepping into the doorway, my aim to slide past him. At least that's what I told myself. Of course, almost immediately, his arms came down on both sides as he trapped me there, stepping into my space. I shivered as his nose brushed over my cheekbone, my breathing hitching at the way the simple action lit up my entire body.

Clearly the years of sexual frustration towards these men were catching up to me.

"Don't be embarrassed," he cooed softly. "I am well aware of how my cousin feels about you, princess."

And how did his cousin feel about me? Because we hadn't truly had that conversation yet. I examined his expression, finding only truth as he continued his little speech.

"I can't exactly blame him. Hell, I can't fault most men for being attracted to you. You're exquisite. However, I *can* kill those other men—"

"King!" I chastised at his dramatics, but then my eyes widened in realization that they may not be dramatics...

He chuckled at my reaction. "Luckily for him, my cousin is exempt from that."

Rolling my eyes, I pinned him with a look. "And I'm not embarrassed, for the record. I just don't know how Dermot feels about me. It's more complicated than that."

"I managed to uncomplicate it for us." He offered a small smirk, his eyes dipping to my lips.

"King, you aren't exactly subtle when you decide you want to make something known."

The man in question flashed a dangerous smile. "And here I thought I'd been subtle for the past eighteen years, princess. You did say you didn't even realize we'd been dating this entire time. That you'd been *ours* this entire time."

Goodness gracious, his words... they should not have this much of an effect on me.

I smirked. "I was more referencing the part where you announced that you loved me."

"Oh, that." He pressed closer, his cock hardening against my stomach as he offered me a thoughtful tilt of the head that didn't match the devious glint in his eyes. "You mean right before I devoured your tight little—"

"King!" I threw my hand over his mouth, blushing a bright red that I was positive was unattractive, as his unexpected blunt words turned muffled. He chuckled as he pulled my hand away and kissed the top of it, the light touch making me dizzy.

"It's true though," he pointed out, his voice a growl. "That was exactly when it happened."

The man was enjoying my embarrassment far too much.

"You can't just say that out loud," I insisted, leaning into him as his fingers slid to wrap around my throat in a firm but possessive hold.

"Why not?" His eyes darted down to my lips again as heat turned his eyes nearly black. "The only people around to hear are far more likely to be jealous they didn't get a taste than to be upset by it."

Good lord, this man was going to kill me.

"King, she hasn't even had coffee yet. Pretty sure that's

taking advantage of her." Sterling appeared in front of us, his lips tilted into a sexy smile. He wasn't wrong, for the record.

"Yeah, King." I slipped from his grasp as he let out a low rumble from the back of his throat, sending me into Sterling's arms. My savior from King's sexiness easily scooped me up, flashing his friend a goading smile before I wrapped my arms around his neck.

When I looked back at King, he was staring at me with a glint in his eyes. Oh, I was going to pay for that later, and I could not be more excited.

I buried my head against Sterling's neck, and a moment later he sat me down at the breakfast table right next to Stratton.

Oh! He was here. In my kitchen. I loved that.

"Morning, angel." Stratton's eyes ran over me, his gaze turning hot despite the concern that still existed there, as he slid me a mug. I eagerly took it, taking a sip and letting out a soft, small moan that had Lincoln groaning from across the table.

I couldn't help but smirk just a little bit, my eyes flashing over to Linc, who was now scowling at me slightly... scratch that, it was nearly a pout. That was just far too funny.

"You slept well," I pointed out to Stratton, his piercing blue eyes hyper-focused on the coffee mug near my lips as he ran a ringed hand through his messy black hair. I could practically feel him wanting to move closer, so I made it easier on him and scooched right up next to him, my other hand drifting over his tattooed forearm. The man was 'bad boy' personified, and I absolutely loved it. I wanted to explore every part of Stratton that I had missed over the years, and I was curious to know how many tattoos he had underneath his all-black ensemble paired with motorcycle boots. If that exploring happened to be with my fingers, and even tongue, all the better...

His hand gripped my thigh as he inhaled sharply, clearly reading where my thoughts had gone. The man was ungodly handsome, and his gauges, rings, and tattoos were a major turn-on. Mind you, one that I'd never considered until Stratton started sporting them. He just had a hard edge to him that I used to be frustrated with because he'd used it to distance himself... but now I knew the truth.

Now I knew that there was so much more to the situation than I had realized, and because of that, something had fundamentally changed between us. Stratton wasn't fighting this anymore. He seemed at peace with it, and I wasn't going to question that at all because he had been missing from my life for so long that it had begun to affect me in ways I hadn't even realized.

Loving someone who wouldn't give you the time of day was painful. But loving someone who you once had but then lost was pure anguish.

I had him back though. I just had to remind myself of that. I also had to convince him to let us help figure out the mess his deceased father had left him to clean up. He shouldn't have to single-handedly bear the responsibility of attempting to reestablish a family business because his father had run it into the ground. Nor to solely bear the responsibility of bringing in enough money to support himself and his grandmother, including her medical bills. That was what family was for.

Not that life wasn't hard, but in times of true trouble, you called on family. And that was what we were, first and foremost. Wildberry Lane was a family.

Stratton seemed distracted by whatever was on my face, his mood a bit confusing to me. He pressed a kiss to my forehead, and I felt a slight split on his lip. I frowned at that. As much as I thought it was sexy when the man fought, I didn't want him to feel like he had to. I didn't want him to have to come into contact with gangs.

"I stopped home to check on MeMaw," he began. "She told me, and I quote, 'What are you doing over here and not at Dahlia's?' I couldn't refuse the woman, so I managed to knock out for a few hours on your couch in the office."

I tilted my head. "You should have come up to the bedroom."

I had a couch up there, he knew that… but I didn't mean for him to sleep on the couch. No, I very much would have welcomed him in my bed.

I nearly shook my head at that. I was a virgin. A virgin who wanted *not* three men in her bed like this morning, but six. Could we say 'in *way* over our head'?

I could feel Lincoln's analytical gaze on my expression, making me far too nervous to look over to see his reaction to my rather blunt statement to Stratton. I hadn't meant it to be so forward, but that was a lost cause at this point, obviously. Luckily for me, his eyes flared with heat, making me know the concept was welcome.

"Probably not a good idea, angel," he mused.

Before I could ask him why, Yates walked into the kitchen wearing one of the stolen shirts from my collection, making me scowl. Unfortunately, he looked ridiculously good in the dark blue shirt along with his dress pants from yesterday, so I could hardly be upset. Looking down at his watch, he seemed to consider something and then looked up at me.

"Bunny, your parents are going to be landing in Naples any minute now and will probably call. I need to run home really quickly, do you want me to wait—"

"I'll be fine," I promised, not wanting to be a hassle if he had something to do. I hesitated before adding, "But can I use one of your phones? I really don't want to use mine right now."

Or ever.

When Kingston handed me his, I clutched it tightly and drained my cup of coffee before getting a second one. My eyes drifted towards the boxes in the office, which were as numerous as my unanswered questions.

It was just going to be a second cup of coffee day.

Chapter Four

DAHLIA ALDRIDGE

"I promise, Mom."

I wasn't lying to her. *I was fine.* Fine being relative to how I could be doing, considering the chaos taking place around me. Although that chaos seemed fairly absent now that I was sitting out by our pool, my back curled against Stratton's hard chest.

The other boys had all run home to get changed or grab stuff for the day, my house becoming the designated spot to be. You wouldn't see me complaining. Due to their absence, though, and my parents not being around, the entire property felt almost eerily quiet, and I was glad Stratton was here. I worried that if I was left alone right now, I would think myself back into a hole of anxiety and panic.

Honestly, this day was already going far better than I expected, and I had managed to keep control over the conversation with my mom, not wanting to send her into a momma bear panic mode. Whether I could stop that or not was up for debate, but I was hoping she would trust my word on this.

My fingers were drawing slow patterns against Stratton's

jeans, and his tattooed fingers were gently combing through my hair that he had tugged loose from its braid. I would have been worried about him being bored, but I could tell he was enjoying this moment of solitude together. Something I wasn't going to complain about since I was very much enjoying being surrounded by his tobacco and leather scent and the warmth that emitted from his hot, hard frame. How did the man manage to make me feel both grounded and like I was having a heat flash? Impressive.

Slowly, I drank my second cup of coffee while examining the morning sun that was glinting off the pool's surface as I listened to her response. I could have put her on speaker, but I could tell Stratton was already listening because he would make certain noises in agreement with what she was saying. The soft rumble that flowed through his chest was so soothing that I was starting to wonder why I had been anxious in the first place.

Except then I remembered very clearly why and what had happened.

"Your father and Mr. Carter are working on handling the legal aspect," Mom promised softly. "We are going to make this disappear and figure out who did this to you."

I believed her. I could hear the determination in her voice, and I wouldn't lie, it did something to settle me. I had no doubt my boys were capable of handling this, but to have my parents not only immediately side with me but also believe me about everything that had been happening was reassuring and comforting. Not that I ever thought they wouldn't, but it was still nice.

"I know, I believe you. But being here or there won't make a huge difference, Mom. I'm going to feel way better knowing you guys didn't cancel your trip with everyone because of me. You know that if you come back, all of them will too, and that would just make me feel even worse—"

"Dahlia, honey, that's ridiculous," she chided.

"But true," I insisted. "Plus, I plan on just doing what I normally do every day. I just want to forget about all of it for a bit, and you know the guys are going to keep me company." *Hopefully in a lot of fun, sexy ways that I never needed to detail to my mom.* "The Labor Day celebration is this weekend, and then I'll be starting school, so I will be crazy busy as it is."

Was that enough reasoning to convince her? I had no idea.

My mom let out a noncommittal sound. "I don't know, Dahlia."

"You know how the guys are." I tried to keep it light-hearted, but Stratton chuckled silently behind me, his hand wrapping around my waist. "They are going to keep me so busy that even if you were home, I wouldn't see you."

The way Stratton's lips were pressed to the shell of my other ear, I had a feeling that he had a few thoughts on how to fill the time. It helped, of course, that I could feel how turned on he was, his hard length pressed against my back. I tried to not wiggle around too much, especially because if Stratton decided to pull something while I was on the phone with my mom, I wasn't confident I would hide my reaction in my tone of voice.

After a moment, she seemed to come to the same decision I did, which was that it wasn't worth it for them to come back. "Okay. Fine. But if you need me there, I will immediately be on the jet."

"I know," I whispered. "I love you, Mom. Tell Dad I love him too."

"We love you. Stay strong. We are going to handle whoever it was that did this."

Was it just me, or did that sound like a legitimate threat for whoever was responsible?

After saying goodbye, I hung up the phone and let out a

small exhale. At least they were staying there until we could sort all of this out. Two weeks would be enough, right? I hoped so. Especially because my emotions were all over the place right now, and I knew without a doubt that if they were here, they would see right through my attempt to keep calm. They would see how much the incident affected me.

Realize that it was part of a much larger problem.

Heck, my mom may have even put together the weight loss from this past year with all the images based around how I looked on that account. That wasn't even including whether or not they would notice the change between the guys and me. I mean, how could they not? Unless they planned to not act like we were together around our parents... crap, what would they think of me? Would they think it was odd that their sons all wanted to be with the same girl? Would my parents be embarrassed that I wanted to be with all six of them?

Holy moly, this was complicated.

"Angel." Stratton's voice was a low, relaxing rumble as I tilted my head back, slouching against him as I let out another slow exhale. "You know you don't have to handle any of this, right? We can handle it—"

"I need to be part of this. I need to handle it. I can't turn away from it, especially because it may be part of something bigger," I pointed out as he examined my expression.

He nodded slowly, seeming to decide to not push right now. I appreciated it, because he had no idea how tempting it was to do exactly that. To let them handle it and to hide away in my metaphorical bubble.

"I have quite a few questions myself," he admitted and then shook his head. "See what happens when I ditch out for a bit? Those idiots get involved with the FBI."

A giggle slipped out as he smiled further, smoothing his fingers over my hair. I let out a small groan of frustration. "I don't even know where to start, Stratton. I feel so over-whelmed."

"I could help distract you," he teased, flashing a charming smile I didn't trust one bit.

"Oh?" I turned into him, my legs hanging off the chair as I ran my fingers over his jaw. "How's that?"

His smile turned wicked. "Probably not nearly as fun as what you are imagining. I was actually thinking that I could teach you some basic self-defense." His confidence faltered slightly as he offered me a more meaningful look. "Only if you want to, angel."

"I love that idea," I assured him, feeling my chest squeeze at the fact that his desire was to take time from his day to teach me to protect myself. I mean... What did I even say to that besides yes? It was incredibly thoughtful.

Stratton let out a satisfied hum before scooping me up and walking across the pool deck, setting me down in the grass. Unfortunately, King's phone and our coffee mugs were abandoned back there, but considering I was so close to Stratton, I figured it was a good trade-off for my lack of caffeine.

The man towered over me, his smile affectionate, as I wondered how we had ever managed to stay away from one another. Well, that had actually been mostly him. I just hoped we would never return back to that. I hoped that he was as much in this as I was. I felt like he was... but you couldn't blame me completely for wanting to wait to make a declaration of love until I had a bit more assurance from him.

Of course there were things outside of our relationship that we still had to work out, from what had been going on with his family to the gangs that were hanging around the fight rings, but I continued to tell myself we had time for that. Time to figure it out. Right now, I was just thankful and happy that he was allowing himself to enjoy this connection between us, one that had always existed from the time that we were young and playing outside all summer. Even though we would argue, it wouldn't stop us from playing from morning until night. It was just the way we worked.

"So how do we start?" I asked curiously, stepping into him as he looked over me, seeming to get caught up on something. He ran a hand over his jaw and let out a small groan of frustration.

"Honestly, I may have made a mistake with this idea. I don't think I'm the right person to try to teach you self-defense," he admitted and shook his head. "Part of me wants to carry your sexy ass back inside and insist you don't need this, and the other part of me wants to pin you to ground until you learn how to fight back."

The pinning to the ground part sounded enjoyable. I voted for that.

I nibbled my lip, getting caught up in my own head as my consciousness snagged on a worrisome thought. "I should learn the basics... I don't want what happened with Ian to happen again. It can't happen again, Stratton. That was far too close."

Talk about admitting my very real fears.

Stratton's eyes darkened as he motioned me forward, his hands coming up to cup my jaw. "You sure? We can wait a bit. I don't want to bring those memories back up."

"I'm fine," I promised. "I will tell you if it's too much."

Before he had a chance to respond, the back door opened and Dermot strode out wearing a fresh pair of jeans and a dark green shirt. He looked absolutely way too good dressed in that color. His eyes filled with interest as he rounded the pool.

"I like that color on you," I chirped, leaning into Stratton. Dermot's eyes lit up with pleasure and his ears heated just a small amount, an endearing reaction that had me falling for the man just a little bit more.

"Thanks, baby girl," he rumbled and then looked at where my sandals were off to the side. "How did the call go?"

"Good." I nodded and added happily, "They are staying there, and now Stratton is going to teach me self-defense. Want to watch?"

Dermot arched his brow and looked at the man over my shoulder. "You think she should learn how to fight?"

He didn't seem opposed to the concept, but it wasn't one that had occurred to him, clearly.

Stratton nodded, his fingers tightening on my waist. "I mean, I'll probably regret it later when she learns how to kick my sorry ass, but she should learn. I don't want another fucker like Ian bothering her."

I couldn't help but smile at the concept of me kicking Stratton's butt. That wasn't even a possibility, but it was sweet that he believed in me that much. I wondered if the man realized just how small I was compared to him?

"Ian shouldn't be a problem anymore," Dermot said vaguely before tilting his head and looking down at me. "I don't disagree, though. Maybe she should learn how to shoot as well."

My eyes widened as I considered what he was saying.

Me? With a firearm? *Oh lord.*

"You want me to learn how to shoot a gun?" I let out the strangled question as Dermot examined my expression, warmth entering his eyes as he offered me what was no doubt supposed to be a comforting look.

"It's not as scary as it sounds, I promise." Dermot stepped closer so that I was captured between the two of them.

"What is the chance of her using that here, though?" Stratton countered as I looked back and forth between the two large men talking above my head. Literally.

You know, it actually didn't surprise me that they got along. I think in some ways they were the most alike out of all my boys. They both tended to stray from the mold of those around them and seemed to purposefully set themselves apart. How they did so was different, and Dermot's was partly because he literally was from a different culture, but it still made an impact.

Then again, I felt like all my men stood out pretty vibrantly against the fairly ordinary background of our small, wealthy, Southern town.

"I am more concerned about the threats outside of Camellia," Dermot hedged as Stratton grunted, seeming to understand what he meant.

"She shouldn't be involved with that shit to begin with." Stratton's voice was laced with something a bit more dangerous. "King knows that."

"Unavoidable at this point," Dermot pointed out, looking frustrated.

"What threats?" I asked bluntly. I may have also been testing this theory about asking questions and getting direct answers.

"The national media has picked the story up, which means not only will there be news trucks here at the gates of Wildberry within the day, but the international media will be notified as well. We may get it taken down, but an heiress to a multi-billion dollar estate being bullied on social media for her appearance and being with multiple men is going to cause a stir no matter what we do. Especially when those men happen to be the sons of families that have a lot of fucking enemies."

Huh? Enemies?

"That is a concise way to put it." I swallowed and pushed, "Why do we have enemies? I mean, who, exactly, has enemies?"

Dermot seemed caught off guard by my question, causing Stratton to laugh, which only made me more confused. The man's voice behind me was filled with authentic amusement. "Yes, Dermot, why would the Ross family have enemies? Why would any of us?"

I really was missing the point here. I could tell.

"King really hasn't told you?" Dermot frowned. "I get why, but fuck is that dangerous."

"Tell me what?" I put my hands on my hips as Stratton tucked me under his chin, amusement still radiating off him as if he found this hilarious.

"We should wait until King is here," Dermot muttered and shook his head. "Ridiculous. Absolutely fucking ridiculous. No matter—we will handle it, baby girl, but you should still know how to keep yourself safe. I can't imagine one of us won't ever be with you, but it would still be a good idea."

I couldn't even be fully frustrated with his lack of answers regarding the Ross family and enemies comment, because two things stood out to me.

One. Dermot and Stratton cared about me enough that they wanted me to be able to keep myself safe. I loved how protective my men were, but the idea that they wanted to go beyond that made me feel valued in a way I never had before. It gave me more confidence in myself, something I needed right now.

Second. The way he was talking made me think he included himself in all of this, which made me ridiculously happy. I hoped I wasn't reading into that too much, but that was how I was thinking he meant it.

"Do you both know how to shoot?" I asked, letting the 'enemies' aspect drop for now. I realized that the concept of my boys being able to use firearms wasn't unfamiliar, which meant that they'd probably talked about it before and I was just having issues pinpointing when that conversation had happened.

"Yeah," Stratton answered as Dermot examined my expression, his own a bit hesitant as if he was worried how I would react to the answer he hadn't given. The man wasn't normally hesitant or cautious, from what I gathered, but when it came to this and the enemies conversation, he seemed both, and I didn't understand why.

"Yes, you could say that," Dermot offered.

"Absolutely not!" Yates called out, walking off of the back porch and towards us.

I rolled my eyes. I had no idea how he had even heard our conversation, but it didn't surprise me when he said, "She doesn't need to know how to do any of that shit, especially shooting. Absolutely fucking not. That is way too dangerous."

His reasoning was ridiculous, and I almost smiled because at least this version of Yates was a bit more familiar. I broke away from the other two, popping my hip and crossing my arms at his insanity.

"How do you even know what we are talking about, you looney?"

"He's a creep, that's why." Stratton chuckled softly as Dermot flashed a smile at him, the two of them seeming to be laughing at an inside joke. One I very much wished to be part of, for the record.

"I know everything, bunny," Yates pointed out vaguely before reaching us and tugging me forward so I melted into his hard chest. "She doesn't need to learn how to fight or shoot. That's not her goddamn job. It's ours."

"Yates," I sighed, letting my head fall back and watching the man with slight amusement, realizing he was annoyed as all get-out with the other two.

"Fucking ridiculous," he growled and then looked back down at me. "How was the call with your mom?"

The change in his tone was almost instant, and I saw from the corner of my eye Stratton throw his arms up in defeat, muttering curses. I understood his frustration, but I also understood how to deal with Yates better than most people.

"Good," I answered before adding firmly, "But more importantly, I have decided that Dermot and Stratton are correct. I need to learn how to defend myself."

Yates's gaze darkened. "No. Not your job."

He seemed almost—no, definitely—offended by the notion of me learning how to defend myself. Clearly, he very much considered it 'not my job,' which made me wonder whose job it was, in his mind.

The back door opened again, and I looked over to watch King making his way towards us. I groaned.

"King, tell Yates to stop being an overcontrolling jerk."

"It's barely nine, how the hell did you manage to piss her off already?" King asked, looking relatively impressed. Although 'pissed' was a bit of an overstatement considering I was still curled into Yates's large chest and his hand was running up and down my back in a soothing motion that didn't match our argument.

See? We could still totally be enemies, verbally at least. Physically, we were going to be a bit less enemy-ish. Maybe enemies with benefits? Sounded promising to me, maybe I should ask him his thoughts on it...

"She wants to learn how to fight and fucking shoot," Yates growled, looking horrified. My lips pressed into a smile at his dramatic outburst. I had to admit, I was a bit glad that King seemed back to his controlled, normal self and Yates was back to being a temperamental jerk. It made me feel a bit more centered. I think Stratton and Dermot both agreed, because they were watching all of this with amusement.

I knew Yates was serious, but I also had been through enough of his 'absolutely not' moments that I'd long ago stopped taking them so seriously. Did that mean I would get my way? Debatable, and depended on how much he was actually against it.

For example, whenever I would go on a date, I would have to manage to keep it a secret, because the one time I told him about one during freshman year it had been such an 'absolutely not' conversation that he had followed me around Wildberry all day until I relented and decided to not go. I mean, Christ, I hadn't even been able to take a shower to get ready because he'd made himself right at home leaning on the bathroom counter.

He had told me I could shower with him there if I was that determined to go, and turns out I was a bit of a chicken because I had given in at that point. I suppose it was good I hadn't gone, because Tyler ended up being a total jerk. He was another one that now hung out with the Brooks twins, signaling exactly what type of person he was, and it wasn't one I wanted to know.

King arched his brow. "Is that true, princess?"

"I think it may be a good idea," I confirmed. "Dermot brought up the point that there would be a lot of attention on me in the media because of everything going on, which could be dangerous, and Stratton wants to teach me some self-defense, just in case something like what happened with Ian ever happens—"

"Please don't." King inhaled sharply, his eyes flashing dark as he seemed to try to shake off whatever my words had conjured. Honestly, the man flipped through his emotional rolodex so fast it was impressive. I think I had just ignored that aspect of his personality most of my life because the intensity of it hadn't been something I was ready for. It should have scared me, but it did everything but.

Yates tightened his grip on me and buried his nose in my

hair, his heart beating a bit faster than before. Was that in response to my comment about Ian?

"I just think it may be worth it," I added softly, not wanting to send King down whatever emotional road he seemed to be pulling himself back from. I had never seen King's temper, not fully, but I had heard rumors about it, and I didn't want him getting that worked up about something that was over.

Ian was no longer anywhere near Wildberry. He couldn't touch me.

"We can't leave her defenseless," Stratton spoke up, his voice edged in authentic concern. "We're good, King, but we aren't perfect."

Yates let out a dangerous sound as I smoothed a hand over his chest, silencing it. Yep. I had been right. He was very much offended at the notion that I would need to protect myself, which meant that... he thought he was supposed to protect me? That was flattering. It was also fairly accurate, considering how he had handled Ian.

"King." Dermot pulled his attention from the look he was sharing with Stratton. "*Really* think about all the attention this is going to bring to her."

"That's not including the apparent enemies that we have that I had no idea about," I chirped.

Dermot's lips twitched as King's head snapped towards me, his eyes flaring with curiosity and concern.

"What?"

"Enemies." I shrugged. "Dermot said we have enemies."

King growled and looked at Dermot. "Seriously?"

"How the bloody hell was I supposed to know that you haven't told her yet?! You have literally been around her your entire life, and you just haven't told her what it is our family does? There is no fucking way I would have known that."

"I would very much like to know what you guys are

talking about," I pointed out as Yates flashed an amused smile at my prim tone. "Enemies sound bad, and King, you keeping a secret from me sounds even worse."

"Damn it," King hissed, his eyes narrowing on Dermot. "If she's pissed at me, you're fucked."

Dermot chuckled, looking very unconcerned with King's threat, as I looked between the two of them. I stared at King until he looked back at me and offered a semi-guilty expression, running a hand through his hair.

King, guilty? This had to be good. Honestly, I should have been more worried, but besides the guys dating someone else, there weren't many secrets that would upset me.

"So..." I prompted.

"Inside," he grunted. "I'll explain inside. As for the other stuff, we should at least look into it."

Yates let out a low snarl, annoyed again, as he broke away from me and stormed towards the house. I rolled my eyes at his antics as King appeared in front of me. I sighed into him as his hand slid around the base of my throat, his thumb running over my pulse point as his other arm wound around my waist in a tight, comfortable hold. I could hear Stratton and Dermot talking, but honestly, I couldn't focus past the way King was examining my face, looking for something. I shivered as his thumb brushed over my pulse again and again, making me blush.

"Don't worry about Yates, he just doesn't want to have to consider the idea of you in danger," King admitted and then groaned as if thinking about something.

"What?" I questioned, going up on my toes to brush my lips over his.

"I just hadn't planned on telling you all this shit about my family until later." His jaw clenched as his eyes darted down to my lips in thought. "Preferably after you were already stuck with me forever."

I blinked and then tilted my head. "Stuck with you forever?"

I liked the sound of that.

"Yeah, marriage, stuck with me forever, something like that," he mused as my eyes widened, his thoughts already elsewhere. "But now I have to tell you, because if I don't, your beautiful head is going to make it far worse than it actually is, which is impressive on its own. So hopefully it won't freak you out too much, at least not enough that you would try to run, not that I would ever let you—"

I kissed King to stop his tangent of vulnerability. I so rarely saw it, and while it was sweet and a bit psychotic, I was worried he was working himself up over nothing. I pulled back as he stared at me with dark eyes and let out a frustrated exhale.

"King," I said as I cupped his jaw, "you're acting crazy. As long as you don't tell me that you are going to marry or sleep with some other woman or love someone else besides me, the chances of it actually upsetting me are pretty low."

King blinked. "Why the fuck would I ever be with anyone but you?"

"Not the point, but very flattering." I smiled, my face heating again.

"Alright," he grunted. "Inside then. We can figure out this shooting thing also—"

"Let's give it a day," I hedged. "Give everyone a chance to get used to the idea."

And by 'everyone,' I meant Yates.

"I need more coffee!" I insisted, turning towards my empty mug. I grabbed it and planned to head inside, considering how many questions I had now added to my list. I pointed towards King's phone as he offered me a head nod in understanding of where it was, his conversation with Dermot seeming to amuse Stratton greatly. I walked towards the house, up the back porch steps, and into the kitchen.

I paused only momentarily, finding Sterling and Lincoln sitting at the breakfast table, a full spread of fruit and breakfast foods laid out in front of them. The sight had the back of my neck heating in embarrassment.

There was no reason for it—it wasn't like they were going to naturally associate food with my problem—but that was what instantly came to mind when I'd seen it.

I poured myself a cup of coffee and sat down casually, trying to not feel like anyone was hyperfocusing on my behavior towards the food on the table in front of me. I knew I had yet to fully confirm the issue to them, but after yesterday, I felt raw and exposed. I wished I had the ability to read their minds, just so I knew what they thought. How they were viewing the situation.

"What is Yates so pissed about?" Lincoln asked, nodding towards the office where Yates was bent over and writing something, indeed looking very grumpy.

"Says it's not my job to learn how to defend myself." I shrugged.

Lincoln flashed a smile, shaking his head as he scrolled through what appeared to be a real estate website on his laptop. Sterling slid a plate of food towards me before he got up and went to grab another cup of coffee, humming a Red Hot Chili Peppers song. It was oddly soothing, but it didn't help the anxiety that rocked through me as I stared at the bagel and fruit on the plate in front of me. I could easily count the calories of this meal and last night's pasta, creating a number that had me feeling nauseous.

I had read an article recently about spotting signs of your friend or family member focusing too much on their weight or having unhealthy eating habits. One of the 'signs' was the overdependence on a calorie counter app. I think that alone had made me realize how bad it had gotten, despite not being able to admit it at the time.

I didn't need an app anymore, though. I knew obsessively how many calories the food I came in contact with contained, and I had a running total in my head constantly, including everything from the five calories that a lemonade packet had in it to the seventy-four calories in the bowl of soup I ate for lunch. Everything was accounted for obsessively, and when I didn't know the amount? I estimated up in value.

It was consuming, this habit. This problem. It consumed everything.

That was the only way I could describe it. It consumed every moment and event. I judged days based on how 'good' of an eating day it was. When considering what to eat, I thought about how I would look in an outfit I planned to wear to events a week away. It was exhausting, and I had absolutely no idea how to adjust my mindset about it.

It was an impossible feat. I was almost positive about that.

"Breathe, Dahlia," Lincoln instructed quietly.

My gaze moved over to him, realizing I'd been staring at the plate. I blushed bright pink and opened my mouth to come up with some reason for acting so weird, but the amazing man simply squeezed my leg and turned his laptop towards me, changing the conversation and allowing me to relax and gather myself.

"That's gorgeous." I pointed at the property on his laptop.

So I wouldn't say that I had a thing for purchasing vacation properties because I had never personally done it, but I did love looking at options when I was bored. And when my parents started shopping around, which they did about every other year? I was always happily part of the process. I popped a grape into my mouth as Lincoln began to show me pictures of the stunning garden estate on the screen. I looked down, noting that it was somewhere in Ardara, Ireland.

The place was made of gorgeous grey and black stone surrounded by thick green fields and a long winding road that seemed to be the only way to access it. The front and back of the property featured large gardens blooming with flowers, and behind it was a mass of dark trees that clearly marked the start of a forested region. I found myself more intrigued by each picture as I realized the place had been redone but kept to appear the same way it had looked when it had originally been built. My smile grew at the dark wood furnishings, large stone fireplaces, and stunning classic art that hung on the walls. I could imagine myself drinking tea and watching the rainy weather while reading in front of the fireplace. It was almost storybook perfect, and I found myself wanting to visit terribly.

"What is this?" I asked finally.

"Yates sent it to me yesterday sometime, I think." He frowned as if unsure of the timing, which I didn't blame him for, considering how crazy everything had been. "He thinks it may be a good purchase and wants our parents to check it out while they travel."

I ate two more grapes, realizing I felt far more relaxed now that I didn't feel as though they were waiting for me to eat. "Good purchase for..."

"A vacation home," Sterling answered, sitting down.

"For Yates?"

"No, for us." Sterling flashed a smile. "All of us."

"We are buying houses together now?" I mused, my smile growing.

King walked in, followed by Dermot and Stratton. Lincoln let out a chuckle at King's eyes flashing over the property on the screen.

"Dahlia just asked if we are now purchasing properties together." Lincoln pointed the comment towards King.

"What the fuck is with everyone busting my balls today?" King grunted as he walked into the office... Well, he started to before turning back and scooping me up. I wrapped my arms around him, very curious about how Lincoln's question was 'busting his balls.' Something that sounded very unpleasant, for the record.

"What are we doing?" I asked as he set me on the edge of the desk and began to pace in front of it. Yates's hand instantly shot out to intertwine with mine, which rested on the wood surface.

"You are about to get all the answers you want and some you very much don't want, probably," he muttered.

I smiled. *Perfect.*

Chapter Five

KINGSTON ROSS

Dahlia's eyes followed me as I paced in front of her, attempting to figure out where the hell to start. I knew the others were spread through the office and the kitchen, trying to give us some space so she didn't feel completely overwhelmed by the questions I would be asking in return to hers, but they were still paying attention. Yates wasn't even pretending to work, his amusement clear on his face as I tried to figure out a way to not dig myself a deeper hole.

How the fuck did I explain to the woman that I loved that most of the men in her life not only had enemies but were probably constantly on the verge of legal armageddon because my family had an extensive history as the leaders of one of the UK's top crime syndicates? There really wasn't an *easy* way to handle this, and I knew I just needed to be blunt, but I was wondering if there was an *easier* way to handle all of this. A softer approach. Honestly, even her witnessing some of the shit that had happened this summer would have been easier, because then she could decide whether or not she thought I was a monster still worth loving.

I didn't regret the shit I had done or would continue to

do, especially to keep her safe, but I didn't want Dahlia to ever fear me. That concept alone was enough to make me sick, which was amusing since I took pleasure in everyone outside of Wildberry Lane being terrified of me.

"King." Dahlia's soft voice instantly had my cock jumping to goddamn attention as I faced her, walking towards the desk and fixing her with a look while caging her between my arms. Her stunning green and gold eyes stared back at me with affection as I examined the way her dark hair laid with a slight wave on her delicate shoulders. The woman was dressed to look nearly fucking edible today, and I'd have absolutely no problem laying her flat on this desk and eating her out, whether people were around or not.

In fact, I would have preferred that over having to explain myself. Not because I didn't want her to know, either. No. I very much wanted Dahlia to be aware of what my life would consist of now and in the future, because she would be part of it.

The difference was that I had to explain why I hadn't told her before now, and the only reasoning was a shit excuse. It was the truth, but it was shit. I hadn't been lying, I had hoped to wait to tell her until I had tied us together more. But now that wasn't an option, and I just had to hope like hell it wouldn't upset or scare her. I didn't want to have to show her the extent I would go to keep her in my life. It was enough that she would find out all too soon how mental Yates was, and I didn't need to add to that.

"It may be easier if you ask the questions and I answer them," I suggested as Yates sat back in the office chair, shooting me a smile and looking way too fucking relaxed.

That's fine. I would find a way to turn this shit on him, and then he would have to explain how exactly he knew so much about what Dahlia was doing and when. Asshole.

"Okay." She nodded and grabbed Yates's coffee mug and

took a sip. He scowled at her, causing a reactionary smile before she looked back at me. I arched a brow at him, knowing she would never see that coffee mug again.

"So, the boxes..." She looked around the room. "Those contain information on everyone in town, along with the electronic files? And you are looking through those, why?"

Thank fuck, that answer was easy enough.

"When the FBI contacted us, we thought they would just want the information we had, but now that they think that Mr. Brooks is possibly working for Glenn, they wanted us to do a review to see if there was anything we could find to connect him to that," I explained simply.

"And did you find anything?"

"Not yet," I admitted. "Besides the fact that he has a ridiculous amount of prescriptions at the pharmacy in town, I don't see a lot of similarities."

"What if he is selling the medicine from the pharmacist?" she asked curiously.

"The amount of drugs being pushed around is far past that, although I have no doubt that is contributing to the problem," I conceded.

"Okay, and the FBI, who is your contact for that?"

"Callum. He was one of the men with India Lexington," I pointed out. Her eyes lightened at that, seemingly happy with my answer. Good. I would gladly give her any fucking answer she wanted to make her smile like that. Especially to soften her for the information she would eventually ask for as well. The not so easy part.

"And why did the FBI contact all of you instead of our parents?"

Yates nodded, seemingly happy with her line of questioning.

It didn't surprise me in the least that Dahlia had started

putting all of this together. I knew last night she had been a bit out of it, but this was the real Dahlia. This was my princess who was always going in a million different directions and put shit together faster than anyone I knew. I both loved and appreciated that quality, because while she had been sheltered most of her life, what was coming was going to be something far different than usual, and it was going to be necessary for her to adapt. I wouldn't risk her safety any longer, and I knew her staying ignorant of what was going on was doing that.

I just assumed we'd have more time.

"Because with the exception of my father, it is far easier for the others to stay out of this shit if they can. It comes with too many legal ramifications if it gets messy," I explained, knowing where her question would go next.

"Why is it different for your father?"

"Because he doesn't care about shit like that," I explained. "And neither do we, frankly."

Her nod was slow as she processed what I was saying, and instead of pushing, she asked another question regarding the investigation.

"And we think that Mr. Brooks is at the center of this? Why?"

"They haven't explained fully," I admitted, "but yes, they think he is essentially conducting Glenn's business while he plays puppet master."

"How bad is the drug problem?" she asked softly, her eyes filling with concern. My chest tightened, not positive she actually wanted to know.

Dahlia had a soft heart and was consistently considering those in Camellia as an extension of our family. They weren't, but I had never wanted to burst that bubble. She had also saved several lives that she wasn't even aware of when she'd forgiven them for stupid or mean shit they'd said. They should be fucking thankful for her. Praising her. Worshipping her... nevermind, that was our job.

"Bad enough it was put on the FBI's radar." I pressed a kiss to her shoulder as she nodded, seeming to understand what I was implying. If she knew just how bad it was—the money being tossed around and the amount of people that had overdosed in this past summer alone—she would have been shocked.

"Wow," she murmured, looking distraught. "This is just so insane."

I squeezed her hand. "I know you are easing into talking about it, Dahlia, but there is a very real chance that Abby's bullying is connected. With the power our families hold in this town, its possible that she was told to target you in order to cause a distraction for all of us so they could do whatever the fuck it is they have been doing."

Like expanding an ever-growing problem. Fucking ridiculous. It wasn't like a drug epidemic needed help spreading... unfortunately, it did so successfully on its own.

Her eyes darkened as she spoke, her voice low and sad. "I don't have proof it was her. It's just a gut feeling."

"It was her," Yates chimed in. "I don't need proof to tell you it was her."

Dahlia looked back at him and shook her head. "It feels wrong to accuse her of something I don't have evidence of."

Yates blinked at her and then ran a hand over his face. "You are way too sweet, Dahlia. That woman is a goddamn monster."

"She's not great," Dahlia admitted and then winced. "Honestly, my head still hurts from what she did at the club Saturday."

Everything inside of me froze as I processed what she was saying, and Yates stood and offered her a confused look. I was glad he could ask questions, because I was working at keeping my anger in check in preparation of whatever the hell she was about to tell me.

I'd always had a temper. Well, 'temper' makes it sound normal, and it was anything but. It was fairly rare that something pushed me to the point of being legitimately furious, but when it did, I had what was easiest described as black-out rages. I'd been close to one this previous Saturday with Greg but had managed to maintain some level of sanity by shutting down those emotions after beating the shit out of him.

There were times, though, when nothing I did helped, and this summer that exact thing had happened when one of the men that my father had led for years decided to attempt to sell us out to the police. Which was ridiculous and showed his inexperience, since in the town of Ardara we had all of the police on payroll. But it had been enough that I'd lost it, furious he would not only betray us but also put my family in danger.

I'd snapped out of it hours later, covered in blood, seeing fear in most of the other men's eyes. Considering I'd brutalized the man in question, it was understandable. I'd nearly killed him, but Dermot had pulled me back. I don't know what happened to the man, but if I saw him again, I would probably follow through and end his life.

Yates's voice was demanding. "Why does your head hurt?"

Dahlia seemed to realize her mistake, her eyes going wide as she looked between us. "We just had a bit of an altercation."

I was going to lose it. Sweet christ. I put my head down, my knuckles turning white on the desk as I considered how anyone in their fucking right mind thought they could put a hand on Dahlia in any way, shape, or form, let alone in a violent manner. I had managed to keep my black-out rages under wraps around her, but the idea of anyone hurting Dahlia sent me absolutely reeling.

"What did she do?" Yates demanded.

"She pulled my hair." Dahlia waved him off and refocused back on me, her flushed cheeks betraying her nervousness.

I stood up and began to pace again, needing to keep myself moving so I didn't go and seek retribution for what happened. I wasn't one to ever enact violence on a woman, but I would find a way to make Abby Brooks pay for hurting Dahlia, and not just for the physical attack. I would find a way to absolutely destroy her until she was suffering more than she could have ever conceived.

Dahlia had no idea how close I was to losing it. I always knew when I was at that point because my grip on reality became tentative at best, and my skin got cold like it was now.

I let out a slow exhale and figured I would move to a different topic, especially since Yates had immediately begun tapping on his laptop, presumably checking the cameras at the club for that day. We would know exactly what happened soon enough.

"When Max confronted you at the courts..." I cleared my throat, shaking myself so I could continue my question. "When Max confronted you at the courts, what did he say, exactly?"

"He said that you were all hiding stuff from me," she explained softly, the hurt in her voice slaughtering me and rendering me useless for a moment, extinguishing my temper. The idea of hurting her in any way left me feeling like absolute dirt. It was why I needed to come clean about everything, including my family.

I moved forward and cupped her jaw. "I only kept it from you because I didn't want you to get involved with the FBI."

Examining my expression for truth, she nodded. "Can I be helpful though, King? Now that I know, there has to be something I can do."

I grunted, knowing that Callum would absolutely love to hear more about her interactions with Abby, especially now that it had gained so much media attention.

"Unfortunately, now that it has gotten so large, there is probably no avoiding it. They are going to want to talk to you."

"Good, then we can do this together." Her eyes were filled with a determination that I found far too sexy.

Then again, this was Dahlia. Everything the woman did turned me on.

She continued, "When should we meet with them?"

I looked at Yates, and he offered me a head nod, letting me know he would set it up. "Yates will contact them and ask." After he located the video he was searching for, no doubt.

Dahlia frowned, her eyes getting a distant glaze to them before snapping back to me. "How bad is the media going to be?"

"There are already local news vans outside the gates," Yates muttered. Her eyes went wide, and I nearly hit him for upsetting her.

I squeezed her hand. "Security will keep them away, and we will just lay low for a bit until they get bored."

"King, why did Dermot think national attention would cause a safety issue for me? What enemies was he talking about?" Her question was soft as she watched my reaction, almost worried about asking.

I hated that. She should feel comfortable asking me anything, even if I was shit at explaining.

An idea struck me.

"Yates, set up that meeting with Callum," I instructed. "I'm running by my place with Dahlia. I want to show her something."

Yates nodded, and I took Dahlia's hand, sharing a look

with the others as I walked towards her front foyer. I knew that I was taking the easy way out in a way, because showing her this was in some ways far easier than explaining it, and at the same time I had a feeling it would probably make it far more real.

Dahlia let out a happy hum as I opened the front door, but it was quickly cut off as her eyes jumped to the gates.

A 'few' trucks my ass.

Fuck.

I shook my head, glad security had put up blockers and forced them back a good amount, but they were still there. Visible enough to be a bother.

I kept her tucked into my side, opposite of the gates, as I led her towards my property. I tried to not think about the overwhelming urge I had to lock her in my house and keep her there forever. It wasn't a healthy or rational thought, but it would keep her safe, and right now that was a major concern of mine.

Dermot wasn't wrong. Dahlia was about to become a large target for most of our enemies, and there wasn't a damn thing we could do about it. Well, besides making it very clear that she was under Ross family protection. There would still be those that attempted to hurt her, and all of them would end up dead.

My lips pressed up slightly, thinking about an incident this summer when I proved just how far I would go to make sure someone respected Dahlia.

"Please!" The hoarse, exhausted voice cracked as I smirked at the clear pain there. Pain that was well deserved in my mind.

"Please what?" I asked curiously from where I sat comfortable in a leather armchair, looking over his half slumped over and bloody form in the wood chair across from me. The binding used to

tie him to the chair was blood-soaked, and his eyes were both swollen shut.

"I'm sorry, I didn't know." His thick Irish accent slurred as Dermot handed me a drink from the bar in the back of the room. The other men in the room were quiet and watching from the walls, silence filled with fear permeating from all directions.

"You didn't know that the woman you were talking about was important to me?" I taunted, knowing it was bullshit. It may have been old-fashioned, but not many people kept photos of unimportant people in their goddamn wallet. I loved the photo I had of Dahlia in there. It was from that previous spring during a weekend trip we took into Savannah. Her smile in it was fucking glorious, and this asshole had not only tried to call into question my authority today, but then made a crude comment about her.

"I just assumed it was some girl you were fuc—"

My fist collided with the side of his head, hating the way he thought he could reference her. Honestly, even if the others weren't watching and I wasn't proving a point, I still would have beat the fuck out of him.

Leaning down, I gripped his hair and spoke softly. "You don't ever fucking talk about her, and when you see her, when she comes here, which she will, you better not fucking look at her, or else I'll remove your other eye while I'm at it."

"My other eye?" His voice was broken as I looked to Dermot, his grin growing as he tossed me the tool I needed.

"Yeah, the other one."

By the end of the night, I had made it clear the respect that Dahlia would be served. All too soon she would need to meet them, though I expected Danny and his one fucking eye to not meet her gaze or else I would make good on my promise. Piece of shit. He had been one of a few that had an issue with me starting to take my father's place. I knew there would be problems since he had stepped back a bit in the past few years, but I planned on doing nothing of the sort. Rather the opposite.

Which was exactly why she needed to know everything. Because Dahlia may be my princess, but she was going to become the Queen of an entire criminal enterprise she wasn't even aware existed.

I just prayed she wouldn't hate me too much for keeping it from her. I would probably burn everything to the fucking ground if I ever felt like there was a chance of losing my small piece of heaven in this atrocious grouping of individuals that we called humanity. Just one more reason I was so protective over my family and her.

"What are you showing me?" she finally asked as we entered into my family's home, the warm decor and soft hues highlighting Dahlia's natural beauty. The woman seemed impossibly more beautiful every single day, and it was enough to drive a man insane. It was getting particularly harder now that Dahlia knew we had feelings for her, knew that she had a little bit of a hold over us, because I could see that coy side in her coming out. The one that was so fucking addictive that she had no idea. If she only realized how drastic her affect on us actually was, she would probably be terrified.

She would also probably hate how much power she held, because she was like that.

Honestly, right now I was just thankful she had accepted the notion that we all wanted to be with her. That was the hurdle I had been most worried about, but she had seemed to accept it easily, probably because she felt what was so clear and obvious to everyone else. How natural it was that the seven of us would be together. Even my cousin, who had been a bit unexpected, but honestly unsurprising.

I should have realized how much Dahlia would have affected him, especially since he and I shared so many similar personality traits. Ones that were a bit obsessively focused on the things we cared about, and in this case, the small pixie-like woman holding my hand with trust as I walked her towards the den of Ross family secrets.

"Something that will make explaining all of this far easier," I said quietly in response. It would also probably make her realize how dangerous it was, exactly, to be involved with the Ross family. Although it was far too late to change that.

As we neared the door of my father's office, I stopped and turned towards her, looking down at her soft, expressive features. I ran my fingers down her throat and inhaled, feeling her pulse and loving the connection it provided me to her emotions, to her thoughts and feelings, even if I couldn't know them exactly. That wasn't even including the overwhelming urge I had to bite down on her pulse, to mark that spot as mine. Such a fundamental part of keeping her alive, and I wanted to mark it as mine, tattoo my name on it like she had branded my heart so long ago.

"I love you," I reminded her and seared my lips to hers in a demanding kiss. Instantly she softened against me, and I found myself pressing her up against the doorway of the office, loving the feeling of her trapped between myself and the wall. The urge to dominate Dahlia ran through me like goddamn wildfire, and I promised myself that after I explained everything, I would finally give into this fully.

I had only ever wanted Dahlia. I had thought something was wrong with me for some time because I didn't find anyone besides Dahlia attractive, but now I knew that my obsession with her only allowed enough space in my heart and head for her.

Which was exactly why I wasn't going to feel bad about letting loose and showing her just how much I've needed her, wanting her from afar for so long.

After all, she was the one who inspired this. It was only fair.

When I pulled back, I immediately opened up the door to my father's office and led her through the dark space, ignoring the neat bookshelves and large, empty desk that faced two large, empty chairs. The entire space smelled of cigars, and I knew the smell would only grow as we entered the next room.

I came to a bookshelf along the back and pulled out a copy of a dark green book with gold lettering that spelled out our last name. Immediately, a nearly silent puff of air sounded as the air seal released, allowing the bookshelf to move back enough that we could step through and to the side, into a hallway.

Dahlia made a confused noise, but when I looked over at her, she not only seemed curious but excited, making me nearly smile. How was this woman so perfect? I take her into my father's dark office and down a hallway on the other side of a concealed doorway, and she's excited. Not scared, cautious, or hesitant, any of which would be acceptable... no, she was excited.

Perfection. This woman was perfect.

The hall was silent and dark as the door behind us closed. Our footsteps were loud, and when we reached another door, I pressed my hand against it, the keypad lighting up as I made a mental note to program her hand in it so that she could always reach this room if needed. It wasn't made to be a safe room, but in the case of an emergency, it would work perfectly, and that was more than enough reason for me.

As the door opened, her eyes went wide, and I let out a small sigh of relief. Now I didn't have a fucking choice. Now she would know, and there was something liberating about that.

When I was younger, my father hadn't let me tell her

because it was too serious for someone who wasn't forced to deal with it, in his mind. Especially someone as sweet as Dahlia. As we had gotten older, I had made the active choice to not tell her because I didn't want to scare her away. But now that was over.

"King..." Her voice was edged in curiosity and hesitancy.

"You wanted to know why the Ross family has enemies?" I asked softly, my lips pressed to her head as she stepped in front of me. "*This* is why."

Chapter Six

DAHLIA ALDRIDGE

I thought I knew every single corner of Wildberry Lane. I had been mistaken.

I hadn't been given the memo on the secret door in the Ross family office that led to... well, whatever in the lord's name this was. It appeared to be a mix between a weapons vault, a command center, and an information storage center. Except really large, and rather comfortable and cozy.

I knew that was probably an odd way of viewing it, but everything from the dark wood floors to the navy walls brought a sense of warmth that greatly contrasted the contents of the actual room. My gaze tracked across the space, starting with the large seating area of leather couches in front of me, seemingly set up for conversation, to the large oval conference table behind that, followed by a dark, imposing desk. At the far end of the massive rectangular room was a large glass-enclosed area that seemed to be split, consisting on one side of enough weapons to militarize our entire town and the other showcasing so many screens that I was convinced they had to be monitoring every street in the freakin' place. *Was that possible?*

Somehow I was gathering I may be closer to the truth than one would assume.

I looked up at King, his expression one of curiosity regarding my reaction, no doubt, along with a vulnerability that I didn't see very often. Of course, growing up together, I'd seen it before, but in the past few years King had grown to have a harder edge, so it was a bit jarring. It also made me nervous, because if he was worried about what he had to tell me, it probably meant I should be worried.

Unfortunately, I was still having difficulty trying to figure out what exactly he was concerned about. Was it that this room existed? That they had a ridiculous amount of weapons? That their family crest seemed to be embroidered or branded on everything in this room? Something that I loved, because it was actually a very cool crest. I just wasn't seeing it clearly... well, except for the fact that I now knew King was cool with the concept of putting secret doors and passageways in a future house.

I nearly smiled at that thought, loving the concept of living with any of my guys... or maybe all of them.

"So, your family likes secret passageways and weapons? And you have really good security? I'm having issues seeing the problem, King," I admitted as he offered me a small smile, motioning for me to follow him across the room towards the desk. Before I could take his hand, I came to a stop, the photographs hanging on the walls catching my eye.

"Holy moly," I mumbled, "is this..."

"Yes," King mused.

I walked down the line of photographs, the consistent figure of a Ross family member in each. First a man I had to assume was his great grandfather, then his grandfather, followed by his father. Each and every one was accented, though, by a political figure, from US Presidents to foreign royalty. Underneath each picture was the date and event, making me realize that King's father had been very busy the past few years considering the amount of pictures that he had. I knew my parents had met some really interesting and important figures while traveling, but this was something else. In almost all of them, it felt like the important figurehead was eager to meet Mr. Ross and not the other way around, at least from what I could read from their body language.

"So the international shipping business makes you popular. Noted," I mumbled.

King chuckled softly, the sound making my skin break out into shivers as I turned towards him, finding him leaning against the edge of the desk, his arms crossed over his muscular chest distracting me momentarily. Honestly though, I was thankful I trusted and loved this man so much, because sometimes he looked very intimidating. I mean, right now, despite the chuckle, there was no humor in his features and his energy felt dark, almost in response to the room. I didn't know what to make of it as I walked over.

"Why?" I asked softly. Both in reference to the enemies question and, more importantly, the reason we were here.

"Because the Ross family has had political ties internationally for generations." He grabbed my wrist and gently tugged me towards him.

"Because of the family business?"

"No," King leveled. "Well, in a way, yes, but not for shipping. Not really."

"King, you are making me nervous." I wrapped my arms around his neck as his fingers slid over my waist. "I need you to just tell me why we are here. I mean, it's fascinating, but I can tell you aren't saying something."

"It's not *what* I have to tell you as much as your reaction to it that concerns me," he grunted, looking down at my expression thoughtfully. "I'm also worried you're going to be upset that I didn't tell you before this."

"I'm getting far more upset with the vague responses," I leveled. "Have a little faith in me, I can handle it."

"I have no doubt of that," he amended. "I just don't want to change how you view me. I've never had an issue explaining this, and now I find myself legitimately worried it could cause you to walk away."

"Hey," I reared back, "don't say that."

The man seemed to consider something for a moment before letting out an exhale and explaining exactly what was on his mind, blowing mine in the process. I was almost positive that this was what the kids referred to as a 'mind fuck.'

See? Who said that I was severely lacking in my ability to connect with my own generation because I was sheltered and surrounded by mostly adults? Clearly that wasn't the case.

"The international shipping business is our legal cover for what we actually do. For generations now, nearly two hundred years and counting, our family has led the top crime syndicate in the United Kingdom, especially in Ireland. We have an empire of resources that stretches into almost every legal and illegal avenue of international government and trade."

Oh.

"Crime syndicate like the mafia? The mob? Like *The Godfather*?"

Did I really just relate this man's serious wording to a movie? *Christ.*

His lip twitched. "Not extremely accurate for comparison, but essentially, yes."

"So you're telling me that the Ross family is part of the Irish Mafia?"

"We are one of the families that rule over the criminal underworld, correct." His voice was smooth while running over my pulse. His words should have sounded ridiculous or made me laugh, but instead I felt a chill roll down my spine, realizing just how serious he was. I inhaled and then nodded in understanding, a few things fitting together for me.

"Well, that would make sense why you have enemies then."

Surprise coated King's face as he shook his head. "I shouldn't be surprised by how you are reacting, but I am. I'm really fucking surprised. I'm also concerned about why you aren't mad that I didn't tell you sooner."

"How did you want me to react?" I questioned softly.

He ran a hand over his jaw and frowned. "You realize what comes with this lifestyle, right? You understand what this means? For us? I can't avoid this life, Dahlia and I am not giving you up. I'm selfish when it comes to you."

I cupped his jaw, understanding in part why he was concerned. "I wouldn't want to avoid this lifestyle, King. If it's part of yours, it's part of mine. I'm upset a bit that you didn't tell me, but I imagine you had a good reason... I think we've been keeping a lot of secrets lately, but we are clearing that up. I trust you. I've always trusted you; that won't change. The fact that you are telling me all of this right now proves my reasoning to."

King let out a low rumble. "I love hearing that you trust me, you have no idea. I want to keep your trust, Dahlia, which is why you have to understand just how bad all of this is. Okay?"

"I'm listening," I promised, leaning into him.

"Our family conducts illegal trade all across the world, so I suppose we do, in fact, do international shipping, but that is mostly a cover and makes it convenient to move things back and forth. We work with other families like our own and government institutions that aren't afraid to get their hands dirty, which are unsurprisingly most of them. Some of the families and groups we work with, though, are far worse than us, and that is what I hate touching you in any way. I know they will have gotten wind of you already by now, and I know they are going to realize how important you are to not just me, but all of us. There is nothing I can do about that, but the idea of someone targeting you makes me see fucking red, princess."

I ran a hand over his jaw in a soothing motion. "How bad are these other families?"

"Each family seems to draw the line somewhere," King began. "We don't fuck with anything relating to human trafficking or sex trade. But some of the people we work with do exactly that, and while we try to avoid associating ourselves with them, it's somewhat impossible. We are all stained and our hands are covered in blood; the only difference is your poison. Ours happens to be large international gambling circuits and weapons."

I hadn't considered what crimes their family would be involved in, but I felt instant relief to hear it was weapons and gambling. Don't get me wrong, obviously none of it was good, but I would take that over sex work or human trafficking.

Christ. Talk about a reality check about how the real world worked.

"Gambling circuits?" I asked softly.

"Fixing large-scale events and the like." He smirked. "That part is more fun than anything."

I narrowed my eyes in thought, "Does that have anything to do with why you took a sudden interest in race horses two years ago?"

King's smile grew. "Maybe."

"And that's the reason why we went to Dubai that one year?"

"Yes," he answered seriously before adding, "We had fun though."

We had, and I totally had thought that it was weird that he was suddenly into horse racing, but now it made much more sense. I nearly swallowed at that, realizing how much money we were talking about. The grand prize had been upwards of thirty-five million... I mean, that was insane, even to me.

"So why did the FBI reach out then? Why would they be willing to work with you?" It was the one aspect of this that was still confusing me.

"We have information on everyone, not just the people in this town, and the American government knows that." He shrugged. "I'm sure it's a case of 'keeping your enemies closer,' but to go against the Ross family would be suicide. Not only do we have information on all of their backdoor dealings, which would damage them far more than us if they got out, but a large amount of the placements in Congress and high-level office positions have been filled by our people. It wouldn't be smart for them to try something."

"And what part do you personally play in all of this?" I had a feeling, but I still needed to confirm.

His eyes darkened. "My father is passing the responsibilities to me, that's why I went to Ireland this summer and why I am working with the FBI and not him. We have officially started the transition of power."

"For you to be in charge of the entire thing?" I swallowed, realizing just how much power he was talking about. How much danger that would put him in. Holy crap. This was becoming more real by the second.

"That is a bit more of the reaction I expected." He winced, looking frustrated.

"I'm just considering all the danger that is going to put you in," I admitted softly as his eyes warmed in realization. "And Dermot? Is he part of all this?"

"Yeah, my uncle was as well, but we have essentially

removed him from the equation because he's a piece of shit," he muttered. "But yes, Dermot knows. He better, since he's my second in command."

"Okay," I murmured, nibbling my lip. "The only thing that scares me about this, King, is that you will be in more danger than ever. But this doesn't change anything between us. Why would it?"

"It changes your life. It puts you in far more danger than you've ever been in, and I fucking hate that." His jaw clenched in frustration. "You are tied to all of this now. Every single stain and bloody action, every death, all of it is tied to you now as well. The guys have made the choice to be part of this, to help me, but you've always been part of it, princess, even if you weren't aware. Now that the media has caught wind, though, we can't—nor would I want to—deny it. You are going to become a target, though, and there isn't a damn thing I can do besides make sure you have the tightest security known to man, and *that* is the part I am worried about changing something between us. I don't want you to realize that I have put you in this corner. That I haven't given you an option. I'm worried it is going to make you hate me."

I paused as I thought through the implications. I'm guessing that's why Dermot warned us to be careful at the club event this weekend. I didn't know a lot about this stuff, obviously because I referenced *The Godfather*... but I was guessing privacy and secrets are a thing? "And here I was insecure about why you wouldn't want pictures of us together out in the media. You were just worried about the ramifications of that much attention into our lives and how dangerous that could be? Honestly, that's pretty sweet."

What? It was! I mean, yes, the man just admitted to being a criminal. A legitimate one. But he also had been worried about the type of attention it could attract for us and what danger that could put me in. The concept made me smile because the man was protective to a fault, I would give him that. What he didn't realize, and something I planned to assure him of, is that I would never blame him for the position I found myself in. Half because I truly didn't think it was his fault, but also because I wanted to be here, with him, no matter what that meant.

My fingers strung through his hair as I pressed our foreheads together.

"King," I soothed, "first of all, it sounds like this wasn't fully your fault. Sure, now that we are together it makes it more drastic, but I am going to assume that I always would have been considered part of this because of our families' closeness. Do my parents know about your dad?"

"Yeah, your dad and the other parents know," he grunted.

"So I would have been in trouble by association," I pointed out.

"You're letting me off easy," he groaned.

"No." I rolled my forehead against his. "Plus, there is nothing you could do to make me hate you, King. Well, if you cheated on me, that would be—"

"I would never cheat on you," he hissed, looking offended. I smiled, loving his reaction. His eyes softened and he shook his head. "Dahlia, I've killed. More than once. I've done a lot of really bad shit, and it's only going to get worse."

"Do you regret any of it?" I asked softly.

"No," he bit out. "Which probably makes me sound horrible."

"Why did you kill?" I bit down on my lip, wondering why I wasn't more upset about this. Was I compartmentalizing? Or was it more that I wasn't surprised because I'd instinctively known how violent he could be? Why didn't that scare me? I clearly had a few screws loose.

His jaw tightened. "Because they were threatening everything we'd built."

"So you were defending your family," I rationalized.

He barked out a laugh and sighed. "That's one way of looking at it."

"You're being too hard on yourself."

"You are being far too understanding considering I just told you I'm a killer." He inhaled sharply, looking like he didn't want to say what came out of his mouth next. "I know you deserve way better than this, princess. You deserve someone who isn't putting your life in danger and has a normal fucking job—"

"Hey!" I poked his chest. "Stop it. What the heck, King? You don't get to tell me what I do and don't deserve. I want you. I love you. So unless you don't want me—"

"Of course I want you," he growled, "but because of me, you are always going to have to worry." His nose traced my cheekbone as my skin flushed with heat, making me feel the opposite of worried.

"Because of you, I am always going to wake up happy," I admitted softly. "I know you are always going to keep me safe. I've always known that. Christ, King, I have been in love with you since we were little. There is nothing that could change that. Maybe that makes me a bad person, but the Ross family is what it is. I know what type of man you are, and as the woman that loves you, I accept the other stuff. It probably sounds pathetic, but there isn't much you can do, King, that would push me away from you."

His sharp inhale had me pulling back as he offered me a hard look. "There is nothing pathetic about you, Dahlia. You're fucking perfect."

He groaned, his fingers wrapping around my throat as I let my head fall back, wanting his lips on me. When they brushed mine in a claiming kiss, a shiver worked its way over me and caused me to tremble slightly. I think he had meant it to be a short kiss, but when he tried to pull away, my fingers tangled harder in his golden hair and I held him against me, deepening the kiss.

A low growl vibrated through his chest as I was suddenly turned, now pressed against the hard wood desk as he stepped into my space. A moan left my mouth at how hard he was against me, and I felt any of the soft vulnerability from moments ago slip away as my skin broke out into a heated flush. King's kiss grew more possessive, and my blood began pumping loud enough in my ears that all I could do was hang on for the ride.

"Dahlia..." His low, vibrating rumble of my name had my toes curling as I pulled back, breathing roughly as his grip on my hip hardened. I moaned softly and nipped his bottom lip, causing him to tighten his other hand on my throat. This side of King was one I absolutely loved. The dominance and the darkness that seemed to envelop me felt like velvet against my skin.

"No biting," he growled, tracing my jaw with his lips as he tiled my neck back further. My knees nearly broke when he bit down on my pulse, sending an electric jolt through my entire body.

"You're one to talk," I whimpered, my nipples tightening against the fabric of the dress I wore, the heat between my legs growing as I tried to shift my thighs together. Immediately King had me on the desk, stepping between my legs and forcing them apart as his fingers slid up my thighs.

"Keep talking like that and I'll put something else in your mouth," he threatened, pressing his lips against mine as his fingers brushed over my lace panties. The delicate material practically ripped under his fingers as he twisted it roughly.

"I like that idea," I admitted breathlessly as he nipped my pulse again.

"Fuck," he snarled. "I need to taste you again, princess. It's been too long."

Suddenly and without warning, he tugged one of my legs forward, causing me to fall back on the desk, his hand coming underneath my head to catch me as he caged me on the edge of the dark, shiny surface. As he pushed up my dress, the cool air-conditioning caused my skin to prickle, the contrasting temperatures making me only feel more needy.

"King." My voice was full of want as he disappeared, kneeling between my spread legs as I heard a snap before my hot center was completely bare to his appraisal. The man didn't give me a moment to be shy as his hands pushed my thighs open and his mouth hit my pussy. My eyes fluttered back as a breathy gasp came out of my mouth.

Holy hell.

This man was way too good with his mouth. The way that he was licking and sucking had me practically shooting off the desk as he locked me in place, his mouth coming over my clit and sucking hard enough that I cried out his name. I could feel how wet I was, my desire coating my thighs, as he continued to devour me whole, his mouth disappearing for just a moment before his finger slid inside of me, causing my entire center to clench around him. I rolled my hips against his face as he started to fuck me with his fingers, his mouth suctioned to my clit, making my climax roar up far faster than I ever expected.

My back arched off the desk as I let out a cry of his name, my climax ramming into me at light speed and causing my entire body to practically seize at the effect of his mouth. My breathing was rough and nearly panting as he licked up my release, his fingers leaving me as I squirmed, needing more from him. Needing him. I didn't care that we were inside this damn room or that it would be my first time.

After everything King had told me? I wanted to show him how much I loved him. How much I needed him. How his family and what they did wouldn't affect that.

"King." My hands found his hair as he appeared above me, examining my expression, an unbridled heat in his gaze. "I need you."

His eyes flared with darkness as he kissed me, hard and unrelenting. "Dahlia, your first time shouldn't be on a goddamn desk."

"I don't care," I admitted softly, clasping his face and putting in every ounce of emotion I felt for the man. "I want you, King. Bad."

A low groan broke from his throat, and I moaned against his lips as he scooped me up and carried me towards the couches. I squirmed against him as he lowered me to the leather and kneeled between my legs, which locked around him as he rubbed a thumb over my clit. The look darkening his green eyes was so possessive it nearly took my breath away. My hands found their way to my breasts, my fingers sliding over the triangles of material covering them as King let out a low groan, surging forward and tugging the fabric aside. I shot up nearly off the couch as his mouth found my hard, needy nipple, his hips rocking against mine so that I was trapped between him and the soft material.

"Are you sure about this?" he asked roughly, his fingers sliding around my throat. "You deserve something way more fucking romantic—"

"Do you want me, King?" I swallowed, my body trembling with exorbitant need.

"Never has been in goddamn question." His growl was accented by him unbuttoning his dress shirt, tossing it to the side as I whimpered, loving that I had the ability to touch his cut, hard muscles now. My fingers instantly found their way to his chiseled abs from where I was trapped under him, his fingers working to undo his belt.

"You are so hot," I mumbled almost to myself. He flashed me a cocky smile and slid his fingers up my waist, pushing my dress over my head and tossing it away, leaving me in absolutely nothing.

When he stood, I tried to pull him back, but he just nipped my finger and tossed his belt to the side, unzipping his dress pants. I found my fingers sliding down my body as I watched him get undressed, no dirty fantasy I'd ever had of this man living up to the reality of how he looked practically naked. I whimpered as my fingers circled my clit, almost embarrassed at how wet I was, but I could hardly care considering my eyes were immediately focused on how hard he was standing in just his dark boxers and watching my action with a low growl.

"Touching yourself again, Dahlia?" he questioned, moving back over me with an almost predatory energy. "I'm fucking positive I told you that was against the rules."

The problem was that I was very interested in knowing what would happen if I broke that rule. I had a feeling I would love it.

"Only if I wasn't with one of you," I reminded him as his hand pulled mine from between my legs. He captured my fingers between his lips and sucked, nearly making me come right then.

"If I'm with you, I am the only one with my fingers and mouth buried in your hot little cunt, understand?" He leaned down to kiss me, my hands gripping his massive shoulders as I nodded, not even caring what I was agreeing to right now.

"What about if I want more than your fingers and mouth?"

I was practically begging here, and his devious smile had me knowing he was well aware of what he was doing to me. Pushing down his boxers, my eyelids grew heavy with lust as his large, tanned hand began fisting his length.

I licked my lips, wanting to taste the bead of moisture at

the end of his cock. I wanted my mouth on him. To know what he tasted like.

"Soon," he grunted, reading my mind. "I'm going to come way too fast if you put your mouth around me."

I flashed him a coy smile as he ran the tip of his cock against my hot center, making me shiver at the sensation. My legs spread automatically to make room for his frame, both of us moaning.

"Are you sure?" he demanded, gripping my jaw in a firm, hard hold. "Are you sure you want to give yourself to me, Dahlia? I was never going to let you go, princess, but if you let me take you, you're going to realize pretty damn quick how insane I am over you. The lengths I would go to keep you in my life. I won't be able to keep that part of me in check."

Oh Jesus, did I love that.

"I want you, King. I've always wanted you," I promised. "I want you to be my first."

My words had him groaning against my lips. "You want me to pop this little cherry, princess?" He snarled, his tip pressing right against my pussy as I tried to wiggle, wanting him further inside of me.

"Yes." I dug my nails into his shoulders hard enough it would probably draw blood.

"I love you." He brushed my lips gently this time, but it was accented by the cry that left my mouth. One that he caught as he surged forward, burying his length halfway inside of me. Immediately my eyes began to water at the feeling of fullness that took over everything else. It hurt. I could feel myself being stretched by his size, but there was something underneath that trying to push through. Something that felt explosive and hotly lethal.

"I'm sorry," he grunted, sounding in pain himself. "I know it hurts, princess."

"I'm fine." I gasped as I moved experimentally, a low growl breaking from his lips. "Holy shit, King, you are huge."

King kissed my face gently but held himself still and buried inside of me, attempting to let me adjust despite the tension and need I could feel in his frame. My body began to tremble as my need ramped up. His voice was like rocks against my skin. "That isn't helping me stay still, princess."

"Move," I demanded softly, my hands slipping into his hair.

His movement was slow as he pulled back and then slid back in but deeper, causing my eyes to flutter shut and my back to arch off the couch. I cried out his name as his pace picked up, deeper and harder each time, until I could no longer feel pain and instead felt a radiating sense of pleasure building deep in my core. My pussy clenched around him as he cursed, his entire body shuddering and his muscles tightening from where he was holding himself over me. His now dark green eyes held mine as he began to piston in and out of me, causing everything inside of me to turn into a sea of heightened sensation that had the corners of the room going fuzzy.

"Fuck," he snarled, "you are milking my cock, Dahlia."

"It feels so good," I admitted breathlessly and then moaned as his hand came to wrap around my throat.

"I'm not sure how much longer I can keep myself in control," he admitted as my eyes widened, realizing he'd been holding back. His chuckle was deep and pained as my legs squeezed around his hips, his pace slowing momentarily.

"I can take more," I promised. I had absolutely no idea if that was true, but I would be damned if I didn't try. I needed to feel all of him.

"Yeah?" His tone was dangerous and caused my skin to break out into pleasurable shivers. "You can take me pounding into your tight pussy as hard as I can? I want to fucking wreck you, Dahlia."

"Then do it," I moaned at his words. He paused only momentarily, inhaling sharply and pulling back before slamming full force back into me.

Holy hell. He had not been lying. He had been completely holding back, and my cries of his name grew as he started to pound into me like a goddamn racehorse. My head grew a bit fuzzy as I relished in the almost high-like euphoric feeling his hard grip offered, his fingers releasing my throat and demanding my climax as oxygen flooded back in. I cried out as it slammed into me like a full-speed rail train, his cock pulsing as King stilled inside of me, letting out a low, feral sound before resuming his pace.

I had no idea how the man did it, but he kept going, kept bringing me to climax and then renewing his efforts. After four times I was getting dizzy, clinging to him, and I wondered if this man was a robot, because this stamina was ridiculous. *This couldn't be normal.* Don't get me wrong, I loved it, but holy crap. His lips ghosted across mine and I felt his cock almost seem to grow larger inside of me.

"Shit, I'm going to come, princess."

"Come." I tightened my hold in his hair as I made the demand, wanting to feel him completely inside of me. It was such a primal need, but the satisfaction at the idea of him coming inside of me was nearly overwhelming.

"I'm going to come inside of you," he growled, nearly reading my mind, and biting my neck as I cried out at the slight sting. I loved his possessive words. I wanted to feel him inside of me, to know that he was still between my legs long after we'd been together.

"King!" I cried out his name as I came. Hard and intensely. He followed, his growl of my name echoing through the space as his hand fisted my hair and he kissed me like a man possessed. I felt my eyes fall shut as my entire body trembled with pleasure, everything inside of me deflating and turning into a melted puddle of content goo. He was buried full-hilt inside of me, and I was pretty positive that he was still coming.

The room was spotted with black as I clung to him, my focus moving in and out as I tried to breathe. King was breathing hard over me as he suddenly rolled us, his arms wrapping around me and tugging me against him so that we were wrapped up in one another on our sides, my head in his chest. My eyes watered slightly, feeling overwhelmed by the intense emotions I was feeling as he reached above me to grab a blanket and drape it over us. I let out a soft hum as he ran his lips back and forth on my forehead.

"God, I love you so much," he whispered softly. "You have no idea."

I looked up at him and offered a sleepy smile. "I think I do. I love you."

His eyes were filled with so much warmth, and as I closed mine, I knew that what had just happened would fundamentally shift things. It was one thing to talk about all being together, but being with these men was going to be intense. I had no idea how they would react, but whatever their reaction was, King and I had just started down a path that hopefully would bring us everything we wanted.

It had to, because I couldn't lose any of these men.

Chapter Seven

DAHLIA ALDRIDGE

"Dahlia." King's voice was warm and soft in my ear as I blinked open my eyes, a golden ray of sunlight coasting across my vision as I snuggled further into the covers and the hard, muscular chest I was curled against. I inhaled King's familiar cigar and vanilla scent as I let out a happy sigh at the way his lips traced my ear. I briefly remembered King carrying me through his home, but I wasn't positive when or how long ago it had been, to be honest.

"We need to get back to the house, princess." His voice was relaxed, but there was a tinge of concern there that had me opening my eyes and examining his face.

"You sound worried, what happened?" I yawned, nuzzling his chest again as he let out a rumble, his arms closing tighter around me.

"National media. It only took them till one in the afternoon to find us." Then he mumbled, "Assholes."

"Really?" I sighed and pulled back, scowling. "Why do we have to get up though?"

His lips pulled into a smile that was filled with a tightness

I didn't like. "Apparently, Callum wants to meet today. As soon as possible."

"Oh." I nibbled my lip and nodded before attempting to sit up. I say 'attempting' because I was almost immediately flat on my back again, King caging me. I couldn't help but smile at the somewhat grumpy expression on his face.

"You said we had to get up," I pointed out, booping his nose.

"I am finding it hard to listen to my own rationale in the face of seeing you in my bed. You have no idea how long I've wanted you here, Dahlia." His lips traced my collarbone. "Now that I have you, I'm all too tempted to lock the door and never let you leave."

Honestly, if it wasn't for seeing the others, the idea didn't sound like the worst in the world.

"Wait." I tilted my head. "Does that mean India will be coming over?"

That concept was actually a bit exciting. My lack of female friendship was something I had been looking to remedy, and while Abby had really knocked my confidence regarding it, making me cautious, I knew India at least well enough to know she was *nothing* like Abby. In fact, I was nearly positive India would eat someone like Abby alive.

"Possibly," King answered and then frowned. "You know India isn't exactly the safest person to be around, right, princess?"

"Seems like a habit of mine." The words came out of my mouth before I could stop them, and King broke into a massive smile, chuckling and shaking his head as he rolled us over so that I was pressed against him. Despite feeling how hard he most definitely was, the tone stayed relaxed and affectionate.

"Why?" I asked in reference to his comment about India.

"I don't have any confirmation, but anyone who surrounds

herself with men like Silas Huntington should be regarded with caution," he muttered.

"Silas?" I tilted my head and then my eyebrows rose, remembering meeting him at brunch a few days ago. I'd definitely gotten a weird vibe off him, mainly because of how intensely he'd been focused on India, which matched up with what King was saying. "What's wrong with him?"

King eased out of bed, my eyes flashing down his body as I nearly squirmed, not used to seeing him completely naked but loving it. He let out a yawn, striding over to the other side of the bed and lifting me out. My arms wrapped around his neck as he walked us towards the en suite, not answering my question just yet. When he turned on the shower and set me down, his answer was half contemplative and half amused.

"It could be nothing, but the rumors I have heard about him are rather telling. Plus, I'm not positive, but I think he may be considered AWOL right now." After a moment, he added, "Then again, if Callum hasn't called him on it, maybe not."

"AWOL?"

"He's CIA," King admitted softly and then smiled. "Although I don't have confirmation on that either. But if he's CIA and he's stateside, it's either for a damn good reason or he's breaking the rules. Either way, when I called in information on all of the people accompanying India and Callum, it was very clear that Silas was not considered safe for interacting with on any level."

"You can just call people and get information?" I stepped into the shower and King joined me, pulling my hips against his so that I was wedged against his hard length, the rainwater showerhead drenching us from above.

"Essentially," he admitted. "Although it's a bit easier when they are government-contracted or military."

"Wow," I breathed out and then shrugged. "Still want to be friends with her."

King shook his head and motioned for me to turn around, his groan filling the space as his cock pressed against my ass and had me arching back into him. His voice was rough. "You're going to get fucked if you keep doing that, and I'm already worried I took you too rough."

I realized then that the man was massaging shampoo into my hair. I had absolutely no idea why the action struck me as so sweet, but when I looked back at him, I was feeling a lot of emotion besides lust. His eyes tracked my expression.

"What?" he asked softer, the heat toned down.

"I just love you," I mumbled, offering a soft smile.

His smile grew. "I don't think I'll ever get tired of hearing that."

I would never stop telling him.

Closing my eyes, I sighed into his touch as he rinsed my hair and then put some conditioner in it. It felt nice to just let King take care of me. It wasn't until my mind began to wander that my eyes snapped open and my heart skipped a beat.

"King..." I looked up at him. "We didn't talk about protection at all."

King's eyes flashed with something much darker than usual and really hot before he shrugged. "What do you want to talk about, princess? I know you're on the pill."

I swallowed, wanting the next part to not even apply to our situation, but considering I had never confirmed it, I figured it was as good of time as ever. I was never going to want to have this conversation.

"But if you've been with someone else..."

I let out a squeak as I was suddenly being backed into the shower wall, his energy turning much more dangerous than moments before, the tension between us growing.

"You think I've been with someone else?" It was nearly accusatory, as if he couldn't believe I had actually stated that.

"I didn't want to assume," I breathed out.

His hand slid around my throat, gentle and seemingly a reassurance to himself. "Dahlia, I told you I've been in love with you since I could fucking walk. Why would I ever be with someone else? The concept of being with any woman besides you is abhorrent."

Oh.

My eyes widened. "So that was your first time also?"

A rumble left his throat as he offered a nod, his other hand running down my waist and across my center, which was now exploding with heat. I whimpered as he circled my clit, his touch gentle on the swollen and sore flesh from his absolutely pounding pace from before. It didn't stop my climax from growing as I flushed, my pulse exploding and breathing growing rapid.

A moan left my throat as he trailed kisses down my neck, his bite against my pulse causing me to jump as a small orgasm rocked through me, making my knees go weak and my eyes close in relief. Kingston Ross was more dangerous than ever. This man should not have this much control over my body.

"More so," he growled softly against my lips as I stared at him in a post-orgasmic daze, "I don't ever want anything between us, Dahlia. I love the feeling of your tight little cunt wrapped around me, and coming inside of you is a goddamn euphoric experience. So no, we didn't talk about protection because we didn't need to. I understand why you're on birth control, but I would be fucking thrilled if you decided to go off that—"

My hand covered his sculpted lips as I squeaked, my eyes flying open. "King, what the heck?"

"It's true," he said through my attempt at silencing him as

he pulled my hand away, kissing the top of it softly. "I hate the idea of anything between us."

"Yes, but I could get pregnant."

His eyes flashed dark again, a small smile playing on his lips. "Like I said, fucking thrilled if you decided to go off that."

I blinked, processing his words as he turned off the shower and grabbed a towel, ushering me forward as I stared at the absolute psycho. Yes, I realized that this was an odd thing to finally realize he was crazy in regards to, but *come on*.

"Your expression is adorable," he admitted softly, amusement filtering in.

"You just said you want me to get pregnant, essentially," I pointed out, my eyes wide and expression probably a mixture of shock and confusion.

King nodded and echoed a sound of agreement while leading me back into his room. I crossed my arms and pinned him with a look, ignoring how his statement made me feel.

"King, you can't just say that."

The man pulled on a pair of boxers, rolling his shoulders back and flashing me a smile. "I'm not sure why this is surprising to you, princess. It's not like I've ever viewed us as anything but extremely serious. You're just privy to my thoughts about it now."

"I have no idea how any of this is going to work," I sighed, looking skyward at his high ceilings. Unfortunately, I didn't find any answers up there.

"Come on, get dressed." He flashed a smile. "You're overcomplicating this in your head, I can tell."

"I am attempting to date six men, and you just said you would be cool with knocking me up, but I'm overcomplicating this?" I sputtered.

"Not attempting, you *are* dating six men, although that doesn't sound like the right word." He frowned and then shrugged. "No matter." Then his expression changed to a smile. "Dermot will be thrilled to know you included him in that."

I blushed and narrowed my eyes, grabbing my dress from the bed and going towards the bathroom, leaving the door open. I let out a huff, finding this version of King extremely attractive and a bit frustrating. He just said all of this so matter of fact, as if he wasn't acting crazy!

Pulling on my dress, I nearly shook my head, feeling completely naked underneath because my bra had disappeared and my panties had been shredded. I scowled, wondering if I should call him out on ripping them, but somehow I felt like that would just turn into King ripping more of my clothes. I ran my fingers through my hair and then came back in the room, finding King dressed in a pair of dress pants and a fitted shirt, his hair messy and damp over his handsome face.

Goodness gracious. How was it possible to get this lucky?

"What?" he asked, amused as I blushed, caught staring. I shrugged as he flashed me a smile, clearly knowing where my thoughts had gone. Instead of admitting what I had been thinking about, I looked around King's bedroom, trying to remember the last time I'd been in here. The space looked very much as I remembered it but with a few different features.

Mrs. Ross had styled her entire house the same as their estate in the Hamptons, which featured high white ceilings with beams, light wood floors, silver furnishings, and white granite. It was accented by blue throughout, and a similar style was reflected in King's bedroom, the large windows bringing a massive amount of light into the space. On one end of the room was the door to the en suite, and on the other end was a sitting area that seemed to function as a workspace for him. That part was a bit newer.

I tilted my head, noticing how the linen couches were covered in papers from where he had sat in the armchair and spread everything out. A cup of coffee sat forgotten, and one of his high school hoodies sat discarded on the back of the chair. *A hoodie that I should steal...*

I wasn't positive what it was about the scene, but it made me smile. When I looked back at him, he was crossing the room, his eyes locked on my expression. Reaching me, he cupped my jaw and pressed a hard, firm kiss to my lips, making me melt against him. When he pulled back, his expression was serious.

"Are you sure you want to meet with Callum?" he asked quietly. "We can figure out a way to keep you more separated—"

"If you guys are part of it, I'm part of it," I said with quiet resolve. "I don't want secrets anymore. I want to handle this together."

His gaze was intense as he nodded and gently pulled me from his room. I looked around the clean and professionally decorated home, deciding that there were elements that I would very much want to pull into my own home one day. Maybe not everything, but something for sure. If it was possible to take all of the homes in Wildberry and make one home as a combination of them, I would have been thrilled.

Oh! I looked at King, wondering if now was the time to ask him about the comment he had made to Lincoln regarding purchasing a house together and 'busting his balls.' Unfortunately, the outside world had different plans.

As we walked out of the house, my eyes widened on the large amount of news trucks I could see and the sound of helicopters overhead. King cursed and kept me tucked to his side as we made our way to my house, the walk seeming far longer than normal. As we walked up the front porch steps and entered my house, I breathed out a sigh of relief, officially back out of the public eye.

"This can't be just about the social media thing," I told King. This was an extreme reaction, even for the nosy media.

"I would agree." His voice was rough as we walked towards the kitchen, the sound of the news echoing through the space.

As I entered the room, I briefly noticed that all the boys were watching the television near the table with varying levels of concern. Yates sat in the breakfast nook, his gaze meeting mine almost immediately, his jaw tightening just enough to let me know that he was worried about something. It wasn't a look I saw often with Yates because normally the man wasn't worried about anything, supremely confident in his decisions, but this was different.

Lincoln and Sterling were sitting across from him, both offering King sidelong glances as the man behind me grunted. I would have turned to look at him, but I was a bit caught off guard by how Stratton and Dermot were watching the screen, one looking interested and the other looking frustrated.

Would any of them comment on my state of undress and wet hair? So far, they hadn't, but I realized pretty quickly that was the least of our problems and why they were all riveted by what was happening on the news.

"We aren't positive who the young man was that they were targeting, or if the Ross or Carter legal teams have been contacted, but this level of brutality is something I haven't witnessed in years." The female news anchor shook her head, looking upset.

"It's awful," the man expressed, looking horror-struck. *"Our correspondent is currently outside of the gated community where both families live as we wait to see the legal recourse that will be taken. I imagine that local law enforcement will be sending someone over, although without knowing who the victim was of such violence..."*

Their words became muted as I watched the video they

were replaying, the screen split between the hosts and the footage. Occasionally, the correspondent's viewpoint would pop up, showcasing the Wildberry Lane gates, our security having created a barrier that managed to block out most of their sightline. I could still hear the helicopters overhead, though.

"Is that..." my voice came across as confused as I neared the television, tilting my head slightly. A range of emotions ran over me, and none of them were nearly as confusing as the level of adrenaline I felt towards the darkness that I was witnessing. The anchor wasn't wrong. This was brutality, and it was at the hands of my boys.

More specifically, Yates and King.

"Greg?" Dermot offered, sounding almost pleased. "Yeah it is, baby girl."

I was starting to realize that my Irish man might have a bit of a darker side. After all, he did have cuts on his hands when he'd first arrived, and I'm sure they didn't come from nothing.

"This wasn't the first issue the Carters have faced. Only this past weekend, their son assaulted Ian McCaffrey at an event hosted by their families' country club—"

"Dahlia." King's voice was strained underneath a layer of cool control.

I continued staring at the footage as I tried to piece together why I wasn't feeling disgust or anger with what I was seeing. Wasn't I supposed to? Wasn't this type of violence supposed to disgust me? Instead, as I watched the dark video play out, King's familiar, muscular frame bent over Greg as he beat the hell out of him, a dark flame grew inside of me.

It was so wrong.

Then again, was it? Greg was horrible.

I truly mean *horrible*. I hated Ian, but Greg made a habit of doing Ian-like actions our entire time in school, and not just with me. A memory surged over me as I considered just one of the many times that the man had attempted to intimidate me.

"Stay right here until I get back," Yates ordered, his scowl making me smile as I shook my head.

I would listen... but only because if I didn't he would probably never let it go. I offered him a sarcastic military salute as he let out a growl but stalked towards his locker. Unfortunately, juniors were separated into two different hallways, so his was in a different section than mine. I began to unpack everything from my backpack, considering what exactly I needed to bring home for the weekend.

When an arm slid around my waist, I instantly knew it didn't belong to one of my boys. The overpowering scent of cologne and the laugh had me knowing exactly who this was. Unfortunately.

I snapped around, backing up against the locker, wincing as my head hit the metal in the process.

"Hi Dahlia." Greg flashed a smile. I had a feeling he thought it was a charming look, but trust me, it was anything but. In fact, everything about him made me uncomfortable. He should have been attractive considering he was tall, muscular, and was even wearing his football jersey, but the man left me with a bad taste in my mouth.

"Hey Greg." I offered a tight smile, my eyes darting over to the turn of the corner where I knew Yates was in the other hall. No one else was around because we had taken our time walking from our last class, arguing about our plans for the weekend. So now I was stuck against a locker with Greg, who was double my size, in my space and offering me a smile that gave me the chills.

I was totally blaming Yates for this one. He better show up soon.

"I heard you were thinking of coming to the game tonight," he said, his hand on the locker next to my face. I shifted on my feet and shrank into myself, not liking how close he was.

"Undecided," I hedged, wondering how he knew that considering

I had just brought it up to Yates moments ago. Then again, it wouldn't have surprised me if he had been listening. Greg wasn't exactly known for being a good guy around school. In fact, most of the girls that he had hooked up with all seemed to note one trait about him.

The man wasn't good with the word 'no.'

Which, of course, scared the mess out of me. I was torn between trying to slip away or offering a set of appeasing words so he would leave me alone. Those were really my only two options right now.

I swallowed nervously, his smile growing as he tracked the movement.

"You should come." His voice held an edge of near warning. "Afterwards, we are going out to the quarry for a party. I know the guys and I would love to spend—"

"Greg." Yates's voice was a low, dangerous hiss as I met his eyes over Greg's shoulder. The man in front of me was large, but Yates was larger, and I immediately felt a sense of security filter through me.

At the sound of Yates's voice, Greg nearly jumped, fear then anger flashing across his face before looking back down at me. He finally turned to face Yates, their feet nearly touching with how close my friend was. I watched as Yates's features went especially cold, making my eyes widen as my heart jumped, not in fear but in something else that I wasn't fully ready to examine.

"Yates," Greg greeted, offering an attempt at a smile. "What's up, man?"

Yates didn't bother with niceties. "I highly suggest you get the fuck out of here."

Greg seemed to debate his next move before he looked back at me, slipping between us and stalking away. My stomach instantly relaxed in the absence of his cologne, but my gaze followed him until he was out of sight.

I deflated against the locker in his absence, looking back at Yates, who looked furious. His gaze snapped back to mine as he seemed to shake himself, grabbing my backpack and throwing it over his shoul-

der. Yates intertwined our fingers and pulled me from the hallway. I
didn't know what to say to the man.

"He's an ass," I pointed out softly, not one for swearing but feeling
like it was needed. Yates's lips lifted in a small smile as he nodded,
seemingly trapped in his head. I tried to think up something silly to
argue about because it seemed to put him in a better mood, going back
and forth, but instead I just tightened my hand in his. I think it did
the trick because by the time we were down two floors, he was
complaining about our plans again, a happy reprieve from the tense
situation Greg and his friends always created.

So was I supposed to feel bad at seeing proof that a man like
Greg got what he deserved, frankly? I hadn't even suffered his
true ugliness, and it was enough, in my mind, to justify it.
Some people were just *bad*. Greg was one of those people. I
didn't need to see proof of that; it was evident in how he
handled everything and everyone.

Honestly, I knew I wasn't the only woman enjoying
watching Greg get absolutely demolished on screen this afternoon. You couldn't see his features completely, but it was
obvious to anyone that grew up with him, his trademark polo
embroidered with our high school mascot giving him away. I
found myself nearly smiling seeing that it was covered in
blood.

Rather than worry about the violence, my brain had
constructed a different concern, one that was frankly far
more pressing in my mind. Whoever had taken this video had
done so from a bit of a distance. I didn't recognize the
setting, but it was lush and green, so most likely by the club?

Who would have taken the video? More so, why? It was
possible it was one of Greg's friends or someone who
followed them from the club when they left with him. I
mean, it had to be someone pretty dumb considering I even

knew that we probably had enough pull to figure out who submitted the file to the news stations.

"Who sent this to them?" I turned to ask King. "Why haven't we gotten it taken down? When did the story break?"

I mean, this was significantly worse than my social media story... Which was obvious, given the number of news channels who'd shown up to cover it.

King's expression was serious as he watched me with a bit of confusion, his eyes darting down to my pulse as if he wanted to run his hand over it. Something I wouldn't mind in the least right now, frankly. His touch was not only familiar, growing more constant every day, but it grounded me, making me know that he was right there with me through all of this insanity.

"Working on that," Lincoln stated. "Story broke about fifteen minutes ago while you guys were... occupied."

My blush hit my cheeks as I offered Lincoln a small scowl, his eyes jumping with amusement. So clearly they had an idea of what was going on. Good to know.

My question: why wasn't this more awkward?

Then again, had anything ever truly been awkward with these men? I was pretty sure each of these men had been with me during an embarrassing moment of my life at some point.

There was the time when I'd been in middle school, throwing up my entire day's worth of food in the toilet because I was nervous about the talent show, and Sterling had held my hair out of my face while Stratton had made sure no one came into the bathroom.

Or when I had gotten my first period in 7th grade during the middle of the day and Lincoln had left school, not asking permission, and walked to the 7-Eleven nearby and picked me up pads and some chocolate. He'd even gotten detention for that one.

Or when I had been running to class during freshman year, trying my best to not be late, and tripped and fell on my butt only to have upperclassmen laugh at me... until King had threatened them. I should have found it odd that it had worked even back then, right? Clearly the man was scarier than I gave him credit for.

Or junior year when I hadn't been able to fit into my planned Homecoming dress because my boobs had decided to appear over freakin' night, sending me into a panic, and Yates had arranged for a personal shopper to come to my house within the hour just to find something I was comfortable with.

No, nothing could really be awkward with these men, not after everything we'd been through.

"Princess." King pulled back my attention as I looked up at him curiously.

"We need to get this taken down," I insisted quietly. "I know we have pull, but with this obvious of proof, if Greg decided to come forward—"

"He'll be dead," Dermot mused as King shot him a look that had me almost smiling. I was starting to realize that confident, never doubting himself King was very concerned about my reaction to his more violent side. What would he think if I told him it turned me on? That probably would be an interesting conversation.

"It could mean trouble," I finished.

Stratton made a noise of agreement that made me feel like I wasn't completely crazy for being worried about this. Although, now that the guys had seen my reaction, they seemed far less worked up, which meant that the only thing they were originally worried about was how I would feel about the video. That was sweet.

A bit twisted, considering they could be charged with assault and battery, but still sweet.

"Right." King frowned and then ran a hand through his hair, pressing a kiss to my forehead. He seemed to snap out of it then, looking and sounding far more like himself. "I'm going to give my dad a call. Hopefully we can handle the news channels on our own. A majority of them should be willing to stop the story, but there will still be those that won't."

"Do we think Greg will come forward?" Sterling asked, his eyes filled with a calculating edge that I wasn't used to seeing from him.

"That would be a mistake on his end." Yates continued to scroll through his laptop while typing something out quickly, seeming rather relaxed.

When King's phone rang, I jumped.

"Shit, it's Callum," he announced as he looked down at it.

I almost followed King into the office but decided to continue to watch the news, wondering if they really would be able to pull the story that quickly. I knew my parents donated to the charitable campaigns of one of the largest media conglomerates in the country, but I wasn't sure about the others or any international media outlets.

"I'm going to give my mom a call," Lincoln stated, standing up and stretching before walking towards me and pressing a kiss to my cheek that I leaned into... before he nipped my ear in a contrasting effort to turn me on.

I let out a small squeak as my body lit up under the action, his wink making my skin flush as he left me with Stratton, Dermot, Sterling, and Yates. My eyes followed their gazes back to the screen, where they seemed to be pulling even more footage. I groaned, realizing they weren't just covering the Ian thing along with the Greg thing, but now pulling in what happened to me... and there was the helicopter shot of King and I walking from his house to mine.

The media was loving this, the Ross, Carter, and Aldridge names getting thrown around. I was just waiting for them to find a way to bring in the Gates and Lee connections as well, because there was no way they wouldn't try to rope them into it. I honestly had very little experience with the media because my parents kept out of it, and any positive media we had was spun by the PR team that our family had on call. So this was different, and frankly a bit annoying.

"I'm guessing this is the type of media that's also bad?" I asked Dermot, trying to gauge how much of a problem this was going to be in respect to what I learned today.

"You mean for the Ross name overall? No. But I expect you know why now. The connection between you and us was already made with the first story, although I suppose this extends the reach. Some of the people we work with may find it a bit frustrating that there has been such direct attention, but that's where it will end." Dermot looked at Yates. "Could be an issue for the Carters, though, considering what your family does."

It probably didn't look good that such an important and well known lawyer's son was breaking so many laws in one weekend.

"I'm not concerned," Yates leveled and then examined my expression. "This doesn't bother you."

It wasn't a question; it was very much a statement.

"The video?"

"Yes, bunny," His tone was slightly softer, as if he was waiting for me to confirm something. He didn't seem concerned like King, just more curious.

King suddenly called Sterling, who got up and walked towards the office, Stratton's arm wrapping around my waist as he rested his chin on top of my head. It was a comfortable hold and one I sank into.

I answered Yates honestly. "It was pretty clear what had happened that night with Greg, Yates. It's not that much of a surprise."

It was at the time—well, I'd also been a bit tipsy—but thinking back through the night, it was clear how upset King had been at Greg... And then to show up with blood on them in the kitchen? After not returning back home with Lincoln and me? Like I said, somewhat obvious.

"Seeing it is sometimes different," Yates stated. When his phone rang, he grunted and immediately picked up, his first words 'I know' making me realize it was his father. I winced at that, hating that this was becoming such a massive issue.

Dermot chuckled, drawing mine and Stratton's attention.

I frowned. "What?"

"I think you freaked King out a bit, baby girl."

"Huh? Why?"

Stratton pressed his nose to my hair, seemingly just enjoying wrapping me up in his arms. He had always been a bit quieter than the others, and maybe a bit broody, but Stratton was a sweetheart at the center of it all. Maybe a sweetheart with tattoos and piercings, but still extremely emotionally open once you broke past that hard outer shell. That thought had me smoothing a hand over his, Dermot's eyes tracking it again as that small bit of what I was pretty sure was envy flashed through his eyes. He had no reason to be envious, though. I very much wanted to touch Dermot, I just wasn't positive where the line lay between the two of us since we hadn't known one another as long.

"You didn't freak out," he explained.

"I mean, they were covered in blood the other night and I was fine. I just don't understand why *this* is what concerns them, especially after what King just told me."

I just had to keep reminding myself to not tell them that their violent sides turned me on. That was weird, right? Acceptance was one thing, but being turned on by it would probably make them worry about me...

But come on! They beat up Greg because of how he acted towards me. Was I the only one that found that attractive?

Possibly. That's fair.

Stratton froze behind me, then he tilted my head up, holding my jaw in a firm grasp. I wasn't positive what it was about the position or him manhandling me a bit, but I felt my body melt into him, allowing him to position me how he wanted. His bright blue eyes darkened as he seemed to momentarily forget what he'd been about to say.

"King told you everything?" His words were rough and a bit raspy.

"About the Ross family? Yes."

Stratton nodded and then let go of my chin gently, my gaze moving over to Dermot, who was looking at me curiously. So I asked a question I was sincerely wondering about.

"So, do you have a secret room also?"

Dermot flashed a smile that was all mirth and darkness. "Not here, but yes. Why? Interested in seeing it, Dahlia?"

I mean, if it yielded the same result as when I saw King's... yes.

When an email ping sounded, Yates ended his phone call, the device sliding onto the table as he opened the message. Almost immediately, a bit of dread seeped in, realizing all too soon what it was that he was looking at. Mostly because there was only one thing that could put that look on Yates's face, one similar to the one I'd seen the night with Ian, violence written across his expression.

He was watching the video from the club with Abby.

Chapter Eight

DAHLIA ALDRIDGE

I was so screwed.

When Yates finished watching whatever part of the video was on his screen, his eyes flicked up to mine and held my gaze for a moment, a swirl of dark emotions there that I didn't want to consider. I made a worried noise in the back of my throat as I tried to escape Stratton's grasp to go find refuge in the office with King. He wouldn't be happy either, but I knew for a fact Yates was going to be upset that I hadn't told him.

Especially after what he had said to me last night about being important to him.

Then I had made the active choice to not tell him the full story earlier, forcing him to find the video himself, an action I was currently regretting tenfold. Stratton grunted as I slipped from his arms and ran almost right into Dermot, his hands wrapping around my shoulders as I heard Yates stand up. Dermot's gaze moved behind me, then he arched a brow and offered me a questioning look. I kept my mouth shut, knowing that saying anything right now would no doubt make it worse.

"Dahlia." Yates's voice was smooth and dangerously soft as he appeared way too close to me, causing me to jump as I offered him a look that seemed to make him even more frustrated.

"What is going on?" Stratton asked, sounding concerned.

"Hallway, now," Yates ordered, his tone brooking no disagreement.

Too bad I was very much not wanting to be alone with Yates right now. Who knew what the man would say or do? I mean, I wasn't afraid of him, but now that he knew I was attracted to him? He wielded *way* too much power.

Instantly my body tightened, thinking about all the fun ways he could punish me instead.

"I would rather not," I pointed out, attempting a sweet smile.

King walked out of the office, talking to Sterling, as Yates looked over at him and then back at me.

"We can have this conversation here then."

That was indisputably a horrible idea.

"I really don't think we need to talk about it," I debated as Lincoln walked back in, his furrowed brow instantly deepening as he caught onto the tension between Yates and me. Which of course drew everyone else's attention.

"One last chance," he warned.

I felt my temper flare, and I narrowed my eyes.

"No."

I wasn't doing this with him.

"Fine." He shrugged, looking nonplussed as he walked over to his laptop. I tried to move forward, but Dermot kept me secured. Sorry, not secured. Trapped. I scowled up at him as he kept his gaze on Yates, his lip twitching up into a smirk that had me knowing he sensed my displeasure.

"What is going on?" Sterling asked, looking concerned.

"I just got the video from the club's security team the day

Abby assaulted Dahlia," Yates explained, leaning against the table, his laptop next to him.

"She did what?" Lincoln demanded.

"What was on the video?" King demanded softly. Dermot's hands tightened on me as he went completely still, causing me to want to turn around and examine his expression fully. Unfortunately, and not so much because I loved it, he had me locked to him completely, not allowing me to turn.

"Not a good idea, Yates," Dermot warned as Yates went to answer. "I would suggest showing and telling him later."

I could feel everyone else getting more tense by the moment, and I knew this was making it so much worse.

I narrowed my eyes in consideration. "They have cameras in the washrooms at the club?"

I didn't like that at all.

"By the sinks and focused on the door, absolutely. We have way too many high-profile and scummy people that come in and out of our club; we need to know what's going on," Yates answered evenly, almost as a secondary thought before he spoke again. "I'll show you later, King. It's for the better."

"No." King shook his head. "Show it to me."

I relaxed back into Dermot, his arm coming across my chest so that his hand rested on the opposite shoulder. There was no stopping this now. I knew that.

"It really wasn't a big deal," I pointed out. "Abby and I had words—"

"Oh, she said some bullshit," Yates snapped, "but words don't include pulling you by your hair so hard you fell and practically cracked your goddamn head open. Not to mention her kicking you in the ribs."

I grumbled under my breath as almost immediately, Lincoln took the laptop to watch the video. I very clearly remembered what he was talking about; no need for the reminder of her calling me trash because of where I'd been adopted from. Oh, and about the guys never wanting me for anything more than sex.

Inhaling sharply, I tried to remove that thought from my head, not wanting to get caught in my own insecurities, especially after such an amazing... that didn't even seem like the right word for it... such a mind-blowing moment with King earlier.

Abby Brooks was wrong. This was so much bigger than someone like her could comprehend.

"Is that true?" King's voice had me flushing with embarrassment at how I had handled all of it, the twins now watching video evidence of how weak I was.

Today more than ever I was seeing the contrast in strength of how I handled situations compared to them. It was practically laughable, the difference. That doubt in my ability to be worthy of this level of happiness started to creep in, replacing the euphoric high I'd been riding on after my experience with King. Damn, I could not get grounded.

"Angel," Stratton urged as I blinked, lost in the moment.

"We got in a fight," I admitted. "I would really rather not relive it."

King inhaled sharply, but before he could say anything, his phone, which seemed to be a bit of my savior today, rang in the office, where he'd left it. This ringtone I knew. It was his father, and I saw indecision flash through his gaze as he looked over at Yates.

"Send me that video. I'll be back out in a minute."

He went into the office as I escaped Dermot's grasp, feeling frustrated as hell with Yates for causing a problem. Ignoring Lincoln's call out to me, I strode through the hallway and up the stairs, wanting to get to my room before Yates could catch up to me, because trust me, that is exactly what he would try to do. He didn't even bother calling out to me, knowing I wouldn't listen as I reached my bedroom and slid into it, closing the door and locking it right as the knob twisted from the outside.

"Bunny..." Yates's voice held a warning tone.

Not answering him, I kicked off my shoes and let out a tired sigh. Face-planting in bed, I looked at the clock, wondering how so many hours could be left in the day. My face flushed as I thought about everything that had happened today. I mean, with the exception of losing my virginity, it had honestly been sort of a hot mess.

I winced, realizing that I was sore from King. I loved it, but I also found myself wanting to go take a long bath or to curl up in his lap and sleep.

"Dahlia." Yates's voice was firm but hard outside the door.

"I need a minute!" I called out and closed my eyes again. I needed a minute so I didn't kill the man. He was so... frustrating. That was honestly the only word I was pulling from right now. Stubborn, also.

Before I could get up and go to unlock the door, a slight shift in the air had me turning around, finding Yates leaning over me on the bed. His expression was not amused, and I looked over at the closed door and back at him.

What on earth?

"How?" I demanded.

He blinked. "You don't have a locked door in this house that I don't know how to get into."

Oh.

Wait, what?

I inhaled sharply and closed my eyes, ready to give him a piece of my mind... but then the man was kissing me. It was far softer and more relaxed, almost apologetic—well, as much as Yates could be—in its tone. I let out a confused noise, my hands slipping into hair as I tried to deepen the kiss. He pulled back and examined my face, his eyes almost cautious.

"You're actually mad at me," he said, looking half confused.

"I'm frustrated with you," I admitted.

"Why didn't you tell me?" His tone was seeped in emotion that his expression wasn't. "She hurt you, bunny. Physically attacked you, and you didn't tell any of us. Why?"

"I mean, there were a lot of things we weren't saying until, like, last night," I mumbled.

He shook his head. "You should have told us; you should have told *me*. And this morning?"

"I don't want you to have to keep coming in and saving the day, Yates," I grit out, sitting up as he crouched down in front of the bed, bringing us closer. "I... it just makes me feel weak."

"You are not weak." He rejected my statement with such conviction I nearly believed him. "Just because you aren't beating the shit out of someone doesn't make you weak, Dahlia. Everyone has their own brand of strength. You are not weak."

"Compared to you guys—"

"More so," he continued as if I hadn't even spoken, his hands intertwining with mine, "stop trying to take my damn job away from me. I protect you, Dahlia. I love doing it, so cut the shit and stop trying to force me to stop."

I arched my brow and smiled. "Yeah, I'm a job now?"

He let out a low hum. "Best one I've ever had."

"Stop saying cute stuff like that."

Yates stood up and grabbed my waist, sliding me forward before crawling over me and caging me between his large, muscular arms. I breathed in his familiar scent, my fingers tightening on his shirt, wanting to run my hands underneath it and up his impressive abs. I swallowed as he brushed his nose with mine, making me melt at the sweet gesture.

This man was overbearing sometimes, and then there

were moments like this, moments where I had absolutely no idea what to do with him.

Well, except love him.

"I don't like it when you're mad at me," he admitted softly.

I offered him a look. "I'm mad at you all the time."

"Actually mad." He flashed a knowing smile.

My hand slid up to his face. "Yates, I'm not mad, I'm just frustrated. Embarrassed about how I handled it and mostly wanting to forget about it. Forget about her. Forget about the bullying. I just want it done. I'm so tired of it constantly affecting my life, and now that you guys know, all I want to do is move on."

Was that honest enough?

Yates seemed to consider his words. "But you can't just forget all about it, Dahlia. It's changed you as a person. Those parts aren't going anywhere."

Leave it to Yates to perfectly point out the problem with my desire.

My throat tightened as I looked down at his shirt collar, pretending to find it interesting. "And I'll have to work through those in time—"

"Together. We are going to work through them together."

My throat closed. "I... I don't know if I'm ready to talk about it."

Yates examined my expression and then inhaled. "I know, bunny. And I know you need time to warm up to the idea of doing that, but we have to talk about it. Sooner rather than later. I need to make sure you're healthy, Dahlia. I can't live in a world you aren't part of, and I am terrified that the way you think about food and the level of control you have over what you eat is going to result in exactly that—losing you.

"I know it's not as easy as telling you that you're beautiful. I know that won't fix it, even though I could say it every moment of the day and have it be true. *You* need to believe it. *You* need to be happy with yourself, and I am going to do whatever the hell I need to in order to help you with that."

Tears were streaming down my face, hot and heavy, before I had a chance to stop them, and I wrapped my arms around his neck, wanting to curl far enough into him that nothing else would ever touch me. Only him. Only my boys.

"Okay," I whispered. "I'll try to talk about it. I just don't know where to start, Yates."

I would have tried something, but the entire thing was overwhelming. I wasn't lying to him: I had no idea where to start, which is why the ramble that followed wasn't really my fault.

"It's not as easy as just deciding to eat. I could eat a week's worth of food in one sitting or nothing at all, but either way, I would be constantly thinking about what I did or didn't eat. It's constant. A thought pattern in my head I can't escape. The only time I feel good or feel in control, especially when we are going through stressful moments, is when I don't eat. Or when I control it to the point that I know at least something in my life is predictable."

I wrenched a hand through my hair and swallowed. "I know how messed up it sounds. I know I have a problem. I know all of that, and the worst part... is that at the center of it all, I don't want to change, Yates. Not because I don't think I have a problem, but because change means correcting my eating habits. I know they are wrong, but there is a part of my brain, the part that is more afraid of those damn pictures and the scale, that tells me they aren't. That my habits are protecting me from being criticized more than I already am. That it could always be worse. That if I stop, I'll truly be out of control and that attribute will make me unworthy of... of, well, any of this.

"The present problem is bad, but the alternatives terrify

me. I know this might not make any sense, but it's the best way I can explain that I don't know how to do what you're asking."

I hiccuped, tears still streaming down my face as I tried to control my breathing, which had heightened. Exhaustion and the overwhelming emotion from earlier were slamming into me like a tidal wave.

Yates cupped my jaw and pressed a soft kiss to my lips, emotion I would have never expected breaking into his gray eyes. "We will just take it day by day, meal by meal, okay?"

I found myself nodding despite not knowing if it would work. I wanted to make Yates happy, but I also wanted to be honest. I didn't want to eat to make him feel better just to turn around and throw it up, and I was worried that would be my default. I felt my pulse pick up as he made a noise in the back of his throat.

"Dahlia, *breathe*. I know this isn't happening overnight. I know you won't start eating how you should right away. I just need you to know I am here for you, okay?" he whispered.

I nodded, nuzzling into his chest as he rolled us so that I was laying on top of him. I worried a bit that I was too heavy for him, just for a moment, but when I tried to wiggle off of him, he just held me tight.

For a few minutes, Yates simply held me to his chest, the sounds of the occasional helicopter passing overhead and muffled voices from below reminding me what was going on. I breathed in his scent as he smoothed his hands through my hair, the moment seeming almost out of context with the rest of the day. Like we were in a bubble. It was just Yates and me. I found myself loving that, and I buried my head in his neck, his fingers running gently through my hair.

"Are you and King going to get in trouble for the video?" My voice was muffled as concern twisted in my gut.

Yates's laugh was soft and a bit dangerous. "What are they

going to do? Legally, it wouldn't be worth the fight. There isn't a clear shot of Greg, so unless he wants to show his hospital records, which would also detail the drugs he was on, he can't prove it's him. More so, if he tries to speak up, there is a lot that will come out about him and his family. It would be a nightmare on his end.

"On our end, the legal battle would be easily dismissed, and on top of that, the higher-ups at these stupid news stations are going to realize the association with the Ross family and back off. Most likely they are being contacted right now—you will see a change in the spin of the story probably by the evening news cycle. They are fucked because they've already aired the story, so now they will have to come up with a way to make it sound better, or else they will get fired by the people who the Ross family practically bankrolls. It will be amusing at best to watch them trip over their own feet, and annoying at worst because the media has a life of its own with small subsidiaries, international, trash media, and social media branches."

I blinked up at him from where I laid on his chest, and his brow arched at my probably surprised expression. My voice was slightly amused as I commented, "I shouldn't be all that surprised by any of this, but I am realizing how little people kept me in the loop over the years."

"Not to exclude you," Yates said, practically reading my mind. "I personally don't think you need to worry about any of this shit. But if you ask, I'll always tell you."

I liked that.

Before I could say anything else, the door opened and Lincoln stepped in, looking exhausted before pinning us both with an amused look. "Must be nice to escape that bullshit downstairs."

Yates chuckled as we sat up and I rolled my shoulders, putting my arms out to Lincoln, who came over and scooped me up in a princess hold. His voice was rough as he looked at Yates. "King is talking to his dad and yours. Callum and them are nearly here. Why has she been crying? Was Yates being an ass, Dahlia?"

"No." I grinned as Yates offered an eye roll. He came up to me and kissed me hard, despite me being in Lincoln's arms, before leaving the room.

Lincoln set me down and looked over me, a scowl coming on his face.

"What?" I teased.

"I don't like how good you look in that dress," he mumbled.

I flashed a smile. "Thought you liked blue?"

"I do." He tugged my hips against him. "I don't like other men seeing you in it though."

"In the color blue?"

"In general," he muttered and kissed my nose.

"I was going to change anyway," I teased. I actually had meant to just put on panties, but I was a bit chilly, so putting on more clothes would be a win-win.

Lincoln let me go, and I slipped past him towards the closet, watching as he went around the room and closed all the curtains, seemingly more upset as he heard the noise of the helicopters overhead.

"What are you doing?" I asked after grabbing my clothes.

"Don't trust them to not use drones or some shit. Security would shoot them down, but still annoys me. They have already been backed up halfway down the lane, but security can only do so much."

"Police?" I asked as I walked towards the bathroom.

"They would do it." He flashed a smile. "Although then they would have to explain why they are providing protection to the people who are supposed to be in trouble."

I couldn't help but smile at that as I slipped into the bathroom, not bothering to close the door. Slipping panties on underneath my dress, I pulled the garment off and once again noticed that I looked a bit paler than normal. Not because of a lack of sunlight, either. No, it was clear I needed sleep and probably food. My stomach rolled at that idea.

Pulling on a pair of navy blue cropped pants and a white and blue cozy sweater that came to mid-thigh, I brushed through my damp hair and nodded, happy with the change. I slipped on my infinity rings and walked back into the room, finding Lincoln sitting on my bed looking over a picture I kept on my desk.

It was one that featured all four of us—unfortunately not Stratton—from prom our senior year, only a few months ago. I smiled at it as he ran his fingers over the glass and offered me a curious look.

"You know life is never going to be that simple again, especially now."

I examined his words and nodded. "Life wasn't simpler, exactly, just more familiar."

I didn't have to add that the bullying was part of what had made it more complicated.

"Everyone is worried about how you are reacting to all of this, even if they don't say it," he breathed out. "We're worried you're going to get some time and space to think about everything you've been told today and—"

"Freak out?" I grabbed his hands as he put the photo down.

"We aren't good men, Dahlia." Lincoln grit out the words like he felt obligated to say them but didn't want to. "You know we will always be good to you, but we have changed a lot over the years, and exposing you to that darkness is probably the only thing that has scared me in a very long time."

"It doesn't scare me," I admitted softly.

"It should."

"You don't scare me, Lincoln." I grasped his face between my hands. "I should be more bothered by it, I know I should. But I'm not. You guys are more important to me than the mortality associated with your actions. If that makes me crazy... well then I am." I shrugged. "Plus, honestly, it does the opposite of freak me out. That video? Especially with a jerk like Greg? Yeah, opposite of freak me out."

Lincoln's eyes flashed dark. "And what's the opposite for you, Dahlia?"

I ducked my head as he let out a low rumble and stepped into my space. I went to answer, but he silenced me with a kiss.

"I lied, don't tell me right now," he decided. "If you tell me you're turned on by violence, I'll have you bent over that bed and screaming my name in seconds."

"Linc!" I squeaked as he tugged my hand towards the door, flashing a devious smile at my reaction.

"Plus, you're probably still sore from earlier," he rationalized.

"Lincoln Gates!" I exclaimed at him calling me out, as he laughed at my use of his full name.

"Come on, Dahlia, we have an FBI agent to talk to." He scooped me up and I scowled, not actually mad. Although I was starting to think this conversation would have been better than the upcoming meeting.

Too late to get out of it? Considering the dark SUV I could see pulling up in my driveway, I had a feeling so.

Chapter Nine

STERLING GATES

"King, you may want to consider heading back to the compound for a bit until things settle down," Mr. Ross's voice echoed through the speakerphone as King leaned back in the office chair, running a hand over his face.

"I'm not leaving," King stated evenly, and I knew it wasn't because he was afraid of getting in trouble for leaving the country during a possible investigation.

"I wasn't suggesting that you go alone. I think Mr. Aldridge agrees that Dahlia hanging around Camellia isn't making this situation any better," he pointed out evenly.

Stratton's head snapped up from what he was looking at near the bookshelf. I arched a brow in surprise because what Mr. Ross was suggesting was... well, surprising. Dermot nodded in agreement as King stared down at the desk, seemingly caught on how to handle this.

"You know what that would mean," King leveled. "Telling her is one thing, but bringing her there..."

"There really isn't a way to backtrack from this, son," his father admitted with a sigh. "They have video evidence. The greater evil is staying there right now. Until we get the media handled, no amount of money can buy off public suspicion, and it's just going to grow. Your presence may even encourage Greg to make the stupid decision to come forward."

Yates entered the room, his gaze conflicted, making me know he had heard the conversation. Probably from one of the many fucking cameras he had in this estate.

"I want to ask her, make sure she knows what she's agreeing to," King muttered in thought, but I was pretty damn sure he had already decided. "Mr. Aldridge isn't going to skin me alive for this?"

A familiar chuckle sounded in the background as King grunted, knowing that wasn't exactly a 'no.' It wasn't the only thing that I suspected Dahlia's father was considering hurting us over.

Mr. Ross continued, "Just get this handled, King; you don't need to be stateside right now. We can talk about everything else later."

Yeah, like how the families were going to have to come to terms with the fact that all their sons were dating the same girl. Although 'dating' seemed like the wrong term, and while I didn't have solid proof besides Mr. Ross, I had a feeling the parents had been aware of something going on for some time. We hadn't been typical teenagers or high-schoolers by any stretch of the imagination, but I'm positive they thought it was weird that we had never dated anyone else and attended every event with Dahlia. Or how we spent our entire weekends with her, avoiding going to any parties outside of the events held by our families. Or making our decisions based around where Dahlia was going to be after high school. Our parents weren't stupid; they had to know.

Everyone had known except for Dahlia, it seemed, and because of that people had tried to prey on the weakness of her not knowing. Specifically people we went to school with. The best part? Because we spent every moment with Dahlia, any rumors that people tried to start at school about us dating or sleeping with anyone were easily proven false. It was almost laughable, the notion of being with someone else when Dahlia was in my life or on this planet in general. Long before I even knew what sex was, the concept of being friends with another girl felt like a betrayal, felt like I would be hurting her. So the notion of sleeping with someone else? Absolutely fucking ridiculous.

"And we are going to be having a conversation later, boys," Mr. Aldridge called out as I ran a hand over the back of my neck. I literally heard my father laughing in the background, and I cursed, knowing that he would throw us to the fucking wolves—also known as Mr. Aldridge—if we fucked this up.

"We can have the jet there by Friday if you let me know by morning," Mr. Ross offered quietly. King nodded despite his father not being able to see it.

I turned my head towards the door, hearing Dahlia make her way through the house, her voice echoing alongside my brother's in the lofty hallways.

"I'll let you know," King agreed and said goodbye, hanging up as I offered him a look. Stratton shifted from where he was standing, his very obvious conflict playing across his face. I think Stratton wanted Dahlia completely isolated from the danger of the world but also didn't approve of the means to do so.

I had to admit I'd missed the bastard, especially because he was so much more rational than Yates, King, and even my own brother. It was a balancing act between us, and when he had stopped hanging out with us, that element had been tilted. Which was also why shit had probably gotten so twisted over the years. Then again, I had no doubt that there weren't many things Stratton wouldn't do for Dahlia, if his behavior at school had been an indicator. He'd nearly gotten expelled so many times for beating the shit out of people, it was shocking he'd ever graduated.

"This is a bad idea, King," Stratton stated firmly. "She shouldn't be part of any of that shit, and you know it."

King tilted his head back and massaged his temple with the hand propped up on the leather desk chair. "Stratton, I know exactly how you feel about the shit my family does. Not only is it way too late to keep her out of it, but she doesn't take the same issue with it that you do."

"Her life is going to be constantly at risk—"

"Either way," Dermot finished. "Whether she accepts this part of her life now or not, she will always be in danger. That's just how it is."

"This is fucked up," Stratton muttered and then grunted, "Her father may actually kill us."

"May?" Yates mused. "I can assure you that he will want to kill us; there is no question about it. Especially once he realizes that it's all six of us attempting to date his daughter."

Dermot nodded, putting his hands in his pockets, looking completely unconcerned. I was going to assume that was because he'd never seen Mr. Aldridge lose his shit. Not much scared me, but King's father or Dahlia's father angry? That would do it.

"'Attempting' isn't the right word," I added.

"Think it will make it any better that I plan on finding a way so that we can all get married eventually? Even if it's just ceremonial?" King asked thoughtfully.

Christ. I mean, this wasn't the first time we'd had this conversation, but in light of everything occurring and the path we were on, it seemed far more serious. Not that I was against that in any way, but it was a bit odd to finally be openly talking about something we'd wanted for years.

Odd, but good. And if Dahlia liked the idea? Well, fuck. That would be amazing.

"Probably worse," Dermot chuckled, not freaked out by the notion of marrying Dahlia, which told me everything I needed to know about his feelings regarding her. "At least if it's casual in his mind, he doesn't have to think about everything that goes along with her being married."

Was it even possible for us to get married? I suppose she would probably have to legally marry one of us and then we could have the ceremony for the rest? How the hell would that work?

You know what, if anyone could afford to find the loopholes, it was our families. Luckily, America's capitalist system did ensure one thing—money could get you anything if you were willing to spend enough.

"Maybe if we get her pregnant he won't kill us," King mused.

"What type of backward-ass logic is that?" I barked out a laugh. I was finding both the notion of marrying Dahlia and having kids with her far too appealing to be rational. I needed some goddamn sleep is what I needed.

"He wouldn't want to leave a child fatherless, right?" He shrugged nonchalantly, as if he hadn't just suggested knocking Dahlia up. I had no idea what she and Lincoln were doing in the kitchen—hopefully getting her something to eat—but I was thankful for it because she would run if she heard King acting like this.

Yates poured himself a drink from the office bar. "Somehow I don't think he would care."

It was true—he was a scary bastard.

King shook his head and smiled. "I think I may have freaked her out a bit today."

"Yeah?" I asked, arching a brow.

He shook his head. "Not because of the family business. No, she's taking that all... way too well, but I won't complain. No, I freaked her out because she realized we hadn't talked about protection and I told her I knew that she was on birth control but that if she wasn't I wouldn't mind. I didn't mean for that to slip out, really, but her expression was pretty fucking adorable."

I stared at him in shock before exhaling. "Fucking shit King, the woman just agreed to entertain the idea of being with all six of us. As in dating. Not getting married and having our goddamn kids."

"I disagree, I think she understands how serious this is," Yates pointed out, leaning against the desk.

"She didn't say no, either. Just thought I was crazy." King shrugged. "Which I am. So that part didn't upset me."

Stratton chuckled, shaking his head and tapping out his cigarette near the open window. I knew he hated smoking around Dahlia, and I appreciated that he avoided it, although I doubted she would mind.

Dermot offered me a look that said it all. It was the 'they are fucking nut jobs and there is no point in trying to reason with them' look. I threw up my hands and fell back on the couch, trying to not think about why I liked her lack of a 'no' in response to such a serious notion. Maybe I was just as crazy as they were.

When Dahlia's voice echoed outside the door, I sat up, rolling my shoulders back, still finding myself a bit sore from the game on Sunday. We had this week off from practice because of Labor Day weekend, and my body had for sure needed it. If we did end up going overseas, we would have to explain it to our coach, but I was hoping he could put together the pieces that it had to do with the shit show going on. I'm sure by now everyone in town was talking about it, not to mention what seemed to be the rest of the nation.

The door opened and Dahlia walked in, laughing at something my brother said as he offered her a smile that I rarely saw. Lincoln was far too fucking serious for his own good, but Dahlia seemed to lighten that. She was good for him.

She was good for all of us, had been from the start.

I nearly groaned at the tight pair of pants she was wearing, her perfect ass on display despite the sweater she wore. The woman made me want to tie her up and explore every inch of her perfect body. I looked at her delicate wrists, imagining them wrapped in a silk tie and pulled above her head as she pulled against them, moaning in response to my mouth on her wet cunt.

Fuck.

"I think the FBI people are outside," Dahlia said happily, coming over to me and sliding onto my lap. I nearly cursed, loving the feel of her ass against me. My eyes trailed over her face, realizing she was flushed, which meant that she very much knew what she was doing and had decided to sit on my lap anyway.

"That would explain why some of the news stations cleared out," Yates agreed and walked back out the door to no doubt let them in. I was glad Lincoln hadn't taken Dahlia to the door—I wasn't sold on her having to be part of this meeting as it was.

"Are you sure you want to meet them?" King questioned quietly.

"Yes." Dahlia nodded.

Christ. I did not want any law enforcement around Dahlia in general, let alone Callum and the crew of people he seemed to carry along with him. A group of people that contained not one person with military training but three, along with the Hearst brothers.

"Come here." King motioned for her and she hopped up, rounding the desk as he tugged her down on his knee. I stayed where I was, my brother spreading out on the same couch as Dermot walked around the desk and stood behind it. This wasn't our first time meeting with Callum, but we also often were part of the Ross family meetings King held. I had been surprised when he had asked us if we wanted to be an active part of it because I hadn't thought there was a question about that, but apparently burying bodies is different than sitting in confidential meetings. To be fair, I knew hell of a lot more than I used to.

Stratton stayed where he was by the window, seemingly undecided on how much of the Ross family shit he wanted to be a part of. Unfortunately for him, he wasn't going to get much of a choice. I had a feeling he would still fight it a bit though.

He stiffened slightly at the sound of male voices echoing through the space as Callum's team arrived. I understood that far too well. Luckily for my peace of mind, I was pretty damn sure that the men in question were with India. Although I couldn't fully read the dynamic, and I would find it both an odd coincidence and a bit funny if they were in a similar situation as ourselves.

The door opened and India Lexington stepped through, making Dahlia smile, which was reason enough to like the woman despite her reputation. Or I should say lack thereof. The Lexington family was old money. Older than ours, and pretty much as old as this country. You would have thought with that type of power there would have been more information about her, but instead it was as if all she'd ever done in her life was go to school. When King was gathering information, it concerned all of us because the woman's dossier was essentially a single paragraph. Although, I suppose it was somewhat fitting, considering the power her family held—as we knew from experience, covering up information was all too easy if you were willing to pay.

My gaze tracked Dahlia as she stood up to hug India, our girl instantly filling the space with a more relaxed and happier tone than would have been there otherwise. Despite her normal stony gaze, India seemed to like Dahlia, and her smile was authentic... Which was good, because if our girl had hurt feelings, that would have been far more of an issue. As they exchanged greetings, my eyes jumped to Eugene Hearst.

The Hearsts were another old money family, and it showed in both his education and way of living that was echoed by his brother Lawson. The two of them were said to be a world apart in personality, the first more rational than the second because of his temper. I wasn't sure I agreed with the statement, though, because Eugene looked on edge as he kept a hand hovering against India's lower back.

I knew everyone was talking around me, but the dynamic was far too interesting to look away from, especially considering the other three men with them. Plus, this is what I did. I was far better at watching than I was at interacting with people. Just like how my brother was far better at finding information on people. My gaze moved to the man walking across the room to greet King.

Callum Reyes. Our FBI contact was far more accessible in terms of finding information regarding his past, considering he was government-connected. A former college football player from Alabama and twenty-seven years old, the man wore cowboy boots even now and offered King a handshake as if he wasn't here to talk business. I had to wonder how he had gotten involved with the Lexington and Hearst families, because there was no way that happened by chance. You didn't even meet their families by chance. They were that powerful. It also wasn't something we were going to question, because this was their business and not ours. If Callum wanted to trust them, it was on him.

My gaze darted over to Silas Huntington, who was seemingly having a silent conversation with Yates. From what we had found on Silas, which was startlingly little, he was a ghost. Rumored to be CIA, but not confirmed, and currently stateside for unknown reasons, his past and present were essentially blank files, and I knew that made King nervous. Hell, it made me nervous. Every piece of intel we received made it clear that Silas wasn't someone we should ever interact with, so him being around Dahlia scared the hell out of me. But if he was crazy, it made sense why he and Yates would get along so well.

I'd always known that Yates was goddamn insane, but last night I realized just how bad it had gotten. What had started as a small hobby—hell, a habit—was now a full-blown obsession, and I knew it wouldn't stay a secret for long.

As Dahlia returned to the desk and King positioned her again, Bishop Vos took a seat across from me. I guess in a way, he was the most surprising. It wasn't very often that someone with so many military accolades after such a short career decided to put themselves in the company of at least three people that I knew didn't have pristine reputations.

It really made me wonder what brought all of this together.

Dahlia's voice pulled me from my musings. "I'm honestly not positive I know much to be helpful, outside of my suspicions about Abby being the one bullying me. I don't have a lot of interactions with Max or his father."

"Just tell me everything about your interactions with them since they moved here." Callum leaned forward, his expression open and relaxed, which was in contrast to the rest of them. I don't think they were attempting to be intimidating on purpose, because Dahlia was willingly giving them the information, but it didn't stop me from feeling defensive.

As Dahlia began recounting the first time she met them, fall of our senior year, I found myself fascinated by listening to her perception of things. I also was sort of blown away by her memory as she detailed interaction after interaction, most regarding Abby, although she did mention Max. She made quick work of the times he'd harassed her, something that had only happened twice, the first being a passing comment and the second... well, King had walked in on that one. I think that was when Max realized we hadn't wanted to be his friend.

Callum had already gathered information regarding Mr. Brooks from us and from what our fathers had told us, although the man seemed to keep a low profile. I didn't know what he hoped to gather from hearing about Abby and Max, but Dahlia seemed to like getting it off her chest, so that was a good enough reason for me.

"The last interaction I had with Abby in person was the night of the bonfire when she came up to our table and tried to talk to all of them." She scowled slightly before adding, "Again."

"And Max?"

Her face went tense. "That was at the tennis court, before... well, yesterday morning, before all the news broke."

"What exactly did he say?"

"That they were hiding something from me," Dahlia murmured before squinting in thought. "I think his exact question was 'How do you handle knowing that the men you love are hiding shit from you,' and I obviously asked him what he was talking about, and then he said something about them 'sneaking behind my back and dealing with shady people'? I think he wanted to know if I was even aware of the situation. He also essentially threatened me by saying that I was going to suffer because of it."

"He did *what*?" King asked, no doubt hating that she hadn't included that part when she told us before. Her cheeks flushed as she shrugged, the rest of the room frozen, half because of King's tone of voice and the rest of us because the idea of anyone threatening Dahlia had us fucking furious.

"Later?" Dahlia's voice was soft, and I could tell she was a bit embarrassed. Luckily, King seemed to stow his anger temporarily, but I had absolutely no doubt that this wouldn't be the last of this conversation. I hated how she didn't view that type of shit as important enough to tell us, or worried it would be a bother, because I knew exactly how Dahlia thought.

I found myself a bit jealous that King had been with her today, and not because of the reason anyone would assume. When we had talked about being with Dahlia one day, as a group, I knew someone would be her first. She would always be my first when I did finally get her in my bed, but the notion of her being with the others didn't bother me. No. I was jealous because unlike me, King now had the ability to fuck the answers out of Dahlia that she didn't think were worth giving.

I groaned, wondering how much she would freak out if I tossed her ass over my shoulder and tied her up to her bed, making her come enough until she decided that moments like that were important because of her safety.

Hell, everything about Dahlia was fucking important.

"Alright." Callum nodded and looked down at his watch, making me realize how much time had passed. "We will stay in touch. We are meeting with a few people that work at the local pharmacy, so if we find anything else or you get any new information—"

"Actually," King drew out, "we may be leaving the country for the weekend."

Callum didn't seem surprised. "You will still be contactable?"

"Yes." King smoothed Dahlia's hair out as she stared at him in confusion. I loved that my sugar's facial expressions were so blatant and easy to read. It made me know when I was doing shit right or when we were fucking shit up.

"Great. If questions come to the Bureau about the incident regarding this weekend, we will just say your location is known or some shit."

"Did you kill him?" Silas asked curiously, his face void of emotion.

"Greg?" Yates confirmed. I frowned, wishing he hadn't given him his name, but if Yates did so, then he didn't consider them a threat.

"If that's his name." Silas shrugged.

"Unfortunately not," King sighed, and I saw Dahlia's lip twitch slightly.

"We will do our best to push the attention of the media elsewhere," India offered, having been silent but causing all of the men with her to look at her. "Maybe we will do something in town to draw attention away from you guys leaving."

Lawson chuckled. "Or you will turn this town into a frenzy."

"Fair," Bishop muttered.

"The police are out front," Eugene commented, looking towards the office door.

"For show," I pointed out. "Just so the town doesn't look bad. They will probably stay there for an hour or two."

"I'll show you all out if we're done here." Yates stood from where he had been sitting on an armchair.

I offered a small wave goodbye as Dahlia gave India another hug, their interaction far warmer than any other in the room. I watched curiously as they walked out the door, leaving the five of us looking at Dahlia, who stood looking out the window with curiosity until they exited the house and neared their car. She turned back to King and pinned him with a look.

"We are leaving the country?"

King nodded, looking suddenly cautious. "My father and

yours suggested it may be a good idea. We would go to the compound in Ardara."

"Oh!" Her eyes went wide as she smiled, looking excited. It was clear she wouldn't take a lot of convincing, and I'm positive that as long as we were back for her classes next week, she wouldn't mind missing the Labor Day Weekend parade. Dahlia loved traveling, so this was right up her alley.

Probably because she didn't fully realize what the Ross Compound was like. Don't get me wrong, it was beautiful, but it was also exactly what it was... a compound that was owned by the largest crime syndicate in the United Kingdom.

Then her smile faltered as she offered a cautious look to all of us. "You talked to my dad? He didn't say anything about everything going on?"

"He had a lot to say." Stratton smirked, looking amused at what Dahlia was trying to get at.

"But about the..." She waved her hands. "The pictures."

"The bullying?" Lincoln played along.

"The social media account ones? He's fucking furious," I agreed.

"No, I meant the pictures with all of us," she finally blurted out.

Dermot laughed as she scowled, her cheeks turning pink again. King sighed. "We haven't talked about it directly, but he will probably kill us when we do."

"He would never!" She offered us a small eye roll as the office door opened back up, Yates standing in the kitchen with the news turned up again. As she walked out there, I offered King a look as he ran a hand over his face.

Mr. Aldridge was definitely going to kill us.

———

Dahlia Aldridge

My fingers intertwined with one another nervously as I sat on the bathroom counter following dinner. I could hear the boys downstairs, their voices drifting up the large, echoing staircase. It should have been a peaceful, almost serene moment, but instead I was left with a sense of panic and anxiety. Maybe it was because I was finally alone... or more likely it was because I was facing a choice.

I ran my fingers over my throat as I tried to talk myself out of being in here in the first place. I had told the boys I was coming in here to shower and get ready for bed, and they were giving me some space to do so. The problem? Following a dinner that I picked at but did eat, I felt trapped now in the bathroom, staring at the scale and wondering if now was the time I should weigh myself.

Despite knowing it would be off because of dinner.

Despite knowing that it was a bad idea.

I just wanted to check.

That was the mantra in my head, and I gripped the marble counter, knowing that eventually someone would come up here to check on me. Already I'd had to ignore the way Yates had been watching me at dinner as we sat around the office making travel plans. It had been a nice reprieve.

No. I needed to just take a shower and get out of here. Or maybe I wouldn't even take a shower—it wasn't really needed after my one this morning and then my second with King.

I inhaled, trying to remind myself of the good moments today had brought. I tried to remind myself that I'd not only learned so much about my boys but I'd had a moment with King that would absolutely always be special between us.

I needed to get out of here.

Sliding off the counter, I gripped it for balance as the room spun a bit, making me realize that in the absence of adrenaline, I was actually hungry. My stomach tightened as I shook it away, feeling that crawling sensation running over my skin that was a tell-tale sign of a panic attack.

"Angel?" Stratton's voice had me looking up to find him in the doorway of the bathroom, his eyes filled with concern as they ran over me.

"Hey." I offered a tight smile and walked towards him, not looking at the scale, afraid he would see through me. "I couldn't decide if I was too lazy or not to take a shower."

That was a thing, for the record. It was also a thing when I was in this state of mind. My anxiety was crippling enough sometimes that brushing my teeth was considered a feat. It didn't last more than a few hours at that level usually, but it could absolutely wreck my day, and I felt sometimes I was at the mercy of my brain and the thoughts it produced. Like I didn't have control over the direction they went. That I couldn't figure out a way to stop thinking... about everything.

In this case, food.

"You didn't eat much at dinner," Stratton pointed out softly, my cheeks turning pink because I knew that he would notice. Sometimes I thought he was nearly as watchful as Yates... although the man would probably be offended by that.

"Do you want something else? We can make a smoothie or something." His eyes were a deep ocean blue, filled with enough affection that it made me feel like I couldn't breathe, the weight of how close we were settling in my chest.

What I loved the most? He wasn't trying to force a conversation about it. Then again, Stratton had always been a 'fixer.' It shouldn't have surprised me that this was the way he was handling what I am positive he already knew about my problem.

"A smoothie doesn't sound bad," I admitted, meaning that.

"Come on." He squeezed my hand, leading me away from the scale as I tightened my grip in his rough one.

"Thank you," I whispered softly, almost hoping he wouldn't hear it. It wasn't an outright admission, but it was pretty darn close.

"I am always going to take care of you, Dahlia." His words were soft and sounded almost like a vow as I leaned into him, not knowing how to respond. Not knowing how to deal with the tidal wave of need I felt for this man.

I wanted Stratton to take care of me, and when I looked up at him, the look in his blue gaze told me that more than anything, he needed it. For whatever reason, Stratton Lee needed to take care of me. The craziest part?

I was absolutely going to let him.

Chapter Ten

DAHLIA ALDRIDGE

Apparently waking up early was becoming a habit. I wasn't positive how I felt about that... no I actually knew how I felt about it. I was absolutely against it. Yet here I was, up bright and early and outside, no less!

The muggy morning air wrapped around my skin as I sat curled up on a pool lounge chair, watching the sun slowly break through the heavy clouds. It almost looked like it was going to rain today, something that I wasn't opposed to in the least. Especially because it meant that the media would probably not be crowding the gate. I still had no idea how in the heck we were going to get out of here unnoticed for the trip overseas tomorrow, but I figured that King would think up something.

I couldn't lie, I was excited about learning more about King's family. Also about where Dermot had lived most of his life. I knew my boys well, but this was like an entire new part of their history that I was unraveling. I just hoped that I didn't embarrass King or Dermot. I had a feeling things would be a lot different where we were going, and sometimes my lack of knowledge about stuff made me sound naive or stupid.

For most of my life I had wanted to be like my mom, and I still did. I looked up to the woman like crazy, but I also found myself a bit envious of India Lexington. The woman was calm, cool, and collected to the point that I wasn't positive if she felt legitimate emotions or not. If it wasn't for the slight smile she offered me while talking, I would think she didn't like me. She hadn't always been like that—at least she hadn't been when our families had vacationed together a few summers ago—but now, something was different. I had to assume it was the result of losing her family; a tragedy like that had the ability to affect even the strongest people.

My brow dipped slightly, realizing how similar we were in that regard. Yates wasn't wrong—the imprint of the bullying was long lasting, and once again, like last night, I could feel myself at a crossroads over the simplest thing.

Breakfast.

Shaking my head and removing the thought from my consciousness until I had more coffee, I started draining my first cup. I hadn't fully gotten dressed when I'd slipped from the room, but I'd pulled on a pair of sleep shorts with my hoodie, figuring that brushing my teeth was good enough for sitting by my own pool.

I did wonder how long it would take for one of them to realize I wasn't in bed anymore. My smile grew as I thought about how I had fallen asleep between the twins but woken up with Stratton wrapped around my center and Dermot laying in bed next to me, his fingers in my hair as if he had been smoothing it over and over again. I'd been half asleep, but when I'd woken up the first time, I was briefly aware of the murmur of the television and the conversation the others were having. It made me wonder when they'd finally fallen asleep.

When I'd slipped from the room this morning, King had been on my other side, and the twins were spread out on the sofas nearby, Yates in the armchair. I wondered if it was possible to get a bigger bed. I mean, it was already pretty massive, but these guys were objectively huge, so we would need at least an Alaskan King... or two. If we put them together, that would work even better. It wasn't like I didn't have the space. Then again, even if my parents were cool with me dating all six men and didn't freak out, or my father didn't try to kill them... I had a feeling that putting that in my room would be pushing it a bit far.

My thoughts began to stray to getting our own house before I shook myself. I was being ridiculous, obviously. They were going to think I was crazy, no matter how serious King claimed they were, if I started talking about living together.

Although... last night was amazing. Before bed we had watched a movie, and I had realized pretty quickly how easy it was to be with these men. As in dating all of them. Originally, the notion had been hard to wrap my mind around... until Dermot tugged me onto his lap and King kissed me on his way to go grab us some snacks from upstairs, wanting a smoothie of his own. Or how Stratton sat next to me during part of the movie while the twins both reclined back in their seats and dozed off. I wouldn't lie, I had crawled in between them about halfway through the movie. Then Yates had stolen me and I'd fallen asleep on him, not realizing how tired I was. Last night had for sure made it a bit more real.

How would it hold up when we left our bubble? Went out on the international stage? Or attended school next week?

Hopefully, the long plane ride would give us enough time to get ready and talk about all of this. Then again, the boys seemed perfectly content with everything. I seemed to be the only one freaking out about all these massive changes. Surprising, right?

"Ms. Aldridge?" My head snapped up as I found a man standing over me, dressed in all black. How the heck hadn't I heard him approach? Better yet, what was he doing in my back yard? I honestly think this was the first time I'd ever seen Wildberry Lane security outside of the gate area.

I put my coffee mug down and sat up. "Oh! Hello, what's up? What can I help you with?" *What can I help you with?* The man was in my back yard. Christ. I was more tired than I thought.

"We need you to come see something we found on the tapes from last night." His voice was professional, but I still found the request odd. Maybe he was deferring to me because my parents weren't here? I mean, in a way, I liked it because I honestly would have assumed he would have gone to Yates, who seemed to interact with security the most out of all of us.

I stood, and instead of stepping back, the man stood in my space, making me move around him awkwardly as I looked at the house. "I'm going to go grab one of the guys, they will want to see—"

"This is rather urgent, Dahlia," he insisted, looking concerned. He then added, "It actually concerns a few of them."

Oh.

Frowning, I nodded slowly. "Alright, lead the way."

I felt myself relax as he walked us around the house and towards the security building near the gate, knowing that there would be other guards there. There were always at least two.

Yet as we approached, I felt my chest seize up, realizing that wasn't the case today. The building sat empty and quiet as the guard opened the door.

Something was very wrong about this. A feeling slammed

into me, a premonition maybe, my gut reaction hitting me like a truck, warning me to take a step back immediately. Something was for sure wrong. Something was wrong about this situation and him.

I tried to take another step back as his eyes focused on my movement. It was all the warning I had before his hand darted out and gripped my wrist, tugging me forward roughly.

I let out a cry, his grip hard, enough that I was worried he would bruise my wrist or break a bone. My cry echoed, and he immediately slapped a hand over my mouth and pinned me against the inside wall of the security office with his arm against my neck, cutting off my air supply. I gasped, tugging on his arm as he offered a sneer, his cologne making me sick to my stomach. He hadn't even bothered to close the door, that was how confident he was.

He loosened the pressure on my neck slightly, enough so I wouldn't pass out, but he kept me pinned and a hand over my mouth. The part that had me freaking out the most? I could feel how hard he was as his head bent down and his breath skated across my face. I felt myself growing nauseous.

"Shut up," he growled in a sharp demand. "I'm here to do a fucking job, so pay fucking attention, Dahlia."

Out of all the emotions I expected to feel, anger wasn't one of them, yet my temper sparked as I nearly kneed this guy in the dick. Well, I would have, but I had no wiggle room, something I found out as I tried to jolt against him. His smile grew as if he found my attempt amusing.

Screw this guy.

At the same time, I was also feeling an amount of fear that had me feeling like I was going to pass out. This thirty-something-year-old man should have been handsome, from his strong jaw and nose to his windswept brown hair. But there was something cold about his light eyes. There was nothing there. Absolutely nothing, and it was horrifying to have directed towards me.

His voice was hard and unemotional as he spoke right next to my ear. "You convince those fucking bastards to stop working with Agent Reyes. Dixon Glenn has a far bigger reach than you can even imagine. He is extending this singular warning to you. *Pull them back or else.*"

"Fuck you." My words were muffled by his hand as I felt my face grow heated with anger at his words. I wasn't someone who swore very often, but this man was clearly the exception.

His chuckle was sharp and cruel as he tightened his grip on my jaw, making my hearing go out momentarily, my heart pounding in my ears as I nearly puked right on him. The fluctuation between anger and fear was a terrifying experience. His hand moved from my jaw and roughly grabbed my breast, making me shrink further back against the wall as much as possible.

"And here I thought you wanted me to fuck off, but I am more than fucking happy to make this job worth it."

A whimper of legitimate fear left my lips as he offered me a smile that was absolutely sadistic, his hand moving back up to my hair, which he gripped hard so I had to keep my eyes on him. Immediately, I made the connection of how much like Greg this man was, and that was absolutely terrifying. His voice was almost soft as he switched gears. "You have one chance, Dahlia. Understand? Or else I'm going to personally make fucking sure that you don't live another day to continue this bullshit."

My eyes darted over his shoulder as my heart began to beat faster, but not in fear, rather relief. I looked back at the man in front of me. "No."

Before he could respond, surprise coating his face momentarily, his body jolted, eyes widening in shock and mouth falling open. Blood began to pool out of his nose as his entire body weight fell on me, the vibration in the air and the ringing through my ears making me wonder if I was dreaming. There was no way any of this was happening.

I stared blankly as Yates pulled the man off me, tossing him to the ground, blood from the gunshot wound in the side of his head pooling on the floor and coating my boyfriend. And me. I had blood on me.

My eyes fluttered as I tried to process what I was seeing, Yates appearing in front of me as he dropped the gun on the ground. The space suddenly filled with *actual* security as I stared into Yates's eyes, shock permeating everything.

Yates's voice was almost a soft coo as he cupped my face. "Bunny, I am going to get you out of here, okay?"

I nodded, and when he lifted me up, I clung to him, my eyes darting over the body and the brains splattered on the wall opposite us in an almost artistic display. I wasn't positive that I would ever be able to look at this security office again. Not without thinking about this.

A small sound broke from my throat, almost a whimper, as Yates's grip tightened on me. I briefly registered that he was walking me towards his house, but I couldn't think about that. Instead I was staring at him, the blood on him, his calm, almost serene expression, and the way he seemed to have already processed what he'd just done.

Oh, he had for sure done this before, that wasn't in question.

But... how he was reacting was such in opposition to the night with Ian. I didn't understand this man. He had such an unbalancing effect, and I felt like I was in a stormy sea just hanging on for dear life.

"You killed him."

Yates let out a noncommittal sound and then chuckled,

the sound startling me as we walked through his front door. "Callum is probably going to be pissed about that."

"Why?" I rasped. I mean, I had assumed he was going to knock him out, not put a gun to his head and blow his brains out.

I was pretty positive I was going to throw up.

"He was threatening you." Yates looked at my expression with concern, and then I saw his temper flash behind his gaze. "He also fucking touched you."

"You killed him for touching me?" My head was spinning as we entered his bedroom, the curtains drawn and the room dark in the early morning light. I could almost pretend none of that had happened.

Almost.

Yates gently put me down on his bed and tugged off his shirt, kneeling in front of me as he began to wipe the blood from my body. I blinked, trying to decide if I wanted to laugh or cry. The first bubbled out of me as Yates regarded me with a cautious yet oddly amused look, his gaze a near charcoal color in the darkness of his bedroom.

"What?" His voice was calm and patient.

"I... I don't know why I'm laughing," I gasped and then closed my eyes, which were growing hot with tears. "Okay, this is okay. What just happened—"

"Is far from okay. He should have died much slower," Yates purred, nipping my jaw.

This was a dream, right? I mean, Yates sounded absolutely psychotic. The man just said he shot a man for threatening me and touching me... That couldn't be right.

Right?

I watched as he pulled his shirt down his face to wipe off the blood, disregarding the drips on the pale carpet that covered his room. It was going to stain.

"How are you fine right now?" I asked softly, my pulse

beating out of control. I needed to find a way to sort through this. To store these emotions away.

"Oh, I'm anything but fine," he said, his voice lethal and quiet. Standing, he cupped my jaw and pressed a kiss to it. "I'm going to run you a bath, and then we are going back to bed."

I nodded numbly, feeling so confused on what was going on right now. The adrenaline of the moment was leaving my body.

"Shower," I suggested as he examined my face and then went to go turn it on. I looked down at the bed I was on and wondered if I would get blood on the sheets. I hoped not. I would feel bad about that.

When he walked back in the room and grabbed my hand, I followed. He pressed a kiss to my forehead and offered me a questioning, concerned look, no doubt wondering if I needed help because I was like a zombie right now. I shook myself and waved him off, and he strode back into the other room after a moment of hesitation, leaving me to strip down. I knew the door wasn't locked, but the closed door allowed me the feeling of privacy to process my emotions.

Except as I stood under the hot water, no emotions came. I scrubbed my body and hair, trying not to get sick as lumps of something fell onto the floor. I eventually had scrubbed every part of me so well that my skin was raw and red.

I stepped out, shaking slightly, as I wrapped a towel around me and walked towards the mirror. Almost immediately, I found myself leaning over the sink because I was going to puke, a piece of... something still in my hair. I couldn't touch it, couldn't look at it, so I gagged over the sink and let out a small sob, realizing I had nothing to throw up.

"Hey, hey." Yates was there then, immediately spotting the issue, removing it and pulling me into his chest, whispering softly in my ear. I wasn't positive if it was helping or not, but eventually the shaking stopped and my eyes felt heavy.

"Yates..." I gripped onto him. "I really don't feel well."

"I know, bunny." His voice was pained, the only hint of emotion I'd heard so far, and it was in reference to me. "Just close your eyes; we will talk when you wake up."

That sounded like a good idea.

I felt him wrap a robe around me before letting my towel fall, my nudity not bothering me in the least in contrast to everything else around me. I melted into the man as I felt an emotion run through me that was unexpected.

Thankfulness.

Yates had saved me. I wasn't positive if the man had really been there to just deliver a warning or not, but he'd threatened me, and for the second time... Yates had saved me.

Except this time, instead of me calming him down, assuring him I was okay, now he was calming me down. Holding me. Comforting me. What an odd relationship the two of us had. I whispered his name before the darkness of unconsciousness closed in around me.

————

The numbness that had kept me from panic cracked the moment that my eyes opened to afternoon sunlight hitting across my face.

Panic. Anger. Gratefulness. Love. And so many other complicated emotions surged through me, causing my breathing to hitch as I realized that I had watched a man die.

No. Not die. He was *killed*. I watched Yates kill a man.

It was terrifying, and yet... I didn't find myself scared of Yates. Or disgusted. Just surprised and in shock. Not at his action as much as the result. A dead body on the ground of the security office, his brain blown out everywhere around me.

A sick feeling worked its way into my stomach as I sucked in air and sat up, realizing that the warm pillow under my face was actually a chest. I clutched the robe I was wearing a bit tighter before turning to look, finding Yates already looking at me from where he lay shirtless and in a pair of sweatpants, leaning against his headboard. The look on his face was relaxed, but his eyes held a dark edge, the man choosing not to say anything as he probably waited for me to either freak out or cry again.

"You got his brains all over me," I accused. In true Dahlia fashion, I'd said the first thing that popped into my head.

Silence hung between us as surprise and then amusement broke onto his face, a strained chuckle coming through his lips as he looked skyward. "Only you, bunny. Only fucking you would find a reason to argue with me after I killed a man in cold blood in front of you."

I offered him an incredulous look. "It was in my hair, Yates."

Yates tugged my waist so that I leaned against his chest once again, curled into his side and looking up at him, his fingers gently resting on my face. "I apologize, bunny. Next time I kill someone, I'll make sure to give you a heads up."

"A *heads* up? Not the best reference, probably." I couldn't help the laughter that bubbled out of me, making me realize that it was possible there was a reason these men and I got along.... Besides the all-consuming, intense attraction, and history. I was clearly mental.

His smile grew at my poor attempt at a joke before his entire face softened. "I was worried about you earlier. Your reaction made me think... well, I didn't know how you would react when you woke up."

"You saved me again," I mumbled and then shook my

head. "I feel so stupid. I realized something was wrong once we got closer to the guard house, but by then he had already grabbed me."

"I know," he whispered, the momentary lightness once again swallowed by the dark void that seemed to surround him right now. Unlike the man who attacked me, the void wasn't absent of emotion; rather the opposite—it radiated with an intensity that reminded me of a black hole, and I was pretty sure I was getting sucked into it. It would explain why I was suddenly accepting things like him killing a man so easily.

Then again... they had nearly done the same thing to Greg, so maybe it was the surprise that was getting to me? Or the brains in my hair. That would do it.

"How?" I swallowed. "How did you know where I was?"

Yates's gaze filled with something sharp and almost cautious. "Dahlia, I always know where you are. I'm always watching you."

A shiver broke out across my arms as I tightened my hold on him. When he rolled us so I was under him, my breathing hitched as my pulse went skyrocket.

"Why?"

"You know why." He nipped my bottom lip.

"Tell me?" I think I did know why, but I needed to hear it.

"The same reason I killed that asshole for touching you, let alone threatening you," he growled, brushing his lips against mine. "Because I love you, bunny. Because you're mine, and he doesn't get to live after touching and threatening to hurt what's mine. He *scared* you. I saw it. I fucking saw how scared you were, and I just lost it."

"Yates." My breathing was tight. I wanted to say those words back to him, and I was in the process of doing so before he silenced me with a kiss.

"Not yet." He shook his head. "Not until I show you

something. Because once you say those words, Dahlia, you don't get to take them back. You're already mine, but you're willingly sealing your fate if you say those words. Before you do that... I need to show you something." The end was said with a bit of trepidation. He continued, "You need to realize just how far all of this goes."

"How far *what* goes?" I swallowed nervously.

"My feelings for you; my love for you," he rasped.

"What do you mean?"

He took my hand, and I followed him out of bed. I considered putting more clothes on, but it was clear the man was in no mood to wait. I followed after, feeling oddly more awake and clear in the head than I had in the past forty-eight hours. I shouldn't have felt like this, but something about the incident this morning had left me feeling far different than I would have expected.

That didn't even include the nervous anticipation I felt because of the tension that Yates held in his muscular, golden back. Christ. The man was legitimately all hard, lean muscle. It was insane.

I frowned as I realized we were going up the stairs, and my heart jumped. *Was this the room he had mentioned the other night?*

Well, now I didn't have to ask, which I had been planning to do for sure. I wondered what was in there that would make him feel the need to stop me from saying 'I love you' back. Because despite Yates being my archnemesis and travel buddy... I couldn't deny that I loved the man. I loved him and probably had for some time. It was a raw and real emotion that surged through me in moments like this, when we were handling an issue or he was comforting me from a panic attack.

As we reached the top of the stairs to the fourth floor, I found myself intrigued by the large lounge space, the dark furnishings and leather couches not particularly matching the rest of the house. There was a large bar across the room and massive skylight windows that showed off the stormy skies and the rain that poured from them. I let out an appreciative hum, wondering what was so odd about this room.

That was until I watched Yates walk towards a heavy black door to the right, opposite of the bar. I swallowed as he motioned me over.

"Intimidating black door. Good. Great. That doesn't make me nervous at all, paired with what you said downstairs."

I swear, if this man had a room filled with bodies or something I would... probably stay and ask him why. Because I was clearly a lost cause when it came to these men. Christ. Did my insanity have no limits?

His eyes flashed with amusement and maybe a bit of concern as he opened up the door, the darkness making it seem all the more threatening. He let me pass, and instead of closing the door, he stayed where he was. A low, vibrating hum immediately started up, and the lights began to turn on in sets in response to someone entering the space, revealing the room in four sections.

My eyes went wide.

I'd watched a man be shot in the head right in front of me, and yet... This was somehow more surprising.

"Yates?" A weird thrill trailed up my spine as I looked around the room, feeling far less nervous than I should, considering the circumstance. Mostly because I could feel his gaze on me from where he lounged quietly against the doorway, his energy anything but relaxed, instead feeling dark and encompassing. I could almost feel him gauging and testing my reaction to what was in front of me. There was a predatory feel to his actions, like he was a lion toying with a mouse... or in this case, a bunny.

It really shouldn't have turned me on, that much I knew.

But none of that could distract from what was in front of me. What he had wanted to show me before allowing me to say the words that I still very much felt. This was a reality that I think some part of me had known but always narrowly avoided focusing on. I mean... the man knew a lot about me, always. I had just assumed or told myself it was because he was overbearing, and it turned out he was.

And so, so much more.

I had avoided this. Mostly because of what it would mean. What it would change between the two of us. What it would mean in terms of myself. That I would be more than okay with this... and maybe actually like it?

Holy moly, I was screwed in the head.

I didn't have that option anymore, to ignore it, and I knew that was his intention. He was laying his cards out on the table and daring me to still make the statement I was going to moments ago. He was showing me the extent of everything and waiting for me to react to this... madness. His madness.

A healthy reaction would have been to run. I clearly wasn't healthy.

"Yeah?" His voice was a low vibration in space.

"What is all this?" I whispered, looking over everything from the screens, to the wall, to the tables. A weird prickle of heat broke over my skin as adrenaline rushed my system, making me feel dizzy.

When the door closed, heavy and loud, my body broke out into shivers as fingers came around my throat and slid up to my jaw, his other hand around my waist. He tilted my head up to look at him, his eyes vibrantly light, almost dangerously so.

"Are you sure you want to know, Dahlia?"

"Yes." I nodded. His hand reached over to press a button

and the screens began to light up, making me know I'd been right about them. He nipped my ear, a breathy sound escaping my lips.

I had known Yates was crazy, and this morning, his reaction to what happened confirmed it... But this... this was something else.

"This is how I always know *exactly* where you are, bunny."

Chapter Eleven

YATES CARTER

Obsession was a funny thing.

The more obsessed and focused you became over some-thing, the more you normalized it. Which was why watching Dahlia's reaction to my insanity was so damn euphoric. Not only because of the high of exposing this type of secret to her, but also because of the array of intense emotions flashing across her face, surprising me with what it inspired in her. The most shocking and the one that put her in the most danger?

Lust.

Dahlia should have been trying to get out the door behind us. It would be the normal thing to do. Not that I would let her, but I would still commend her efforts. Then again, Dahlia was far from being normal, mundane, or anything that could ever be considered average. No, Dahlia, my bunny, was extraordinary and fascinating, two things she no doubt didn't consider herself. That was fine. I had more than enough time and ability to focus my attention on proving otherwise. Besides, who else would be the best to convince her than the man who watched her literal every move?

Like a fucking stalker.

I nearly ran a hand over my face and groaned at that thought because there was nothing *like* about it. I very much stalked Dahlia, and she was no doubt going to think I was absolutely psychotic after this. Did I think she would still love me? That she would say the words I had seen on her lips downstairs? Honestly, I didn't know.

There was caution and fear I felt towards the notion of her rejecting me, but it was a risk I was taking because I needed her to know what she was committing to. This obsession wasn't going away, and if anything, it would get worse now that she knew. By telling me that she loved me, it was essentially handing me a free pass, and the woman was smart enough to realize that.

My eyes ran over the way she stood, her hands grabbing my arm that was wrapped around her as her breath caught at my words. I could see a flush on her skin, and I was all too tempted to rip that robe from her body and fuck her over all the surfaces in here. I had imagined it far too many times, and the times that I'd stroked my cock to the video feed of her floating around her house in practically nothing only made the fantasy all that much more real. I wanted to fuck her in here, badly. But I needed to make sure she wasn't about to lose it after the day she'd had.

Hell, after the *week* she'd had.

Fury threatened to take over my lust for a minute but I shut that down, instead focusing on the way her lips parted as she focused in on a mug that sat on the table.

"That is..."

"Your mug from yesterday," I hummed knowingly.

"And these cameras..." she whispered.

"All over your house, the rest of Wildberry, as well and pretty much wherever else in town you would go," I admitted, my lips tracing her neck. "Convenient that everyone trusts me to install security equipment."

Dahlia blinked up at me and stepped forward out of my grasp as she tilted her head at the screen that was currently set to the guard house. I had all of it transmitted to my phone and other devices, but this was the main hub.

"And what's this?" she asked, her tongue darting out to touch her lips as she moved to a different screen. I inhaled sharply, trying to not focus on the action or think about how her mouth would feel wrapped around other parts of me. How her lips and tongue would feel against my skin.

"The tracker I have on your car and purse, although you don't use either as much as I assumed when I put them there," I admitted.

"Which was when?" she demanded, her eyes darkening with heat.

Fuck. Mad or turned on, it didn't matter to me. I loved Dahlia worked up, especially if it was because of me.

"These? Replaced the old ones a few months ago."

"How long have you been..."

"Stalking you?" I chuckled, sitting down at one of the many tables that contained an assortment of Dahlia's belongings. There were a lot more on the shelves along the walls, right next to the obsessive amount of photos I had of her that I liked to have just for when I was working in here. Somehow made it feel like she was with me.

I tilted my head, trying to remember how and when it had started.

"Honestly, I don't know." I watched as she walked the perimeter of the room, looking over everything. "It started with just wanting to make sure that you were safe around freshman year after that one asshole tried to convince you to go to Homecoming and wouldn't let it go, so I convinced the school to let us pay for a new security system... which I had access to. Then it sort of escalated because I would watch you all day long, going class to class, wanting to make sure no one bothered you."

"Yates," she mumbled, seeming to process all of it before turning to look at me. "You acted like you hated me."

I barked out a laugh and then offered my hand as she hesitantly walked over, relief filling me that she'd still touch me. I spoke in a soothing tone as if I wasn't showing her what a goddamn psycho I was. "I never hated you, Dahlia. It's impossible for me to hate you. I'm obsessed with you."

I stated it casually enough that you would almost not believe that it completely consumed every waking moment of my life. That *she* consumed every moment of my life.

"Obsessed with me?" She seemed to try the phrase out on her lips.

I pulled her down on my lap and kissed her neck, speaking softly. "Absolutely consumed. I would take any reaction from you, from happiness to anger, because anything is better than nothing. So if arguing with you got your attention, then we would argue all the fucking time. I love watching how heated you get as it is; you're fucking stunning when you're upset or turned on."

"Yates!" Her blush had me groaning as I nipped her throat.

The action seemed to draw her out of it as she stood up and ran a hand through her hair, looking around again.

"Shit, Yates."

I let out a hum and stood, closing in from behind as I grabbed her hips. "Bunny, there isn't anything you do that I don't know about. I have integrated myself so far into your life that even if you told me to fuck off right now, I would still be here, watching you day in and day out."

There was no point in lying to her. She could reject me if she wanted, but this wasn't something I could stop.

Her breathing hitched. "Holy hell."

I rested my lips against her shoulder and tried to ignore the overwhelming fear that she would reject me that was pounding through my head. "You can probably understand why I wanted you to wait to say anything. I didn't want to hide this from you anymore."

Dahlia turned into me, tilting her head back as she examined my expression. "Yates... this is insane. I mean... I don't even know what to say..."

"You don't have to say anything." I tried to not be disappointed over the notion of this fucking with her head enough that she wouldn't feel comfortable telling me how she felt. At the same time, I could hardly blame her. It couldn't be easy realizing that you were in love with a goddamn psychopathic stalker.

Murder and stalking all in one day. I was surprised she wasn't screaming.

No, I wasn't surprised, actually. Nothing about Dahlia surprised me because the way she reacted to stuff was absolutely unique.

"But it doesn't change the fact that I love you."

Her words hit me as they shattered my faux calm, my pulse quickening and body hardening against her as I considered what exactly she was saying.

My voice came out rough and raspy. "What?"

She stepped into me, her eyes shining with heat and truth. "I said it doesn't change that I love you, Yates. You're insane, like *I should be more worried* type insane, but—"

I seared my lips against hers, backing her up against a hard metal table as a wave of need crashed into me. Holy fuck. I couldn't believe the words that were coming out of her mouth. I pulled back, grasping her jaw as I demanded her full attention.

"You love me? After everything I've just fucking shown you?"

She was sealing her own fate, and I wasn't going to stop her.

"Yes." Her voice was firm and soft, pupils dilated and skin pink, making me know she felt the same surge of want that was coursing through me.

She let out a soft whimper as I examined her face, searching for truth and finding something so much more, realization slamming into me at how exactly Dahlia felt about all of this.

"Do you like knowing how obsessed I am over you, Dahlia?" I hissed, my cock pulsing in the confines of my sweatpants, the bastard impatient as hell. Her chest was rising rapidly in response to her breathing as I let my other hand travel down to tug on the tie of her robe. My eyes immediately dipped to her hot little frame as the material parted to reveal her perfect breasts, her pink nipples hard and making my mouth water as her hands fidgeted as if to cover herself up. Instead I wedged a knee between her legs as my fingers skimmed over her tight wet heat, a whimper escaping her throat.

"You like knowing that I spend every single fucking day watching you? Constantly? That I obsess over every detail of your day from the moment you wake up? That I collect your goddamn stuff like a psycho because I want to be near something that you've touched? That I stare at photos of you while I work during the day, just to remind myself how fucking perfect you are? Not that I could ever forget. Do you like knowing that you are the center of my fucking world, Dahlia? Not part of it. Smack dab in the fucking center of it. I do everything based around you. Everything."

"Yates..." Her moan was soft as I circled her clit, her entire body shaking with need as I considered getting her off right away but kept my touch teasing, wanting her drenched and craving me. Like I constantly needed her.

I leaned in and sucked hard on her neck, causing her to cry out, knowing I would leave a hickey. Bending down slightly, trailing my lips across her breasts, I tugged one of her hard nipples between my teeth, causing my bunny to grow more wet against my fingers.

"You do, I can feel it," I growled, feeling almost fucking dizzy with relief that she wasn't rejecting me. "I can feel how much you get off on this, bunny."

"Yes." She nodded, fingers jumping into my hair as I came back up to her lips and kissed her hard, demanding every moan and small sigh of my name from her.

"My little bunny who loves her stalker. *Say it*."

"I love you," Dahlia whispered.

"Fuck. I love that," I snarled against her lips and gripped her jaw harder. "Do you know how hard it is to watch you from a distance all day? Without touching you? Tasting you? To see you smile at other people when the only people who should be so fucking lucky are the ones you come back to here? Do you know how fucking hard it is to not kill every bastard that tries to take you from us? Thinking that they have a right to take what's ours and always will be?"

"Oh, wow." Dahlia's voice was shaky, and I could feel how close she was to coming, her entire body clinging to mine.

Which was why I leaned down to kiss her hard before pulling my hands away from her body, turning her sharply away before pulling her against me. I groaned as her ass pressed against my cock, her body pinned against the metal of the table as my hand found its way back to her jaw in a possessive hold, tilting it back so that I could see her gaze. Her heated and lust-filled gaze. I had to imagine the bite of the metal table pressing into her thighs hurt, but she only spread her legs further, squirming against me.

I used my other hand to slowly pull the robe off each arm until she was standing completely naked in front of me, her head tilted back and throat exposed submissively. Fuck. I could come just from looking at Dahlia, that was how bad this was. Everything about her spoke to how much she needed my touch, and I found I couldn't help myself, circling her clit again as I nipped her ear.

"I was going to make you wait to come until you were begging, but you need it, don't you? You need me to fix it?"

Mine. So fucking mine. It was all I could think about, seeing her like this.

"Yes," she hissed as if in pain.

The woman had no fucking idea. I'd been in a constant state of pain for goddamn years now.

"Then you're going to come with me inside of you. Are you going to let me between your legs, Dahlia? You've already said you loved me, so I'm never letting you go, but will you let me claim you completely? Fill you with my cum until it's dripping down your thighs?"

"Please?" Her whimper had me chuckling softly, sliding my hand from her jaw down to her hip as my other squeezed her perky ass, causing her to spread her legs more, arching her back against me. I let out a low groan, loving the view of her nearly bent over one of these tables. I spent all day imagining this shit, and now I had Dahlia naked and in my arms. I felt like the luckiest bastard in the world, especially since she knew I fucking stalked her.

"Are you sore?" I nipped her shoulder as she bent further over the table, her ass rocking back against me as I considered just how hard I could take her. Because I wanted to fuck her hard. Really goddamn hard. But I also had no intention of my bunny remembering this as anything but fucking amazing.

"A little," she moaned as I ran my fingers over her slit once again, "but I need this, Yates. Please?"

Goddamn it, this woman was going to kill me. I loved how vocal she was. I smiled against her neck as I considered sinking my teeth into her skin. Marking her.

After all, if she was a bunny, then I was the big bad wolf she was letting fuck her.

"My greedy little bunny." I licked the side of her neck, tasting her sweet skin. "Don't worry, I won't let you suffer. I plan on fucking you, sore or not."

"Yates." Her whine of my name had me sliding both hands to her waist and pressing her forward as I pulled out my cock, fisting it and running the hard tip against her hot cunt. I couldn't deny the low moan that broke from my throat at the feel of her against me. This woman was sent to fucking destroy me, I was absolutely convinced of it.

I took half a second to look over her, to memorize the sight, brand it into my subconscious. Because it was also the last thing I would see before I lost all of myself in Dahlia. It was my last rational thought for the rest of my life, because the moment I was buried in her and came inside of her, I knew my obsession would grow into something insatiable. Predatorial. More twisted than it already was.

There was no helping it. No stopping it. No preventing it.

She looked back at me, hunger in her green eyes, trusting me to fix it...

I slammed into her, balls deep, without asking and without warning. I watched pleasure, surprise, and a tinge of pain flash across her expression as she cried out my name. I kept one hand on her waist as I wrapped the other in her hair, fisting the soft locks as I began to pound in and out of her. I didn't wait for her to get used to me. I was a bastard for it, but I also craved her. I needed her like nothing else, and she said she wanted me, so I would give her all of me. Plus, the way she was arching and pushing back against me, moaning and gripping the table, told me she didn't mind one fucking bit.

My pace only grew harder and more unrelenting as her knees practically gave out, her body fully bent over the table as she called out my name, her frame wracked with shivers as the cold surface contrasted her hot temperature. I pulled back on her hair just slightly as she cried out, an orgasm slamming into her hard as she tried to grip the table underneath her, the smooth metal causing her hands to slip. She couldn't brace herself, she just had to take all of me, and the sound of her ass hitting against my pelvis with each thrust was like music to my fucking ears.

"Goddamn it," I snarled, "You feel so fucking amazing, bunny. You were made to be fucked. Hard."

My hand came across her ass and she jolted, tightening around me. I knew I wasn't going to last much longer, so I tugged her back against me, my hand probably bruising on her throat as I continued to slide in and out of her.

"Say it," I demanded against her ear, biting down on it. "Say it while your tight little cunt milks my cock. I want to stuff you so full of cum—"

"Yates!" she screamed, climaxing again as I groaned, loving how she was doing exactly as I told her. Well, mostly...

"Say it," I growled. "I'll fucking stop if you don't."

I wouldn't. Nothing could pull me out of her.

"I love you," she moaned. "God, I love you, Yates."

Love was too small of a word to describe how I felt for Dahlia Aldridge.

Her words were a trigger for me, my name on her lips paired with the notion of this amazing woman loving me causing me to bury myself to the hilt and groan out her name into her neck as her entire body shuddered against mine. My release seemed to continue on forever, dripping back down onto my cock from where it overflowed her tight cunt, both of our releases mixing. I shouldn't have been surprised by how much it was, considering I'd never come so hard in my life and for sure never inside of anyone, let alone Dahlia. But holy shit would I be coming in her more often. As in every single goddamn day.

I pulled out of Dahlia, her whimper causing me to feel a sense of satisfaction that was bone deep as I turned her towards me, her perfect ass on the table as I stepped between her legs and slid back in, wanting to feel that connection with her. She clung to me, her breathing rough, as I rocked inside of her, loving how she seemed to squeeze me in the aftershocks of her climax. After a moment, she let go of me and fell back against the table with a sated smile, her eyes closed as her fingers intertwined with mine that were smoothing against her hips. I felt mesmerized by the gorgeous creature that let me between her legs even after admitting some shit that I was positive could get me institutionalized.

I had given her fair warning though.

"So you never hated me," she mumbled and opened her eyes, offering me a small, smug smile.

I couldn't help but laugh. "Hated you? Oh no, Dahlia. I fucking love you. That should scare you far more."

"Maybe I was being honest." She sat up, her fingers smoothing over my bare chest as her legs opened wider, allowing me to sink in further. "Maybe I love that you're obsessed with me. That you stalk me."

I couldn't help the smile that grew at my twisted bunny. She may not have been as dark as we were, but I knew that was because of the bubble she'd been in. The more she was exposed to the life we led, the more it would become normal. We all had dark souls, and I could feel our shadows and our sins infecting her innocence.

The best part? The woman didn't seem to mind. She was

sinking willingly into the shadows, and it made it all the more hot and maddening to watch.

Dahlia Aldridge consumed me.

"You better hope that's not the case." I ghosted my lips over hers.

"Why?" she asked breathlessly.

"Because you don't realize the things I would do for you, especially if I knew you were okay with them," I admitted, nipping her bottom lip.

Before she could respond, a knock on the door had her blushing as I smirked. Pulling out, her eyes flared, watching where we had been connected, her little pussy looking absolutely wrecked and messy with cum. I let out a low rumble and helped her slip back on the robe before adjusting my sweatpants. I was already missing being inside of her. I caught her up in my arms as a second knock sounded.

"I love you," I whispered gently.

"I know." Her smile was coy and had my cock hardening... which shouldn't have been possible after how much I had come minutes ago. I groaned, watching her walk towards the door and swing it open to find Sterling and Stratton.

"Hey guys," she chirped.

Sterling offered her an amused look as Stratton narrowed his eyes at the room behind us. The room he was no doubt a bit shocked by. Only King had known to some extent how bad my obsession had gotten in the past year or so. I didn't care anymore if they knew.

Plus, the room also had a shit ton of file storage for other stuff, so they should have access. It was extremely secure. I wouldn't want anyone else to be able to get access to all that information about Dahlia, after all.

"How are you doing, sugar?" Sterling mused, unsurprised by her reaction.

"Wonderful." She then offered me a teasing smile. "Just

finding out all about Yates being obsessed with me. Extremely flattering, honestly."

I chuckled at that as she led Sterling towards the stairs. What was I going to do with her? She was never going to let me live this down, that much was clear.

"She isn't scared of what a lunatic you are?" Stratton asked.

I flashed him a smile and shook my head. "She was into it," I said smugly.

"Crazy. All of you are crazy," Stratton muttered, looking partly amused as we made our way downstairs. I frowned, suddenly thinking about what had happened this morning.

"Did security tell all of you—"

"That you shot someone this morning?" Stratton took out a cigarette and lit up. "Yeah. King was somewhat upset about that one, mostly because he was worried about Dahlia. Seems like she's fine though."

"Eh, the murder part might have freaked her out," I admitted.

"Well I hope it's not too bad, because she's going to probably be freaked out again when she sees King."

I grabbed a shirt quickly from my bedroom before we kept walking down the hallway, following the sound of Dahlia's voice. "What do you mean?"

"He may have lost it a bit," Stratton hedged.

Fuck.

Chapter Twelve

DAHLIA ALDRIDGE

"Angel, I do not expect you to go tonight, not after everything. In fact, I never expect you to come to this stupid shit." Stratton's voice was gruff as King tensed underneath my fingers in response to the reminder of what had occurred this morning.

I continued to smooth his hair as we lay on my bed, King's large frame between my legs, his arms wrapped around my center and head pressed against my stomach. To say the past hour had been interesting would probably be surprising considering everything I'd been through today. But it was true.

Honestly, at this point, I was somewhat just rolling with it... between witnessing a man get shot and finding out Yates was legitimately obsessed with me, something had just snapped in my head. My rational reactions were absent, and I wasn't positive if it was a coping mechanism or I had just compartmentalized it already. Either way, I actually felt rather good right now.

Personally? I think I'd just hit my limit and now I had broken into 'if you can't beat them, join them' mode.

I would put a pin in that for now.

When we had left Yates's house, Sterling had led me over to King's, still in my robe as he 'apologized in advance' but didn't explain why. Well, I realized pretty quickly why when I walked into the Ross family office and found King absolutely furious, more mad than I had ever seen him as he berated security for allowing that 'motherfucker' onto the property. They had looked terrified, and I would have to say rightly so considering the glass shattered on the ground—apparently from when he had first come in here, furious beyond words—and the look he was giving them, his chest heaving.

While I wasn't used to King being that angry, it felt essential that I calmed him down. It felt like he was hanging on the edge of something that was more vicious than his fury at the time. So I had crossed the room, not caring that he was in the middle of yelling at them, and wrapped my arms around his muscular frame.

I hadn't known what would happen but I was extremely happy when he seemed to snap out of it, backing away from that dangerous ledge. King was done after that and ordered them from the room, the disgust with their performance very obvious. At that point I'd taken his hand and brought him to my house, the others following. I could tell all of them were exhausted, so we all relaxed in my bedroom as half of them dozed off.

Well, until Stratton mentioned leaving for the fight.

"Oh, I'm going," I assured him as King let out a low rumble in his throat but pressed a gentle kiss to my stomach. When I'd gotten into my room, I'd changed into an oversized shirt and sleep shorts, and he had managed to push up my shirt so he could lay his face on my bare stomach. I had no idea why I found the action so endearing.

"Dahlia," Stratton warned, his face filled with concern.

"I'll take her." Dermot let out a yawn from next to us.

King relaxed a bit, making me know he trusted Dermot to keep me safe at this fight.

I imagine he would want to go, but Yates, King, and the twins were going to meet with Callum and show him the video of what happened today, considering the man had threatened me about getting involved. I think King was going because he worked with Callum the most, Yates clearly had videos of *everything,* and the twins were going to do 'damage control.'

Which translated into mitigating King's reaction to seeing the video... Although, as I looked at Yates speculatively, I wasn't positive he would be any better.

My lips pressed up again, thinking about Yates and how insane he was. It did make me wonder where the cameras were.

Suddenly, I blushed, thinking about all the times I'd laid in bed whispering their names as I ran my fingers along my wet heat until I came at the idea of them touching me. Not just one of them, either. *Christ.* Had he seen that? I wasn't positive if the thought embarrassed me or turned me on... no, I did know. It was very much the second one.

Clearly he didn't have one in the bathroom, because then he would have realized just how much I weighed myself. How much I'd thrown up. Thank god for that.

I should have been more upset about the insane invasion of privacy... but instead I found it sort of hot. I liked that he was always watching me. I liked that his feelings bordered, or completely bulldozed into, the notion of 'unhealthy.' Was that wrong of me? *God.* Clearly something was wrong with me, right?

"Princess." King's voice was silky and calm, way more calm than I knew him to be. I looked at him as his green eyes inspected my face curiously, the anger from before thinly veiled as he tried to appear relaxed for me. It was a sweet effort, but I also knew that it was probably just going to make this worse in the long run. Maybe there was something else we could do to get his frustration handled...

"What are you thinking about?" he questioned

My cheeks turned pink as I considered the array of thoughts I had just run through. I nibbled my lip. "That is a complicated question. I am thinking about a lot today, and honestly attempting to not think at all."

There. Honest. Right?

"That sounds dangerous," Dermot rumbled.

"Me thinking?" I turned my head.

"Dahlia is always overthinking," Yates pointed out from where he sat with Lincoln, both of them looking over something.

Sterling nodded from where he sat at the end of the bed watching the television. "It's true, she is."

I shrugged and turned my head to look at Dermot. "It's nothing bad."

Because if I really let everything that happened today seep through, I could end up screaming, and that wouldn't be good.

"Unlikely," Yates quipped from across the room as I narrowed my eyes.

"Sassy, Yates, especially for someone who just..." I let my words trail off as he offered me a dangerous narrowed glance, daring me to continue.

"Who just what?" Stratton asked, amused.

"Oh, nothing." I continued to run my hands through King's hair as he chuckled. I knew he and Dermot would protect me. Hopefully.

Yates stood and walked across the room, leaning over the bed as I squeaked, sinking against the pillows. "What, Dahlia? What did I do?"

Admitted to loving me.

Stalked me.

And then fucked me in your little stalker cave.

"Help!" I used my spare hand to tap Dermot's chest and he chuckled, pulling me by the hips and out from under King, who made a disgruntled noise. I curled against Dermot's chest and smiled at Yates.

"I'm waiting, bunny," he stated, unperturbed.

"Dahlia," Dermot warned.

I smiled against his chest. "Someone who just told me they loved me."

"That wasn't what you were going to say," Yates immediately snapped back.

I laughed because he was right, but if you think I was about to get myself in that much trouble in a room of all of them, you were sorely mistaken.

Before I could poke fun at him, our banter clearly and unfortunately not leading in the sexy direction despite earlier, Yates's phone pinged with a notification. He eyed it and then looked at King. "Jet will be ready tomorrow, we are set to leave around three."

"You mean the afternoon, right?" I demanded, my eyes widening. "Please say you mean the afternoon."

His smile grew as he chuckled. "Unfortunately not, bunny."

"Don't worry, we can take a nap once we are on," Lincoln said, his face nonchalant and not matching the heated look he pointed in my direction. Right, a nap... sure. Somehow I just did not believe he meant that.

"Fine." I scowled and rolled off Dermot, my face flushing as I felt just how hard he was, a low groan escaping his throat. I walked towards my closet and immediately began pulling out what I wanted to wear.

"Wear a hoodie." Stratton was right behind me, the voices

of the others in the room giving us a moment of privacy as I looked up at him.

"A hoodie?" I asked, half amused by the serious look on his face.

"And anything else you have to cover up," he grumbled and then wrapped an arm around my waist. "I hate that you're going to be around any of these fuckers."

"I'm there to support you," I defended softly.

His eyes warmed as he nodded and then nipped my ear in his warning to wear a hoodie. I didn't mind—after what I experienced last time, I was happy to wear comfortable, dark clothes that wouldn't get me noticed. I shouldn't have to worry about that. Heck, no woman should. But after everything that happened today, I was ready to bury myself under layers of clothes and blankets to keep myself comfortable.

I was just waiting for it to hit. The moment where all of this became too much.

Because I wasn't dumb. I knew how my anxiety worked, and I had a feeling that the moment of reckoning was coming, waves of desperation that would berate me. I was trying so hard to keep the other demons at bay, the ones that relished in my suffering.

I wasn't positive how long it would work for, and that terrified me.

Trying to remove those thoughts from my head, I began getting ready, the process not taking very long considering I was just braiding my hair and applying some light makeup. The others, with the exception of Dermot and Stratton, each said goodbye before heading downstairs to go to the meeting with Callum.

Almost instantly I was missing them, their absence removing some of the warmth from me. Then the sound of Stratton and Dermot's quiet conversation from inside my bedroom soothed me. I never realized how lonely my space was without them constantly in it. Now that I had that—had them—I wasn't positive I could return back to that other state.

"Angel." Stratton's voice was soft and commanding as I looked to the door, finding him looking over me with a heat that didn't match the oversized hoodie and leggings I'd chosen. I would probably be hot, but that was okay.

"Like it?" I turned, showing off the hoodie I'd stolen from him some time ago.

What? The man had left it on my armchair one morning our sophomore year... and he'd totally done that on purpose. I nearly face-palmed at how oblivious I could be.

"I didn't realize you'd kept it," he grunted, stepping forward and pulling me against him. "I fucking love seeing you in my shit."

I smiled up at him. "Well, I figured if you were going to be bossy about what I'd wear, I would wear your stuff."

"And you listened to me, despite me being 'bossy.'" His pleased tone seemed to flare with a dominance I didn't expect as his grip tightened on me. I held my breath as he seemed to snap out of it and pressed a kiss to my forehead. "I wanted you to have a piece of me with you even though we weren't talking."

"I slept in it pretty often," I admitted and then nibbled my lip. "But you stopped coming to sleep in my room around that time."

His eyes flared. "I didn't trust myself. I felt—*I feel*—way too much for you, and with you inches away in bed, sleeping and blissfully unaware of me watching you... I just didn't trust myself."

I saw that, and yet his words caused my body to heat as I pressed closer to him.

"What would you have done?" I asked softly. A dark look seemed to fill his gaze, his hand sliding up the back of my neck to angle my head. A small whimper left my throat as he brushed his lips against mine in a soft caress.

"Maybe I'll show you sometime," he mused quietly. "Show you what I imagined doing to you. How I wanted to wake you up. How I wanted to take my frustration out on you after spending all day wishing you had talked to me. Or fuck, even looked my way."

"Stratton..." My voice sounded almost breathless at what he was implying. I was extremely interested in far more details or an example on him waking me up, for the record.

His smile was still dangerous, but his touch softened, caressing my skin and surrounding me with affection. "But right now I need to get my ass to this fight. Be safe on the drive over, okay?"

"Okay." I nodded, feeling completely off balance but absolutely enamored with this broody, confusing, sexy man. I sincerely considered speaking the words that were at the tip of my tongue again, the ones that I had admitted to at the last fight when I indirectly told Stratton that I loved him. The man had yet to return the sentiment, but I was trying not to think about it too much... and clearly failing.

As he walked out, I let out a small sigh and looked at myself in the mirror, wondering how so much had changed in the span of forty-eight hours. Hadn't it only been Tuesday when I woke up to go to my tennis lesson? I may have been stressed then, but now... well, now was much different.

"You ready, baby girl?" Dermot pulled me from my thoughts as I flashed a smile at the man, an authentic one, his stunning green eyes and handsome face making it easy to forget where my thoughts had begun to go.

"Yes." I nodded and walked towards him. Before I could slip out the door, he caught me by the shoulders and dipped his head down, surprising me with a searing kiss then had my knees going weak. I blinked hazily as he pulled back, his smile cocky as I tried to not find that ridiculously attractive. His hand gripped my one braid and tugged lightly, examining my expression as his own turned more serious.

"Are you actually okay? After everything that happened today?" Dermot's eyes were shaded darker as he switched tones on me so fast I had to take a moment to fully process what he was saying. I could see the concern there, and I didn't blame him. I imagine after what he experienced with me the other day, he was worried I was going to have a mental breakdown. Which probably wasn't far from the truth.

"Am I okay?" I asked and frowned. "I am right now."

"And in the future?" He tilted his head thoughtfully.

"I honestly don't know. I have a feeling this is all going to hit me, and then I may freak out a bit," I whispered and then offered him a smile. "But right now? Now, I'm good."

Dermot examined my expression as if he didn't fully believe me before nodding slowly, seemingly lost in memory as he considered his next words. "Seeing your first death like that is hard."

"I think it's more of the shooting his brains out part, not the death," I stated rather bluntly.

Dermot's smile grew, looking amused at the dark humor that had accidentally slipped out of me. I hadn't even meant to be funny, but I did appreciate that he found me so. Then again, Dermot may smile and laugh at my jokes even if he didn't find them funny. The man was sweet like that.

Tucking me under his arm, we walked through the house in relative peace as I considered how comfortable the two of us were. I had no idea how that was possible considering we hadn't even known each other a week. Yet here I was, tucked under his arm and feeling as if I'd known him for years rather than days.

I think there were just people like that, though. People that you connected with on an unexpected level almost immediately. Despite our lack of a history, I felt like I knew Dermot. I figured the best move with him was to just trust my instincts.

As we walked out of the house, Dermot paused momentarily, his eyes looking skyward for helicopters or drones most likely, before tracking towards the gate where security was posted.

My stomach tightened as my vision narrowed on the guard house. I tried to shake myself, but I didn't realize I wasn't walking forward until Dermot was holding my face and talking to me in a gentle tone.

"I need you to breathe, Dahlia, and don't look at the guard house." His tone was firm and calm, almost commanding. I nodded, breathing in through my nose, before exhaling. I could feel sweat breaking out on the back of my neck, but I kept my eyes on him as he gently led me across the street.

I was distracted enough that I didn't have time to appreciate his stunning brick colonial estate that I'd not so secretly lusted after for years or his gorgeous Aston Martin, both of which I would have usually spent copious amounts of time appreciating. Instead I let him place me in the passenger seat as I tried to pull out of the weird sensation coursing through me, almost like panic but darker.

I gripped the seat, trying to ground myself. Looks like I hadn't been completely wrong. I had been fine around my boys as a group and without seeing a reminder of what had happened today, but now there weren't distractions. Now I was faced with the truth of the guard house that we would be driving right past. I swallowed nervously as he backed out of the driveway.

He ran a hand over my leg as he drove towards King's driveway instead of the gate. I felt like I could breathe again, the temporary threat of going past the guard station gone as I stared at him in confusion. It made a bit more sense, though, as he drove down the long driveway that looped towards the back of the house. I felt my eyes widen as security stood near another long, winding road that clearly was used for them patrolling the Wildberry grounds. I found myself feeling much better as we began driving down the lane, music playing through the car in a low, steady rhythm as my ears rang with the effects of the emotions I'd felt moments ago. I don't think I fully pulled out of it until we exited through a gate that led to a road out back. The moment we were on the main road, I looked over to Dermot, who was watching me with concern.

"I'm fine," I promised. *Especially since he went out of his way to make sure we didn't go past the guard house.* I didn't want him worrying that I was going to freak out at every single turn. No one deserved to live feeling so on edge.

"Don't pull that shite with me," he said calmly as my eyes widened. "You're not fine, and I don't expect you to be. Yates shot someone right in front of you, baby girl. I would be shocked if you were fine."

I nodded, sinking into the expensive seats, examining the dark storm clouds above as twilight filled the space around us. It was a beautiful, stormy night, and honestly, if it wasn't for the mounting tension in my shoulders and my headache, I probably would have found it romantic. Instead, I closed my eyes and intertwined my fingers with Dermot's, his grip on my thigh comforting and a bit possessive. I felt a surge of heat roll over me that did a lot of good to pull me out of this haze.

Was that the key to my anxiety? Sexy men doing sexy things? Well, I had that in spades here, fortunately.

"You know, I've never been to Ireland before," I mused softly, rain starting to speckle the windshield as I thought about leaving for the plane so early in the morning. "Which is weird, considering that everyone else has been there. But I've only been to London, and that was once. I'm excited for tomorrow."

Dermot offered me a look, seeming to gauge something, and then squeezed my leg. "That was on purpose. You haven't been to Ireland because no one wanted to risk your association with the family."

My mouth popped open as I blinked and ran a hand over my face, offering a small laugh. "Well now I just feel stupid."

"Not stupid," he argued, his tone serious.

I nodded, realizing he didn't like when I said stuff like that. I turned in my seat to face him and realized that something was bothering him. Something more than my words.

"Are you excited to go back? You just left; I can't imagine you are."

His voice was a low rumble. "The compound doesn't bother me. My father's estate next door? I would be happy to never set a foot in that disaster again."

"You don't get along with your father?" I asked, my tone gentle because I could see pain there despite him being a serious pro at hiding it.

Dermot's chuckle was soft and dangerous. "Understatement, Dahlia. The man is an absolute bastard. One of the many reasons he has been removed from a position in the Ross family business."

"And your mom?" I was hoping for a better story there. Despite knowing who Dermot was, King never really talked about his family in Ireland, and well, I was starting to realize why now.

"Walked out on us."

"Oh my god," I squeaked, feeling horrible. "I am so sorry—"

"Happened forever ago, Dahlia, you didn't know." His voice was soft and patient, his gaze finding mine as he offered me a small smile. "Probably for the better. Plus, I don't blame the woman for leaving. My father is a piece of shite. "

I nodded cautiously, not wanting to offer an opinion of that because I was already worried I was messing this up. "Is there any chance we won't see your father while we're there?"

"No," he sighed and then tensed, "Well, you won't, but he will make a point out of seeing me. I'm keeping him far the fuck away from you."

I frowned. "If he's a jerk like you said, you shouldn't have to see him alone."

Something soft passed across his features as he picked up my hand and kissed it gently. "I don't trust him, and I *really* don't trust him with you around."

I blinked and nodded. "That bad?"

Dermot seemed to disappear in his memories for a moment before he inhaled and nodded. I didn't push it, instead tightening my grip on his hand and leaning my head against his arm despite the center console between us. Closing my eyes, I let the hum of the car serve as a relaxing moment before the insanity I knew that would be at this fight.

I wasn't wrong.

As we pulled up into the grass and mud parking lot outside of the quarry, I noticed that there were far more people than last time. It was also drizzling, which made it harder to see, but from what I could tell, it was also more rowdy. Dermot made a noise in this throat that sounded vaguely threatening as he parked his car in the dark near the far edge of the trees. I didn't blame him, considering people were jumping on cars in the parking lot.

He leaned over, and I thought he was going to kiss me, honest to god, which of course caused me to be truly shocked when he opened the glove box and pulled out a gun. My eyes widened as he opened up his jacket, a dark zip-up, and holstered it against his chest. When he finally caught my expression, he grew amused.

"Better safe than sorry, baby girl. I would love to say that I can protect you completely on my own, but there are a lot more of them than me." He kissed me then and hopped out of the car, causing me to shake my head as I wondered just what type of crazy these men were.

Well, clearly I knew the type. I also was clearly attracted to the type.

"I wish he wasn't even doing this fight," I admitted softly.

"You should tell him that."

I shook my head. "I have, but I can only tell him so much, especially considering the circumstances."

Dermot nodded in understanding and pulled up my hood as he put his large, muscular arm over my shoulders, passing a couple pressed against a motorcycle doing... Well, I'm not positive what they were doing. From what I could hear, though, they both seemed to be enjoying it, so that was good, right?

"Fucking bastards," Dermot muttered after we had passed another group of guys smoking something. It wasn't pot or cigarettes, and it had Dermot looking tense as all get-out, so I curled further into him. This wasn't my scene at all. I was here for Stratton, so it was worth it, but I had never felt as much of a contrast as I did currently.

As we neared the ring, people cleared out of the way for Dermot, and I didn't blame them. Looking up at the man, I realized just how intimidating he was. His dark hair was damp from the rain, making him look even more dangerous as he kept an eye on everyone around us, his expression calm and calculating. Practiced.

Yeah, I was a bit out of my league here. At least when it came to whatever the Ross family was serving up. I suppose it had been a bit easier to ignore those elements with King because I'd known him for so long, but Dermot was different. I could see the tension rolling under his skin, and the way he held himself had me wondering just how quickly he could pull that gun out.

I was going to take a bet and say extremely fast.

"You can't keep looking at me like that, Dahlia." His voice was low and vibrated through his chest, against me, as his eyes flashed down.

"Like what?" I asked softly, knowing how he probably saw me looking at him. Because as I was learning, it seemed the things that should have scared me with my boys didn't. They turned me on. They also made me feel safe, which after everything that had been going on, was really nice.

"You know, baby girl." He pinned me with a look as I offered him a small smile.

I looked up as we reached the main ring, my eyes immediately spotting Stratton, who was standing outside of the ring, his arms folded as he ignored the man next to him, offering small answers or non-responsive nods. I examined the man in question, his worn leather jacket featuring a massive amount of patches. His tanned face and long black and gray hair put him at a slightly older age, and his clear attempt to goad Stratton, based on his mannerisms, had me feeling angry.

Stratton's eyes met mine before moving over to Dermot, seeming to convey something, before snapping back to the man trying to talk to him. I looked up at Dermot, who kept us exactly where we were. I offered him a questioning look on why we weren't going over there.

"I have a feeling that is the exact person that Stratton doesn't want you to meet," he admitted quietly. "Let's stay right here for now. Are you good with that?"

I nodded, not wanting to mess anything up as I wrapped my arms around his waist, keeping my head hidden from the rain as the current fight wrapped up. I desperately wanted to be over there in his corner supporting him, but Dermot was right. I didn't want to trivialize Stratton's concerns, so I stayed wrapped up in Dermot's arms.

When Stratton's fight began, I straightened up further, watching as my tattooed, *way to hot for his own good*, motorcycle god stripped off his shirt after dropping his jacket in the corner. I noticed the cool level of calculation in his gaze, and it made me feel confident in this fight despite the size of the man he was going against.

I frowned, realizing the older man that had been bothering Stratton was in his opponent's corner, the fighter featuring a massive tattoo that was the exact same sigil that the older man had on his jacket. A moth? Hadn't Dermot said something about Denim Moths? Made sense now. Although —and I knew they probably didn't care—if they were the Denim Moths... wouldn't it make more sense to wear denim, not leather?

No? Just me? Honestly, that was completely possible.

When the announcer started the first round, my eyes widened as the opponent bulldozed forward, making Stratton dart out of the way. I watched as Stratton easily moved around the man, and Dermot chuckled as he landed a blow so hard to the side of the man's head that he stumbled. It seemed like the guy he was facing relied completely on brute strength. I tensed as he moved forward again, and this time Stratton was more prepared, hitting him not only in the side but then in the face, sending the man stumbling back and onto the ground. Apparently that was enough for them to call round one.

I was thrilled and also concerned. My eyes darted over to the Denim Moths, who looked furious, the older man yelling in the ear of the massive guy, who looked like he had a broken nose. Stratton didn't seem nearly as pleased with his first round win, his eyes narrowed on the interaction in the corner as if he could read their lips. Maybe he could. The crowd was growing increasingly rowdy as people were jostled around us, Dermot moving me in front of him as he pulled me firmly and tightly against him.

His chin rested on the top of my head, and I would say it was cute because it felt that way, but I had a feeling the man was trying to keep me away from everyone else as much as possible without tucking me into his jacket and zipping it up. I leaned back into him as round two began.

"Come on, Stratton," I murmured, wishing I could cheer for him. Dermot squeezed me slightly and I looked up, his eyes narrowed ahead and to the right. When I looked, my chest tightened, realizing that it was the guys from the grocery store. They were talking to the older man, looking over at me.

Crap.

"We are leaving," Dermot ordered softly, his hand on my back as he began to edge me towards the back of the crowd, people parting immediately. I could feel his hand hesitating near his jacket, and I honestly wouldn't blame him for pulling out his gun right now considering the amount of weapons I could see on people.

The crowd cheered behind us as suddenly we were tugged back... Well, Dermot was yanked back, and I snapped around, finding a massive man holding Dermot around the neck with his large forearm. I panicked, moving forward to move his arm, or at least try to. Dermot released a dangerous noise in response to the man's threat as I froze, realizing that there was a gun pressed to his head.

Oh my god.

"Go to the car," Dermot said evenly, his voice rough from the pressure the massive guy was putting on him.

No. I wasn't going to do that.

Another cheer went up as I realized Stratton had been

knocked on his ass. My stomach sank. How much did we want to bet it was because he was distracted?

"We need to borrow Dahlia for just a minute," someone spoke from behind me, causing me to jump as the older man's bony but strong hand clasped around my forearm. Dermot let out a low growl as the man led me forward, something that I suspected was a gun pressing against my back as the crowd moved for us, everyone seeming to ignore what was going on as Dermot went unusually quiet. I had no idea what he was thinking, and honestly the threat of a weapon pressed to my body was having me blank out slightly, though my panic rose as we drew closer to the corner. Stratton, who was wiping blood from his nose, immediately met my gaze from across the ring.

I had thought I'd seen every emotion on Stratton's face before, but the authentic fear and fury there had me feeling almost like I'd had the wind knocked from me. The older man wrapped a hand around my neck as the hard, cold object moved to the back of my neck. Realization dawned on Stratton's face as the announcer began talking the crowd up for the final round, which would determine who would win. I honestly thought I would be crying or something in response to the threat to me right now, but instead I was completely focused on Stratton. I had a feeling that he was the one really in danger and we were just pawns.

"You better hope he throws this round," the older man mused.

Dermot cursed as the man tightened his grip on his neck. I realized then his hands were being restrained by the man at an angle that almost made them look broken. Instead of looking like he was in pain, though, he looked furious. It was actually terrifying, his gaze meeting mine as he looked at the hand around my throat, his jaw tightening to the point I worried it would break.

This day... This was one for the books.

"You're doing all of this for fucking money from a fight?" Dermot demanded softly, his voice laced with something truly lethal.

The older man let out a low growl. "No, you Irish fuck, I'm doing this so the boy learns some goddamn respect. You don't refuse an invitation from the Denim Moths, trust fund piece of shit."

"We were going to go after his grandma before the next fight, but you showed up at just the right time," he growled in my ear. "Now tell me, Dahlia, does Stratton let just anyone fuck you? Because from what I saw on the news, you seem to be into that."

Christ.

"I would sincerely suggest you stop fucking talking to her." Dermot's voice was icy as the man tensed slightly but ignored him.

Both of us looked up as round three started, and I watched as Stratton pretended to fight. When the larger opponent landed three fists to his head and two in the ribs, authentic pain blossomed on his face. He dropped heavily as the man hit him one more time. I had a feeling that he hadn't needed it, but it ended the round quickly.

Stratton struggled to stand before he grabbed his shirt and jacket and strode across the ring, hopping over the rope and down into the mud, his blue eyes lit up with an amount of anger that I hoped to never see again as he stormed over to us.

"You won your fucking match, get your goddamn hands off her," he snarled. The blood that covered his face caused him to look authentically terrifying, his body vibrating with an energy that rivaled the turbulent night sky.

The older man released me, and Stratton tugged me forward against him. Dermot grunted as the large man released him, and he immediately went for his jacket before the older man laughed.

"I wouldn't do that, boy," he warned.

Dermot seemed to pause, his temper nearly getting the better of him before he reined it in, a seemingly wise choice considering almost everyone around us had weapons of some kind.

The man looked to Stratton. "You go up against any of our guys, you lose. You want to win more, then I will be waiting for you to accept our invitation." He flashed a smile. "Either that or I will be paying a personal visit to Dahlia and maybe that sweet grandma of yours."

Stratton was shaking with fury but he kept quiet, leading me out as Dermot walked ahead of us, both of them seeming to want to get out of here as soon as possible. Oddly, I found myself rather calm, more worried about them than myself. When we finally made it to the parking lot, Stratton crushed me against him.

"Never fucking again," he growled. "You can't come to these anymore, understand?"

"Yes." I nodded, not wanting to set him off more because I could see how freaked out he was. The man wrapped his arms around me further as Dermot talked quietly on the phone. How much did we want to bet it was King?

I ran my nose against Stratton's neck as he lifted me up, his arms underneath my butt.

"Fuck, that was terrifying," he said through a strained voice.

"Did he hurt you?" I pulled back and examined his face, a dark bruise forming on his nose and cheek.

"Doesn't matter," he growled before kissing me softly, making me want to pour everything into it. Every ounce of concern and worry about him. The taste of his blood exploded between us from the injury on his lip, and I let out a small moan of surprise, mostly because of the pulse of heat that hit my center.

Stratton let out a low growl and pulled back, still looking extremely upset. "Get in Dermot's car and let's get back home. I'm over this shit. I don't know what I'm going to do, but this is clearly not working."

I watched as Stratton got on his motorcycle and strapped on his helmet, making me breathe a sigh of relief. When I looked back at Dermot, he was hanging up his phone and ushering me around the car, the lightning illuminating the mud pit that served as the parking lot.

I was distracted enough by the storm that until we started driving, I didn't realize the tension that was running through Dermot's frame. My gaze ran over the white-knuckle grip he had on the steering wheel and how his gaze was focused ahead, the tick in his jaw making me almost nervous. I hadn't known the man long, but I had never seen him this worked up.

I swallowed nervously and slid back into my seat, turning slightly to keep my gaze on him.

"Dermot?" I asked softly, his eyes snapping over to me.

"Yeah?" His voice was rough and raspy.

"Are you okay?" I whispered softly, repeating the question he'd asked me earlier.

"No."

Chapter Thirteen

DAHLIA ALDRIDGE

His answer was the last time he spoke until we had reached the back entrance to Wildberry, his mind seemingly a million miles away. If this were any of my other boys, I could have told you what they were thinking, but this was Dermot. I had no idea if he was pissed at what happened, pissed that we went, or pissed at me. I didn't think he had a reason to be pissed at me... then again, because of me, he got a gun put to his head.

My fingers went to run through my hair, but my braid stopped me. I considered taking them out but I was already semi-damp, and I didn't want to ruin his car with my wet hair. I really was trying to avoid making him any more upset than he already was.

It wasn't normally my style to walk on eggshells, but something instinctual told me that an angry Dermot was a bad thing. A really bad thing. Not that I was in danger or that he would hurt me, but just to be cautious.

"I'm going to drop you at your house—"

"Where are you going?" I asked instantly, both worried about why he wouldn't be with the rest of us and insecure about why he wanted to get away from me. At least that's how it felt.

Dermot looked at me, his eyes nearly black in the shadows of the car, his voice strained as he responded. "Going on a drive to calm down."

I examined his expression and frowned. I wasn't positive that I believed him. As he finally pulled up to my house, Stratton's motorcycle pulling into his driveway, I reached forward to grasp Dermot's hand. He looked at our intertwined fingers and inhaled sharply before offering me a look that sent worry, fear, and a bit of desire running through me.

"Go inside, Dahlia." It was a warning laced with something almost hot. No, I didn't think he was mad at me right now, but he was for sure something. I just didn't know what to call it.

I did know tonight was not the one to push him, so I nodded and leaned forward, pressing a kiss to his cheek before getting out of the car. Dermot made a soft, almost upset sound, but when I looked back he was focused on the rainy street ahead. I closed the door softly, wishing I didn't have to leave him.

I walked towards the porch as Stratton made his way over, both of us watching as Dermot drove off towards the exit. I shook my head at how insane tonight had been as Stratton led me into the house, his temper one I was more familiar with. Which was why I wasn't surprised when my back hit the wall right inside the front door, his frame caging mine against the cold, hard surface.

"Breathe, Stratton," I reminded him softly.

His nose was tucked against my throat as he let out a soft noncommittal sound, his hands squeezing my waist on either side as if he was reassuring himself I was there. There was absolutely no way I could forget how close we were with how good he smelled and how hard he was, my center tightening despite the completely inappropriate timing.

"I could have lost you tonight," he mumbled, his voice raspy and pained. "Fuck, that was way too close, angel."

"Hey." I captured his jaw between my hands. "I am fine. You're fine. Dermot is... well, I think fine. Let's go tell the others what happened and then head to bed, okay?"

Stratton pulled back, examining my expression, before he nodded. The man kept me tucked against him as we headed towards the back of the house. I wasn't too surprised to find King and Sterling in the office, although I did wonder where Lincoln and Yates were.

"Sugar, you're soaking wet." Sterling frowned, coming up to me and wrapping me in his jacket as I laid my head on his chest. Stratton was already on an angry tangent, King's gaze running over me before going back to Stratton and seeming to absorb everything he said regarding the incident with the Denim Moths.

Now that he was here, I had a feeling King hadn't been the one on the other end of the call with Dermot, which begged the question, *Who had been?* Also, was now the time to mention the all-important detail Stratton had left out about a gun being pulled on me as well?

Actually, instinct told me he had left that out on purpose.

"He pulled a gun on Dermot?" King clarified, standing up. "Where is he?"

"Said he was going on a drive," I whispered.

King froze and cursed, tugging on his suit jacket and striding past us. I blinked up at Sterling, who just pulled me further into him. Stratton left the room as well, following after King, as I considered doing the same.

"Should we?" I asked softly.

Sterling shook his head and then frowned. "What exactly happened? Fully."

I had a feeling he would want details. I loved Stratton, but the man had given the CliffsNotes version of everything that had occurred. So I told him, his eyes turning cold and dark like an icy tundra as I explained that I'd had a gun pulled on me as well.

I winced. "Should I have told King that part as well?"

"No," Sterling hissed through clenched teeth. "I am very glad you didn't. Right now there is a chance he can calm Dermot down before he starts some shit, but if he knew that? Well, we probably would be in a different situation."

I inhaled and nodded. "Today has been weird."

He chuckled softly, but the darkness was still there. "Yeah, yeah it has been."

I didn't ask where Lincoln and Yates were, deciding that I was going to sit this one out. I think I was hitting a wall, because as we neared my bedroom, my eyes grew heavier and Sterling picked me up in a princess hold.

That was right about when I fell asleep, exhausted from the day.

Though 'exhausted' was clearly an understatement because my sleep was dreamless, a bone-deep fatigue invading everything. I was still dressed in my oversized hoodie and leggings when I finally blinked my eyes open, Sterling's calm breathing making me feel relaxed as I squinted my eyes at the clock, realizing it was nearly one in the morning. The television was on, so I could see that Stratton was sleeping in the armchair spread out and Lincoln was on the other side of me. I frowned, not liking that I didn't know where Yates, King, and Dermot were.

Slipping from bed, I toed on some slippers and made my way out of my room and down the large marble staircase. I figured I would check the office first. I wasn't disappointed to find King sitting at the desk, his forehead propped up by his hand as Yates sat in front of him in one of the leather chairs with its back to the door. He was saying something quietly, but that wasn't what caught my eye. No, it was Dermot, who was currently knocked out on the couch, his lip busted open.

I stepped into the office and offered King a wide-eyed look, his gaze both tired and angry, something dark brewing under there. My gaze darted to Yates, who was now looking back at me, my eyes narrowing with concern.

"Holy crap!" I slapped a hand over my own mouth, wincing at how loud I was, but thankfully, Dermot didn't wake up.

"He's not waking up anytime soon," Yates mused as I crossed the room and gently grasped his face, looking over the bruising on the side of his jaw and the dried blood from under his nose. Luckily, it didn't seem to be broken.

"What happened?" I demanded.

"We had to 'convince' Dermot to not start a full-out gang war," Yates mused, tugging me down onto his lap and burying his head against my chest. "You smell like rain; I like it."

I almost smiled at that, the man seeming both sleepy and somewhat adorable. Maybe he needed to get hit in the head more often. *Obviously joking*. I was sincerely concerned he now had legitimate screws loose.

My eyes darted to the bottle and empty glasses between King and him.

Ah, that made sense.

It was also part of the reason King was so quiet, because a slightly drunk King got super quiet, and it was honestly a bit eerie sometimes. His eyes ran over my face as he let out a slow exhale.

"I'm fine, he's fine, Stratton's fine," I assured him quietly. "We're fine, King."

He inhaled and nodded. "I'm still going to slaughter them."

I didn't respond to that, not willing to clarify if he was

being serious or not as I looked down at Yates, his eyes closed. I had no idea if Dermot had told him about them pulling a gun on me, but I felt like that little detail didn't need to be brought up currently. If it came up later, fine, but right now they needed to go to bed.

"Was he really going to try to take them all on?" I murmured.

King snorted. "I don't think he'd thought through it that far. Dermot has a... temper. Not the same as me, but for sure a temper. He's a bit of a hair trigger when he feels like someone is threatening something important to him."

"Oh." I swallowed.

"That would be you, princess, if you didn't realize." He took a drink of the amber liquid in his glass. Lightning flashed outside, thunder rolling in the distance as the sound of rain pattered on the window nearby.

"He went because of me?" I clarified.

"Yes." He nodded and then sighed. "He is assuming responsibility for your safety and what happened tonight. I told him that it wasn't his fault since the bastard pulled a gun on him, but I don't think that's valid reasoning in his mind."

I blinked and shook my head, running my fingers through Yates's hair. "That's insane, King."

The man laughed darkly. "After all of this, that's the insane part?"

To be fair, it was a valid question.

I watched as he reached to pour himself another glass, and I moved to stop him. I had a feeling that King would want to be sober for our trip, and currently he was on his way to being wasted.

"We have to be on the jet in two hours." I reached over and slid the bottle down the desk, Yates making a noise of complaint at my movement. King watched the bottle until it came to a stop and looked back at me, his smile turning a bit lighter.

"So responsible, princess." He offered me a heated look.

"That's me," I laughed. "Super responsible." And not crazy, clearly.

Yates let out a soft sound, nuzzling against my chest that was currently covered in a hoodie and making me turn ten shades of red. King flashed a smile at my embarrassment as I narrowed my eyes. I stood up and nodded towards the door. "Come on, both of you need sleep. Let's go."

"This reminds me of when we got drunk sophomore year and Dahlia tried to make sure we didn't get caught." Yates flashed a smile. The memory had me almost smiling.

To think I had considered them good influences. They had owed me for that though, and had been fantastic babysitters when I had finally decided to drink for the first time, keeping track of me as I attempted to explore all of Wildberry drunk on champagne. It was only fair after trying to keep all of them from getting in trouble that night.

"And we still did," King grunted. "My dad was so pissed. Mostly because my mom was upset, so of course he made it far more of a big deal."

"To be fair," Yates measured, "if our kids did something stupid and Dahlia was upset, I would probably be more mad than if she wasn't."

My mouth fell open as King offered him a nod, the two of them both walking out the door as if... I mean, I wasn't crazy, the man had just said... Were they being real here? I tilted my head, watching them walk towards the stairs, laughing about something, as I ran a hand over my face and looked back at Dermot.

... who was sitting up now and offering me a pained expression.

"You okay?" I walked towards him as he stood up and ran a hand over his face, wincing when he touched his busted lip.

"I fucking hate Yates," he stated with no heat. "Bastard nearly busted my face open."

I leaned forward and cupped his jaw, my touch seeming to jolt his memory, guilt passing over his features. I was really glad that King had given me a heads up about where he was mentally, because when he sat down, detaching from my touch, I probably would have been offended.

"Dermot." I sat on his knee, and he looped his arms around me almost automatically. "You have to stop. That was one hundred percent not your fault. If anything, it was mine. I wanted to go. I put us in that position."

"I should have predicted that," he muttered, inhaling and exhaling slowly.

"You did. You were trying to get us out of there," I pointed out as he grunted. "Seriously, D. You did everything you could. The guy had a gun to your head and was choking you out. We got out of there, and that's all that matters."

"I want them handled." He inhaled sharply and stood up, lifting me so that I was in his arms as he walked out of the office, keeping me against him.

"Where are we going?" I asked curiously.

"Bed for at least an hour," he muttered. "I need a clear head."

My smile grew. "Yeah, wouldn't want you thinking taking on an entire gang on your own was a smart idea."

His chuckle was authentic as he kissed my neck gently. "I would still do it. I'd do it for you, Dahlia."

I believed him, and that was the scary part.

Chapter Fourteen

LINCOLN GATES

"Shit, I'm exhausted," my brother admitted, running a hand down his face as we sat in the private airport terminal, the jet in the process of being readied for us.

I grunted in agreement, Dahlia making a soft noise against my neck as I pulled my jacket more securely around her. She'd fallen asleep on me in the car and I hadn't bothered to wake her, just deciding instead to carry her in here. Her tight little frame against me, though, wasn't doing anything to help my state of being perpetually turned on around her, plus now I was exhausted. How much sleep had we even managed to get?

Not enough, clearly.

"Once we get on the plane, I'm crashing for a few hours," I told him.

King, who came to join us, handed a coffee to Sterling. I hadn't even bothered with that shit; right now, I would take any excuse to go back to bed, and not having coffee was perfect for that. Dahlia murmured something against my neck as I brushed my lips against her forehead, loving the way she was melted against me.

I wouldn't lie, there was a small part of me that had worried about how things would change once we actually enacted this plan. I worried that her being with one of us would change the dynamic with the others, but I was finding it was the opposite. Instead of backing away from physicality with others, it was almost as if she'd given herself the freedom to act how she had always wanted to. I loved that. I loved that there was no sense of hesitancy when it came to us anymore, not that there had been a ton to begin with.

As I watched Stratton cross the airport next to Dermot, the two of them holding bags from the main terminals, I wondered how it was that Stratton hadn't insisted on Dahlia eating way more since the other night. I know we hadn't talked about it yet, but it was fairly easy to piece together the change in her weight and eating habits along with the timing of the bullying. It infuriated me that Abby could fuck with her head that much, and it killed me that Dahlia could ever doubt how fucking gorgeous she was. But I would do my best to reinforce the latter sentiment, even if I had to remind her every single fucking day for the rest of our lives.

"Ms. Lori's friend just arrived," Yates offered, removing the headphones he was using to talk to security back at Wildberry. The security team that was in a lot more shit than they even realized.

Although, to be fair, the man that had attacked Dahlia wasn't anyone they had ever met. He had somehow gotten a hold of a uniform and slipped in, but he'd never been vetted or put on security detail, so the most we could be pissed about was them letting someone into Wildberry that didn't belong.

Which was the exact fucking opposite of their job description.

It didn't change the fact that I was jealous Yates had been the one to fucking kill that asshole. I winced slightly, thinking about Dahlia's reaction on the security cameras. The way she paled, pure shock the only stark expression on her beautiful face. I knew that she had compartmentalized the incident, but I had no doubt it would affect her in time.

I also knew that it was probably better that she had seen that before we arrived in Ardara. King, of course, disagreed, as did my brother and Stratton, but I think they were all forgetting about how violent the interactions got when we were there. How we wouldn't be able to just hold back if someone was disrespecting everything the Rosses had built, even if Dahlia was in the room. Plus, I had to side with Yates on this one—I think she was strong enough to handle it.

Fuck. I hoped she was, because there was no backing away from this now, and I think that reality freaked King out, which is why he was still trying to fight it. Dahlia had been in a perfectly constructed bubble for so long, and while I preferred that bubble, I also knew that it was delicate. The only way to ensure that she was safe was to surround her with fortified goddamn steel. For that to happen, it would have to be forged with blood, and people would have to die. It was a pretty straightforward fact.

"It feels fucked up that I left," Stratton grunted, upset about leaving his grandmother.

"First of all, I'm pretty sure she insisted you go," I pointed out, recalling the conversation this morning when I had gone with him to his house to grab some shit.

"That's because of Dahlia," he grunted.

"Something about worrying that if you didn't go, she wouldn't get great-grandbabies, right?" Sterling chuckled.

"So don't worry about it." I tightened my arms around her. "Ms. Lori doesn't want you to put your entire life on hold for her, Stratton, I know that for a fucking fact. Taking one trip out of town is perfectly okay."

Stratton looked like he was on the verge of arguing before

his gaze darted down to Dahlia and he offered a nod, running a hand through his hair in stress. I was glad the bastard was back, but I was still pissed at him for not telling us what was going on with his family's business and financial situation.

Something we were looking into, because it just didn't ring true to me that he had nothing left. I am positive he believed that, but I also remembered how Mr. Lee was with money, and I found it hard to believe that he didn't have a separate offshore account. The Lees were older money than we were, so while I fully believed that he had fucked up the family business, I didn't believe there was nothing left. Stratton would probably be pissed when he realized we were digging up the past, but he could deal with it. We would do the same for any one of us, so he would need to adjust.

"Just have security keep me updated," Stratton told Yates.

"Will do," he confirmed. "Honestly, I am looking into new companies as it is, but they are good until we get back. Plus, I know you're worried about the retaliation from those Denim Moth fuckers."

Dermot let out a low sound and shook his head, making me nearly smile, something I hid against Dahlia's silky hair. I knew Dermot losing his shit shouldn't have been funny because Dahlia in danger is definitely not humorous, but watching King try to calm down his cousin? That had to have been amusing.

"You're not fighting anymore, right?" King asked.

"Nah," he admitted and then looked at Dahlia. "I don't want her involved in that shit, and no matter how much I tell her no, she will still probably show up."

"Stubborn," Yates muttered as I smiled, because that was accurate. Dahlia was pretty easygoing until it was something that mattered to her, and then the woman was one hundred percent focused. Extremely stubborn and determined.

Personally, it was one of my favorite qualities about her.

"I just need to figure out what I'm going to do," Stratton admitted, more to himself, looking out the private terminal window in thought. King leaned forward, looking like he wanted to say something, but then stopped. I already knew what he wanted to say, and I agreed it wasn't the time.

I had absolutely no doubt that King wanted him to help with the Ross family shit. He was already involved to an extent, but the issue was that Stratton had a lot more moral lines than the rest of us did. He also was stubborn as hell, and the bastard probably wanted to figure out a way to fix his family's reputation and company on a matter of principle.

"Mr. Ross." The attendant for the flight suddenly appeared, offering us a tired but friendly smile. "We are ready to leave."

"Dahlia," I whispered against her ear, "I need you to wake up, beautiful."

"Beautiful?" she hummed sleepily, "Well, if that's the way you're going to wake me up, I'm more likely to become a morning person."

I chuckled, hiding the strain in my voice because I had a million far better ideas on how to enhance her mornings. As she slid off my lap and stretched her arms above her head, I nearly let out a low groan. The woman was wearing a pleated white skirt with a tennis jacket, an outfit I'd seen a million times before, and each and every time I imagined what she would look like bent over with red hand marks on her perfect ass.

Not knowing what she was doing to me, she offered a sleepy smile and walked towards the tarmac. I followed after, offering the attendant a nod of thanks for letting us know.

The Ross jet wasn't very different from our own, but while ours was suited a bit more towards business with the amount

of trips our parents took, this was more suited towards pleasure. The cream-colored seats were embroidered with a green
and gold family crest and a large door at the back of the plane
led to what I knew to be a master suite. *With a bed.*

Fuck, that sounded amazing.

Luckily, it seemed that Dahlia and I were on the exact
same wavelength because she threw open the door and fell
face first into bed, making me laugh. I grabbed her waist,
trying to not rub against her pert ass, as my cock jumped at
being so close to her tight heat. She let out a soft sleepy
sound as I moved her into the center of the bed and leaned
down to take off her tennis shoes. I slipped off my own and
offered King a head nod as I closed the bedroom door,
knowing that he would have to spend the majority of the trip
focused on the shit he had to handle when we got there.

Our number one concern?

Ian.

We had arranged for Ian to be taken care of, but it seemed
that no one could find him. Considering our contacts, that
was a goddamn feat on its own. Part of me hoped he was still
alive because I would much rather handle it on our own and
draw it out. Then again, we already had so much attention on
us that the death of someone Yates beat the fuck out of at
our country club only a few days ago would probably seem
suspicious.

Which was why I was really hoping that the media would
get their heads out of their asses and realize that trying to go
up against our families was a horrible idea. I couldn't even
blame the smaller news stations because our last names
weren't extremely recognizable, but the corporate owners of
all those media companies would know exactly who we were.
Especially considering the amount of money that the Gates
family alone sent annually to each one. Money was an easy fix
to most things because people as a whole cared more about

lining their pockets than they did about their jobs. It was that simple. *Usually*.

"Lincoln," Dahlia sighed softly as I slipped under the covers with her, realizing I'd gotten stuck in my own head again. As I pulled her against me, I breathed in her soft scent and ran my fingers along her waist where her jacket had ridden up. Despite it being a simple—if not ordinary— moment, a pulse of emotion hit my chest as I realized just how much I loved Dahlia. How important she was in my life. Fundamental. Down to the fact that I could recognize the intoxicating scent of her perfume anywhere.

"I love you," I admitted softly against her ear. I had said it before, but this was different, or at least it would be to her.

Turning into me, her green eyes warmed as she offered a small smile. "You love me?"

"You know I do." I ran a thumb over her lip.

"That was different." Her tongue darted out to touch my thumb as my cock jumped against the press of her soft body on mine.

"Not for me." I'd always meant it this way from the time that I knew what it meant to feel love like this. I slid my other hand to her lower back as I pulled her tight to me, her eyes flaring with heat at realizing how turned on I was. Not that I was trying to hide it. "I've always meant it exactly like this, Dahlia."

Rolling her so that she was underneath me, her legs parted slightly as her skirt rode up, showing off a pale pink pair of lace panties against her hot center. Fuck.

A low groan escaped my throat as I looked up, finding her offering me a somewhat coy smile, her arms wrapping around my neck. Her large green eyes darted down to where I was hard, painfully so, and her smile grew, her eyes dancing with heat.

"Do you think my suffering is funny?" I mused lightly,

dipping down to kiss her soft lips, hard and bruising, my cock rubbing against her panties. The action had her jolting slightly as her back arched off the bed and a moan left her throat.

"Is that it, beautiful?" I wondered curiously. I wanted to play this game with Dahlia. I wanted to hold her on the cusp of coming until she was sobbing and begging for release at my hands. Only then would I let her come. I needed her to feel the same frustration I'd felt for years now, even if it was only for a moment in time.

"No," she whimpered as I pulled back. Her grip tightened, causing me to flash a smile. My finger pulled down her athletic zip-up, and the fabric fell apart to reveal a pink lace bra cupping her perfect tits, the transparent material highlighting her hard nipples. I immediately was pulling back the cup of the right one and teasing it in my mouth, unable to stop myself from tasting her.

That was my weakness when it came to holding out on Dahlia's pleasure. It was how much I craved her release. How I wanted her limp in my arms after coming so hard she had tears streaming down her face. I was normally a patient man, but when it came to her, that was a hard fucking feat.

"I think it is. I think you love how frustrated you make me." I nipped the soft skin of her breast as she tightened her legs around me, seemingly worried about me going somewhere. *I wasn't.* I couldn't.

My fingers teased over the soft lace of her panties, the material wet, causing me to groan. Her hands tightened in my hair, and I teased her nipple with my teeth before soothing it with my tongue. Her cry of my name had me letting out a low groan against her skin, wondering how loud she would shout it if I was buried inside of her.

"That's okay, because I'm going to show you *exactly* what it feels like to be frustrated, to suffer like all of us have been these past few years," I growled against her lips, pressing down on her much smaller, soft frame. I could keep her safe like this, trapped underneath me. I fucking loved that concept.

"Linc!" Her gasp was music to my ears as I rolled her over onto her stomach in a sharp movement. Almost instantly her back was arching as she went up on all fours, my fingers brushing up her silky legs to grip her ass, the smooth skin on display from where her skirt had fallen to her hips. Goddamn, she looked even better than I imagined.

"Oh no," I warned with a dark laugh, stopping her movements as she tried to rub against me. I brought my fingers back down to her tight, covered little cunt and continued to pet it, her thighs shaking slightly as she tried once again to rub against me, a frustrated sound leaving her fuckable mouth.

"You didn't think I would let you off that easily, did you? After all this time of you teasing us? Now you want to get fucked and don't expect any punishment? For someone to fill you up and pump into that hot, spoiled little pussy? No, beautiful, you deserve a bit of a punishment for the hell you put us through."

"Oh shit," she whispered as I flashed a smile she couldn't see. My fingers pulled down her panties, leaving them around her thighs so that she couldn't spread her legs fully. I let out a low growl, wanting to bury my tongue in her cunt but deciding to continue to play with her, loving how soaked she was. My fingers continued their pattern as her fingers gripped the pillows, looking back at me with frustration.

She didn't even know half of it.

"I'll make you come, Dahlia," I promised. I leaned over, pressing my hard length against her center. "But only when I say so. We are going to do this my way. Understand?"

"Yes," she moaned as I pulled back and slid two fingers

inside of her, causing her to cry out my name into the pillow. I pumped in and out of her as she squeezed around me, causing me to nearly come at the idea of my cock being lodged inside of her.

I could feel her climax building, so I pulled out, smiling at her sound of protest as she looked back at me with a sexy little pout. "Linc, come on—"

My hand came across her ass hard enough that she jolted forward, but the moan that left her lips had me seriously considering if I could marry this woman right here and now.

It was one thing for her to find the darker parts of our life attractive, but I fucking swear, if I found out Dahlia didn't mind a bit of pain at my hands, I would lose it.

"Did you think I was about to let you come, Dahlia?" I nipped her ear as I slid my fingers back in, causing her to let out a sound of relief as she pressed herself further against me.

"Maybe," she whimpered as I used my other hand to fist her hair without warning, pulling it back just hard enough that I knew it would sting. Her small cry was filled with heat, pain, and a bit of surprise as I leaned forward to nip the shell of her ear.

"No," I chuckled softly, the sound sounding dangerous to even me. I continued to pump into her before stopping and pulling out, her protest smaller this time. I still slapped her ass hard enough that I knew it stung, her legs attempting to slide further apart. She wanted more, and fuck did I want to give her more.

"Do you like a little pain?" I asked, my voice rough as she offered me a look over her shoulder that had me nearly slamming into her. Her lips were parted and pupils blown as she looked at me as if I could solve her frustration.

I could. But I also wasn't done.

"Do you?" I tightened my grip on her hair as she whimpered, her pussy drenched against my fingers as I circled her clit and caused her to tremble.

"Yes!" She exhaled as I pumped my fingers back into her.

I knew she was getting closer. Damn it, this woman was so responsive.

"Good girl," I praised, my voice raspy with need. I increased my speed, and when I could feel her getting even closer, I let go of her hair and brought my hand across her ass, harder than before. She flew apart as I watched with a sense of fucking awe. She cried out my name, and the sound was enough that precum leaked from my cock, making me want to take it out and come on her tight little cunt, wanting to mark her.

No, I didn't trust myself to do that.

Instead I drew my fingers out and popped them in my mouth as she collapsed onto the bed, letting out a small moan. I rolled her over and kneeled above her, looking down at the fucking goddess that I somehow got to worship in this lifetime.

Her hair was messy and tangled, eyes closed and face flushed. My eyes trailed over her pushed-up skirt where my fingers were now circling her wet heat in a gentle, almost teasing way, her body trembling at the oversensizitation as a flush covered her bare breasts, her bra twisted and practically ripped.

Fucking hell. The woman was perfect.

"That," she exhaled and opened her eyes, "What the heck was that? That was amazing, Linc."

I loved this woman. I seared my lips to hers as I cupped her jaw and realized that loving my best friend was possibly the best thing that had ever happened to me. I loved how comfortable she was around me and how she had me practically laughing one moment and wanting to bend her over my knee and spank her the next. It was fucking perfection.

I pulled back and let out a small rumble. "That was what I wanted to do every single damn time that you wore a skirt to class."

"I wouldn't have minded." She flashed a smile and squirmed, a small whimper breaking from her throat.

"Stings?" I asked, referring to her perfect ass, and her eyes flared with heat.

"I like it," she admitted softly. "Every time it hurts I'm going to be thinking about what we did."

That was it.

That was fucking it.

I turned towards the door as Dahlia tugged me back down, her smile knowing.

"What are you doing?"

"I'm going to find a fucking priest before we take off so we can get married," I grunted.

Her laugh was amused and also a bit sleepy, then she let out a yawn. "After a nap? Plus, it may be difficult to have a wedding with multiple people."

We would make it happen.

"Fine, after a nap," I muttered as I tugged her against me underneath the covers.

After tossing off her bra and pulling back on her jacket, Dahlia was out almost immediately, leaving me with her firm little ass pressed up against my still hard cock. There was nothing I could do about that, and I knew that I probably wouldn't be getting any more sleep, which was unfortunate, but it was worth it just to hold her. I tilted my head up and looked at the ceiling.

I hadn't been lying to Dahlia. I wanted to marry her. I'd always wanted to marry her, though. When Sterling and I used to play 'house' when we were eight or nine in the back yard, both of us were always married to Dahlia. She never picked one or the other, and maybe that was where we had gotten greedy because I never expected her to choose.

We both wanted her more than was rational, so we would just have to figure something out, and soon, because the years of wanting her from a distance meant I was absolutely done waiting for Dahlia to be completely ours.

Chapter Fifteen

DAHLIA ALDRIDGE

Oh, why you so obsessed with me
Boy, I wanna knowwww—

"Did you just turn off my music?" I pouted, hiding my smile as Yates offered me a searing look, making me almost lose in my attempt to act like I didn't know why he was upset. Well, *one* of the reasons he was upset.

Apparently, he hadn't slept, and then on top of that he had to listen to Lincoln and me in the other room, which left him in a bad mood.

Oh, also probably because I kept playing Mariah Carey's 'Obsessed' just to mess with him. Not that he knew that. For all he knew, I was just getting ready.

"This is my getting ready playlist," I pointed out, applying a moisturizing primer before turning from the mirror. After nearly eight hours of sleep, I was feeling fantastic and using the master suite to get ready for our arrival.

"No, it's not." Yates sat back down on the bed and typed something out. "Your playlist doesn't have any Mariah Carey on it. You don't even like her Christmas music, let alone that song. Especially since you found out it's about Eminem."

"Because she did him dirty!" I exclaimed and then frowned. "How do you know—"

His look had me smiling as he put down his laptop and walked over, backing me up against the bathroom counter. "Dahlia, if you think it's surprising that I know what each of your playlists have on them, then I'm not even going to enlighten you about all of the other shit I have memorized regarding you."

My smile grew as I reached over to his phone, holding his gaze as I pressed play on the song. It started blasting as he let out a low rumble, snapping up the device I'd been using and striding out of the bedroom, leaving me laughing.

"What did you do to Yates, princess?" King asked, leaning in the doorway as I ran a brush through my blow-dried hair and began to apply light makeup.

"He didn't like that I was playing Mariah Carey's 'Obsessed,'" I smirked.

King let out a bark of laughter as he ran a hand over his face. "The man tells you that he stalks you—"

"Watches!" Yates called from the other room.

"That doesn't sound any better," King called back and focused on me. "So the man tells you he is obsessed with you and you tease him about it?"

"Was I not supposed to?" I tilted my head curiously and then smiled. "This is Yates, King. If I didn't tease him about it, that would be weird."

"Accurate," Sterling called in passing as he grabbed something from the closet.

"See?" I mused. "Plus, he knows I don't mind."

"She's into it," Stratton pointed out, walking in with a cup of tea. I smiled at him as I pressed a kiss to his cheek and thanked him for the sweet gesture. Sweet man. Sweet, grumpy, broody man.

"Is that true?" King asked once it was us two again. I

sorted through the lipsticks I had, wondering which would be the best. Heck, I hadn't even decided what I was going to wear yet, so this was probably going to be a bit difficult.

"Yes," I nodded. "I would say that's accurate. It is a bit flattering."

King chuckled and shook his head. "Dahlia, I have no idea how it's possible that you still manage to surprise me after all these years."

I turned towards him and smiled. "What should I wear to this special compound?"

His lips pressed up, his own suit matching what most of the others were wearing, a well tailored, dark custom piece. In fact, the only one who wasn't wearing a suit was Stratton, and I knew it was a very purposeful choice on his end. Plus, the man hated dress clothes more than the twins.

"You can wear whatever you want, princess. No one is going to tell you different."

"So I could wear a bikini?" I deadpanned. Honestly, it felt really good to relax and be a bit sassy after everything that had happened. Plus, I was riding on some good sleep. I wouldn't lie, a large part of my ability to relax was my detachment from my phone. If I didn't see the problem online, then it wasn't happening, right?

King's smile turned dangerous as he shrugged. "Sure. I'll have to find replacements for anyone who sees you, but I won't tell you no."

"Replacements?" I arched a brow.

"If they saw you in a bikini, I would have to kill them," King admitted, that dangerous coolness invading his eyes before snapping back to warmth.

Goodness gracious.

"You would kill them for seeing me in a swimsuit?" I asked curiously, leaning against the counter.

"I would kill for a lot less than that." His tone was

cautious, but instead of scaring me, it somewhat excited me, which was totally messed up.

"I'll wear something different, then, to save you the trouble." I let out a small laugh as warmth invaded his gaze again, his lips tweaking.

"May have to kill someone anyway; you look beautiful in everything you wear." His lips ghosted my forehead before he disappeared back into the main cabin.

I knew King's words should have scared me. I mean... almost everything in the past three days should have, and some of it did. The biggest element? My reaction to the violence my boys exhibited. I couldn't blame being a bit tipsy like that night in the kitchen, either. I was sober and accepting their behavior.

No. Not just their behavior. I was accepting them and loving them just as they were. Like I had always done. Like they did for me.

My boys might have been a bit darker than I thought, but I still knew they were good men. I saw how they treated those who were important to them, and the ones they hurt usually deserved it. At least that was what I was telling myself.

As I sorted through the clothes we'd brought with us, I looked at the temperature for where we were landing. Raining and semi-chilly, which meant that absolutely nothing I owned would work. *Wonderful*.

"King," I sang his name out, the man strolling back in with a questioning look.

"It's going to be cold there," I pointed out, "which means nothing I packed works at all. Especially not the bikini idea."

He chuckled. "Damn, that's unfortunate, princess."

Narrowing my eyes, he motioned for me to follow him across the master suite where he opened a wardrobe.

"My mom won't mind," he explained, and I nodded, knowing she wouldn't.

Haven Ross was by far the most fashionable woman I knew, something my own mom could attest to. Which was why sorting through even a limited closet of hers was a freakin' joy. Luckily, we were pretty similar in size and wore the exact same size shoe, so I easily plucked out a silk skirt, sweater, and heels in a monochromatic cream.

Getting ready in the bathroom, I slipped off the robe I was wearing and pulled on the silk skirt that was high-waisted and came to mid-shin. It was almost romantic looking, but paired with a gold designer belt and thin, oversized cream sweater, it became elegant. I slipped on a pair of cream stilettos and added a pink lipstick to brighten the outfit up a bit. With a nod, I walked out of the room, and King looked up and smiled.

"What?" I asked a bit self-consciously.

"I don't think my mom has ever worn that, actually," he admitted. "You should keep it. You look beautiful, Dahlia."

"Oh." I blinked at the sincerity and almost sweetness in his tone. "Thanks, King."

He kissed my forehead and motioned for me to follow him out into the main cabin. Instantly, I could see the terrain we were flying over had changed, water surrounding us in all directions. A small thrill of excitement ran through me as I sat down on a bench next to Dermot, his body tense and his face void of emotion. I felt bad being excited when he wasn't, so instead of saying anything, I simply slipped my hand into his much larger one and hoped that it helped. He tensed at first but then slowly relaxed back into the seat.

"You should show me around tomorrow," I suggested as I looked over to find him watching me, his eyes riveted to my face. I blushed at his direct attention and continued, "I know everyone else is viewing this as business, but I have never been here before."

"I could show you around," King offered, sounding wounded. I looked over to find him nearly pouting as Dermot let out a chuckle that was almost his normal, relaxed tone.

"I'll show you around, baby girl." He kissed the top of my hand, and I smiled happily.

See? Sure, Dermot and I were still getting to know one another, but I seemed to be doing alright just based on instincts. I leaned into him as I realized we were descending. I felt my toes curl as that sense of excitement hit me again, thrilled to be traveling and away from the nonsense back in Camellia.

"Princess," King said after a moment, his tone more serious as I found him standing. "Before we land, come here."

I let out a small yawn and stretched before following him back towards the master suite. He sat down on the bed, his face far more clinical than the lighthearted King from only moments ago. I closed the door and sat on the bed, knocking his shoulder playfully as I offered him a questioning look. He wrapped an arm around me and tucked my head underneath his chin.

"I am just going to give you a heads up." His voice was low and almost velvety, dripping in soothing tones despite his words. "This is going to be a different environment than you're used to. A lot more dangerous."

"Even in the compound?" I questioned softly.

"Always a possibility." His jaw clenched. "Especially with all the changes going on. People hate change."

They did.

He continued, "If I ask you to do something tonight, just trust me, okay? I promise I'll explain the reason for whatever it is later, but at the moment I just need you to trust me."

"You know I trust you." I squeezed his hand as he nodded and then grunted.

"Also, just ignore the security I am going to have on you. They are part of the deal," he muttered and shook his head. "This is going to be interesting."

"Isn't there something we can do to make it easier? Why is it going to be a problem?"

"The family business runs on the notion of family, so they are going to be uncomfortable not only with a group of men they don't know well, but me not giving them a clear directive on what we are," he explained softly. "Especially since our situation is unique."

"And if we tell them that I am dating all of you?" I asked softly.

"I wasn't planning to hide that you are ours," he said, "but it could produce some negative reactions."

I nodded in understanding. "Seems like how most of the world feels about it."

I nibbled my lip, almost admitting my insecurity that there was something wrong with me but knowing that he would assure me that wasn't the case. I just needed to believe it. After all, my love for these men was extremely real. Extremely right. So how could it be wrong? It was something cemented deep inside of me.

Suddenly, a flash of something went over King's face as he stood and walked over to the bedside table, opening it and pulling out a fingerprint safe that was the size of a book. He opened it easily and called out to Dermot, throwing him something as the handsome man walked in. Dermot nodded in response, sliding it onto his finger before sending me a wink and walking back out. King adjusted something on his hand and then closed the safe, his other closed around something small.

"This may help," he said softly, adjusting his suit jacket as

I realized he had not only a chest strap on for the gun at his side, but I was nearly positive he had another gun at his hip. Damn.

I blinked, refocusing as he took my right hand and slid on a ring that matched the gold and emerald one that he wore on his right hand. His ring was more masculine with a thick, gold band and the family crest on top, standing out in a bold and dominating way.

The ring he was sliding onto my finger was more delicate, but it also featured the family crest surrounded by emeralds. I tilted my head, loving how it looked as he stopped halfway down my finger and pulled it off, offering me a smirk and sliding it onto the ring finger of my left hand instead.

My eyes widened and my mouth opened, words not seeming to form.

"Not the ring I want on there, but should make a point." He flashed a devious smile as I blinked, staring down at it, pretending that I wasn't absolutely in love with it.

"A point?" I murmured.

King was backing me up against the bed. I squeaked, falling back as he caged me from above, his hand bringing mine up to his mouth, where he kissed the ring gently. I whimpered as his other hand closed around my throat, running over my pulse as he brushed our lips together, causing everything inside of me to turn molten.

"Yes, a point. That you belong to us, of course," he murmured and then nipped my lip and stood up. I watched him in shock as he went to the closet and pulled out a tailored tan trench coat for me, motioning for me to stand.

Naturally I did, moving in a silent daze... like a twit. I sincerely didn't know how to react to this.

King chuckled, and when he kissed my lips softer this time and walked out, I just shook my head and followed.

Chapter Sixteen

DAHLIA ALDRIDGE

I think what surprised me the most about our arrival at the private airport was the amount of people waiting for us. Specifically, people dressed in dark suits with dark SUVs like we were in some type of... well, mafia movie.

I mean, to be fair, the reference was obviously fairly accurate, and despite being next to King, his hand in mine, a bit of fear trickled down my spine. There was a charged sensation to the air, and I could see the tight security around the airport, making me wonder how much of a threat faced the Ross family on a daily basis. If that was the case, then Wildberry had been very much a bubble for them to escape all of this.

As we walked down the staircase that led off of the jet, I went to put a hand up to shield my eyes from the sun, only to have an umbrella appear in front of me. I grabbed the handle and looked up to find three men in black suits—who seemed to appear out of nowhere—greeting King and Dermot. My ears rang, overwhelmed by the sudden change in atmosphere.

King placed a hand on my back, something none of the security missed, no doubt, as we walked across the pavement towards one of the cars. It was then that I noticed the other cars were positioned throughout the airport along the fence, all the men having guns drawn and facing outwards.

"Um, King?"

He looked down at me, his eyes filled with curiosity. "Yeah, princess?" He mussed my hair lightly, taking my umbrella and holding it up so I could cross my arms over my chest. How he knew that I felt more comfortable doing that right now was beyond me. I swear the man was a mind reader.

"This is intense. Are these the people..." I didn't know how to finish that sentence.

He chuckled lightly and shook his head. "No, this is security."

"Security for the freakin' president," I mumbled as he flashed me a smile and helped me up into the SUV, dismissing one of the men who offered a hand to help me. I curled into the leather seat and breathed out a sigh of relief, glad there was a partition up between us and whoever was driving.

As the boys started talking around me, seemingly far more relaxed than myself, I kept an eye on what we were passing, curious about the place the Ross family still seemed to call home, to an extent. Dermot was positioned on my other side, placing me in a sandwich between King and him that I absolutely loved.

What I didn't love? The tension rolling through Dermot's frame, his hand gently squeezing my thigh every so often as if to remind himself that I was there. I kept looking down at it, loving how massive it was compared to my leg, his grip possessive and commanding without him even meaning to be. I snuggled into him, and he looked down at me with a soft affection. Still, there was a coolness to his gaze underneath it, and it worried me. I felt like the man was drifting out to sea, and I had no idea how to bring him back to me.

Maybe I needed to instead swim out to him. I just didn't know how.

It wasn't long before we were pulling past a massive stone wall that spanned as far as I could see along the road, appearing seemingly out of nowhere. When we reached a solid black gate, there were four guards who greeted us and called out for it to be opened from the other side. I sat forward in my seat as it opened to reveal a forested road that stretched forward seemingly forever.

I was finding that Ireland was not only thick with greenery, but everything here was damp and vibrant. It smelled different as well. Not in a bad way, though. Actually, I really rather liked it.

I hadn't thought to bring my camera. Something that I was completely regretting right now. My eyes scanned the different angles that I could shoot from, the way the muted sunlight tried to break through the lush greenery. I could imagine just how beautiful the photos would turn out.

"I wish I had brought my camera," I admitted.

"It's packed." Sterling offered me a surprised look as if confused that I didn't know that. "Sorry, sugar, I should have told you that. I clearly was more tired than I realized."

"Thanks, Sterling," I offered him a soft smile. The returning wink he offered had my cheeks flushing with color as I turned back towards the window. Why did he have to be so thoughtful and sexy?

Trying to distract myself, my thoughts moved back to that vacation home that Lincoln had shown me. Maybe we could go see that while we were here.

The car was silent, and after a few minutes, King adjusted his jacket and leaned forward, knocking on the partition. It rolled down so he could speak to the driver, allowing me to see forward far more clearly as we circled the driveway.

Damn. I didn't say that lightly, either. I watched as we approached what I had to assume was the Ross family compound, and holy moly was it a compound for sure.

First of all, it had to be well over ten thousand square feet because it was nearly commercial sized, yet it looked like an oversized home. More like a castle.

Wait, that was exactly what the compound was. A castle.

Lord.

The stone exterior was covered in moss, barely disguising all the security measures that had been added. The windows looked fortified, and the front of it appeared to only have one entrance, located near the grand driveway that could easily fit twelve or more cars.

I legitimately didn't have words for this. I mean, this was... this was insane.

As I got out of the car, the doors to the estate opened, and an older man that was not dressed like the security team at all strolled out. King was relaxed next to me, so I assumed the lanky guy dressed in shades of brown and gray was okay in his book? Or at least not a threat.

"Mr. Ross," the man's voice rang out in a clear Irish accent, "welcome back. Everything has been prepared for you, including the extra bedrooms."

King led me up the stairs and offered the man a small smile, clasping his shoulder in thanks as he led us into the massive home. *Castle.* It was totally a castle. I had the urge to go back and introduce myself to the older man like I would back home, but apparently that wasn't a thing here?

The thought didn't distract me for long, though, because suddenly I was staring up at the massive foyer we had entered into. *Wow.* It was absolutely gorgeous. The ceilings were domed, painted with what looked like different renditions of the family crest. The walls that seemed to border an outside courtyard in the center of the estate featured stained glass windows that portrayed scenes that I couldn't fully understand because I wasn't close enough. There were people moving about dressed in similar colors as the older man, and the entire place had a rather comfortable and somewhat cozy vibe to it, especially with the two massive fireplaces that were roaring at either end of the foyer.

"Princess." King came up behind me, wrapping a hand around my throat and tilting my chin back. "I have to handle a few things. I know you will probably be bored—"

"I'll be totally good," I promised, looking around. "Can I explore?"

"Absolutely." King pressed his lips to my ear. "Just don't leave the actual building." Then he turned to the guys. "Lincoln, Sterling, I may need both of you. Stratton, you know I want your help, but I understand if you don't want to."

Stratton stared at him for a minute, something seeming to pass between them as he finally let out a slow exhale and nodded. Walking over to me, he wrapped a hand around the back of my neck and kissed me hard and deep before following King and Dermot towards a long, dark hallway. I had absolutely no idea what had just been decided, but I felt like it was important. My tongue darted out, tasting his kiss on my lips, and I looked back to where Lincoln was now in front of me, his smile a bit wicked.

"Be good, beautiful." He cupped my jaw and kissed me, making my knees nearly break in the process. Him saying the word 'good' would always be associated with the orgasmic experience that he gave me on the jet. I felt like I was in a daze as Sterling kissed the top of my head before following his brother... leaving me with Yates.

"You're leaving me with Yates?!" I called out as Sterling's laughter echoed through the space.

I turned to look at Yates, who was leaning against the stairwell offering me a heated, amused look. I blushed as I walked forward, not feeling nearly as sassy without the others nearby. As if he knew, he tugged me forward by the hips and dipped his head, hesitating right above my lips.

"Don't like hanging out with me, bunny?" He tugged on my bottom lip.

"You're okay." I flashed a smile, and as he let out a low rumble, I leaned against his chest and frowned. "Wait, why didn't you go with them?"

"I try to stay out of official meetings as much as possible so that I'm not biased," he explained. "I'm King's legal counsel when it comes to more official shit. My dad did it for Mr. Ross, and I have to say, it beats sitting through those damn meetings with the other families."

"And you get to hang out with me," I pointed out, "*Exploring.*"

"I would love to explore you some more." He offered me a dangerous smile as I offered a mock gasp and stepped back, his eyes narrowing at the distance.

"You don't want to show me around this super cool castle?" I even batted my eyelashes for full effect as he barked out a laugh and shook his head.

Allowing me to lead him through a set of halls opposite of where the boys had gone, I let out a soft hum. "So if Dermot is second in command, and you're legal counsel, what do the others do?"

"I don't think any of us really have figured that out yet," he admitted. "We thought we had a bit more time. We were going to wait until the holidays to have an official meeting and bring you with."

"Oh yeah?" I teased, "That positive that I would go along with all this craziness?"

His eyes flashed with slight uncertainty. "No, actually. I

know almost everything about you, Dahlia, but I still couldn't be one hundred percent sure."

"You had to know all this time how much I love you guys," I whispered. I wasn't even paying attention to the halls and rooms we passed, my eyes focused on Yates.

"I knew how much you loved them," he admitted roughly. "I wasn't sure how you felt about me besides being attracted to me."

"Yates." I stopped him, grabbing his hands. "I know I say we are archenemies, but we literally spend every day together. We freakin' vacation together."

"Our families vacationed together," he pointed out.

"If I didn't love you, heck, if I didn't *like* you, do you think I would have gone along with all your crazy plans?" I smiled. "You woke me up, *on vacation*, at six in the morning! You should have realized how I felt when I willingly went with you."

His laughter bounced off the walls around us as I smiled, unable to stop myself. When it suddenly cut off, I turned to look at a group of men who had just walked into the hallway, my own expression slipping into something more serious. Yates let out a quiet curse as the main guy, followed by two other men that seemed to slip into the background, flashed a smile that seemed far too familiar. He was older— if I had to guess, I'd say he was in his forties, maybe fifties —but very handsome. Yet there was a look to his green eyes as they ran over me that made me uncomfortable, his perfectly styled dark hair adding to his cold and calculating look.

Why was his smile so familiar? It was going to drive me crazy!

"Yates Carter, when I heard King was back, I was thrilled, especially since we didn't get to handle our business last time he was in town." His Irish accent was thick, and once again, sounded familiar. Or maybe it was his voice that sounded familiar.

"Yes, we had some business to handle." Yates didn't extend a hand shake as the man stopped a few feet away, looking over the two of us with interest. I instantly knew this guy was bad news, and he hadn't even said anything bad yet.

"Now that's not completely true. I heard you were skipping town because my nephew and you fucked up." His eyes moved over to me. "Amongst other reasons."

"It's not your business," Yates said firmly, his voice cold. "King is in the office—"

"You must be Dahlia." The man stepped forward and offered a hand. Instinctively I met it because of the manners I'd had ingrained in me. His lips brushed over my hand as he offered me a cold smile, causing me to feel sick to my stomach. "I am understanding the appeal now. Also, why exactly King would risk all of this because of some woman."

What was King risking?

"Enough," Yates bit out, pulling me back.

"You as well?" He arched a brow. "And here I thought it was just King who had fallen so far. An Aldridge, nonetheless."

"What?" I demanded softly.

His eyes slid over to me. "I bet my son has also shown interest, hasn't he? You don't have to tell me. I know he has. You remind me of his bitch mother."

His son?

My eyes widened in realization as Yates let out a vicious sound. I kept a hand on him to keep him still, Dermot's father, I presumed, letting out a laugh that was almost nervous.

"Just in looks, I promise."

"Fuck off." Yates stepped forward into his space, overshadowing him. "You know how limited my patience is. If you want to go see King, do it, but don't fucking talk to her. Don't even look at her. Understand?"

The man paled as he grunted and offered a nod, storming past with the two larger men following him.

I swallowed, watching him disappear as I looked at Yates. "That was Dermot's father?"

"You can't call that piece of shit a father," he growled and took my hand, leading me around a bend and through a set of doors. Instantly, mist hit my skin as I found us standing outside in the courtyard in the center of the estate. Between the stone path and lush greenery, it almost reminded me of a faerie garden but full size.

"He was horrible," I whispered and shook my head. "Holy crap."

I couldn't quite process that that man was related to Dermot.

Yates nodded in agreement. "I have been waiting for an excuse to get rid of him."

"I am assuming you don't mean like 'kick him out of the building'?" I offered a small smile.

"No, I don't mean anything so temporary." His eyes sparked with something dark as his lip twitched. "Unfortunately, family is different than some fucking bastard trying to corner you. Although if he keeps looking at you like that, Dermot may take care of his father for me."

I rolled my eyes. "He wouldn't kill his father for looking at me."

Yates arched a brow. "Right, and he didn't want to take on an entire gang by himself after they threatened you. Rational action isn't really a trait in the Ross family, not that I have a right to talk."

I tilted my head in thought because he wasn't wrong... and that would mean Dermot felt something for me that was far more serious than I had considered.

"Well, that and their temper." He shook his head.

"King doesn't have that bad of a temper. I feel like his anger at security the other day was more than justified."

Yates brushed his hands through my hair as my head tilted back. His eyes were a dark charcoal shade, and his expression was serious. "Absolutely more than justified, but that was King angry. I'm not talking about him being angry. I'm talking about him losing his shit, something I hope you never see. Although, the way you managed to pull him back from that was fairly unusual, so maybe if he blacked out you could do the same then."

Blacked out? He had the ability to get that angry? I tried to imagine that but couldn't fully. Hadn't I seen him angry yesterday? I thought that had been bad, but if I was to believe Yates, then there was something far worse. King was such a steady presence in my life, and the idea of him being so furious that it would upset someone like Yates made me wonder how bad it really was. Before I could ask him for more detail, the garden door opened and out strolled Dermot, shaking his head and looking really annoyed.

My eyes widened as he took out a cigarette and lit it, not noticing us as he sat down on one of the stone benches, leaning his forearms against his knees. Yates kissed the top of my head and urged me forward, and when I looked back, he was gone.

What the heck?

I heard a door shut in the distance as I shook my head, needing to have a talk with that man. How did he move like that?

Dermot was murmuring something to himself, looking stressed and honestly a bit shaky as he inhaled on the cigarette and blew out the smoke around him. I sat down next to him on the bench without a word, his gaze snapping to my heels before crawling up my legs, his eyes nearly black as they met mine. I considered asking him what was wrong, but assuming it was his father's presence, I just ran my hand up his back in a soothing motion. It worked for all of a minute.

Then the man seemed to snap. I let out a squeak as he tugged me onto his lap, my skirt riding up so that it was tight across my hips as I straddled him. His arms circled my back and his lips pressed to mine in a tobacco kiss that shouldn't have turned me on. I could taste whiskey on his lips also, making me practically purr. My fingers dug into his hair as he let out a low growl that vibrated against my mouth.

"Fuck this place," he muttered and pressed his forehead to mine. "I heard you met the bastard that calls himself my father."

"He seems like a jerk," I offered quietly.

"He likes to pick on those smaller than him, specifically women. It's why I don't blame my mum for leaving us," he admitted softly. "If he treated her anything like he treated me growing up, then I don't blame her for running."

"How did he treat you?" My voice was raspy, afraid of what his answer would be.

Dermot's eyes were shaded dark with pain as he shook his head. "Doesn't matter, baby girl. He can't pull that shit now, and that's all that matters."

"Why is he here?"

"Because he wants back into the family business and King refuses to let him in, just like his father did." He chuckled. "When your own brother doesn't want you to be part of something, you think he would get the hint. I don't know why he complains; he gets more than enough money from the legal trading business we do."

"Maybe it isn't about the money?"

His eyes darkened. "It's always about the money for him."

I froze as I heard the garden door open. I knew we

weren't doing anything wrong, but I still felt like we were in a compromising position. Dermot didn't move me though; he simply gripped my hips tighter as any expression disappeared from his face, making me know exactly who it was. Guess that meeting was rather short. Not that it surprised me—it seemed like this guy was really pushing his luck being here.

"I see America is treating you well." His father's voice was more of a sneer now that Yates wasn't around, his eyes running over me as he approached. Dermot gently moved me off his lap and stood, blocking me from his view, his body tense despite his calm voice.

"You're not welcome here, and I know King made that clear," he said evenly, the warning clear.

"You have always let King handle everything for you," his father bit back. "One of the many reasons you're a disappointment as a son. You should be the one in that fucking office."

Dermot tensed but relaxed a tad as I ran a hand up his back and stood with my head against his spine, trying to offer my support. It was all too clear just how bad their relationship was, and I didn't know what exactly to do.

Well, I had thoughts on what to do, but they weren't legal and I honestly hadn't realized I was capable of having such violent urges. Then again, the idea of someone hurting Dermot not only seemed impossible with how imposing he was, but made me absolutely furious.

"You're just mad because he won't give you what you want." Dermot's accent was thicker with both amusement and frustration. "Like I said, you're not welcome here."

His father stepped closer, and my eyes widened at the anger and pure hatred on his face. *Holy moly.* He really hated Dermot. I had never thought it was possible for a parent to hate their child like this.

My arm wrapped around Dermot's waist as I plastered myself to his back further.

"You can't even get your own woman, fucking the same whore that your cous—"

Dermot cut off his father's words with a hand gripping his throat. My eyes widened as Dermot literally tossed the man back out of his space and gently removed my hands from around him, stepping forward and into his father's face as he staggered to his feet.

"Do not talk about her. Do you understand me?" His voice was terrifyingly cold.

I shivered, my toes curling at his tone, as his father rubbed his neck but let out a cold, hard laugh. He was a big guy, but Dermot was huge.

"I will talk about her how I want; she's on our family land," he growled. "I'll even have her back to my fucking quarters if I want. What's one more person between her legs — *Oh, fuck.*"

My face drained of color as Dermot grabbed his shoulder and punched him hard in the gut, whispering something in his ear. His father's eyes went dark as he jolted back, and Dermot stood there, seeming to wait on something. After a moment, his father turned as if to leave, and Dermot took a step back, looking at me almost to assure himself I was still there. Of course that meant he didn't see the crap his father tried to pull.

"Dermot," I whispered, my eyes wide.

I could hear the sound of the slap so clearly through the garden as my own body trembled. The action was so hard and cold. Practiced. This wasn't the first time he had hit someone like that, and if I had to guess from the way Dermot's entire body went frozen, it wasn't the first time his father had hit him. I had seen far more extensive violence lately, but this was different.

A red mark appeared on Dermot's turned cheek, my throat failing to produce any noise as I noted the haunted look passing over Dermot's face as he finally looked back at his father. I couldn't see his expression, but from the way his father paled, I was going to guess it wasn't good.

I tried to move forward, wanting to stop Dermot or maybe to help him... I honestly wasn't positive at this point. I let out a small grunt as an arm locked around my waist, my head snapping up to find King, holding me to him unyield-ingly. Almost bruising. But he wasn't focused on me, his eyes dark and cold on Dermot's father. My hands tightened into fists as I looked back, watching his father start to tremble in realization that he'd messed up. The energy in the garden was absolutely venomous.

"You have one chance to leave." Dermot's voice was darker than I'd ever heard it. "I don't want to kill you in front of Dahlia, so I am giving you one fucking chance."

I wanted to tell him that he didn't have to hold back for my benefit.

"This is my fucking house, I should be living here—"

Dermot stepped forward, grabbing his throat as I heard the click of a gun, which Dermot pressed against his abdomen. My chest tightened and my breathing went fast, both worried and fascinated about what would happen. I couldn't help but hate this man for hurting Dermot. I also wasn't positive if I was ready to analyze the part of me that was excited to see him suffer.

"I would suggest you leave, Patrick." King's voice was smooth and dangerous. "Now."

Dermot let go of his neck and the man stumbled, his breathing rough as he shot a hateful look, before practically sprinting from the courtyard. I swallowed, not liking the tension in Dermot's back as I tapped King's grip on me. He released me almost immediately, and I crossed the space and wrapped my arms around Dermot once again, a shudder seeming to run through him.

I didn't hold back, trying to infuse affection and love into the grip I had on him. I didn't worry about being rejected or him pushing me away. I knew he wouldn't, and when he turned towards me and wrapped me up further, his nose pressing into my hair, I knew I was right. I didn't think twice as he lifted me up, my butt on his crossed forearms as he carried me inside, his chest letting out a low rumble.

I couldn't tell you where King had gone or where the others were. None of that mattered right now. I was trying to be an emotional space heater for Dermot and warm him up completely.

"Dermot," King called out.

Dermot paused, looking back at him silently.

"I told our teams I want McCaffrey in the basement by tonight."

Dermot finally let out a soft, dark chuckle. "I'll be there."

McCaffrey?

"Like Ian McCaffrey?" I asked softly. "You're bringing him here?"

I couldn't lie, panic surged through me at that, and as if knowing, Dermot let me slide down his body and walked me back against one of the stone walls near the stairwell.

He grabbed my waist and spoke softly with a dangerous heat. "To kill him, Dahlia. We are bringing him here to kill him."

"Oh," I whispered.

"Afraid?" he asked, looking resigned to my reaction.

Was I? I shook my head. "I'm more afraid of being in the same house as him, not the other part."

It was true. I hadn't known for sure what King and them had been talking about the night of Ian attacking me, but I was piecing together that they were supposed to have him 'taken care of.' So where was he now? I didn't like that he was out there. I shouldn't have supported their plan... but I wanted it handled. I wanted him gone.

I blinked, realizing it was the first time I had actively wanted someone dead.

Was I changing? What was happening to me? Was it a bad thing?

"Don't overthink it," Dermot warned softly.

"I wasn't overthinking it for the reason you would assume," I murmured, my brow dipping in confusion.

"What do you mean?"

"I mean that I think... I *want* Ian dead."

Chapter Seventeen

DERMOT ROSS

Dahlia's approval of Ian's possible murder should not have made me this happy. Then again... her approval in general made me fucking thrilled. It wasn't surprising. I was already bordering on the edge of obsessing over her.

Right... On the edge. That's what we were calling it?

Despite everything that had happened in the past few minutes with my father, a smile formed on my lips as I considered pinning her up against the hallway wall and showing her how fucking happy her words made me. Then I remembered that there were others who could come across us, like security, and my possessive side had me scooping my baby girl up and carrying her towards my bedroom.

The one that I'd been living in the past few years to avoid my father and all the stupid shit he involved himself in. I could have taken her to a guest suite, but I wanted to see her in my room. In the space I'd inhabited for so long, even if it wasn't really mine anymore. I'd never brought anyone back here to the compound, and the amount of nights I'd spent alone and thinking about something needing to fucking change probably stained the space with a level of sadness that I hadn't felt since moving to Wildberry Lane.

I knew that Dahlia noticed the tension and stress that I exhibited while here, but what she didn't realize was that this was my normal. Who I was with her was someone far happier than the man I'd grown up to be. It was probably why I clung to her despite her being in my arms.

"Is that bad?" she whispered, her voice soft and hesitant.

"No."

She nodded, and I tried to find the words that wouldn't showcase just how thrilled her words made me. "I want Ian dead as well."

There. That was normal, right? Well, more normal than telling her what I wanted to do to him and how much I wanted him to suffer for ever even thinking about attacking her. I may not have been as bloodthirsty as my cousin, but I still had a list of people that I wanted dead. I think this place brought it out in you, and that was why Dahlia's approval of it, even to the smallest extent, was extremely dangerous.

It also had me knowing that she was far more suited for this lifestyle than she realized. Dahlia may have lived in a bubble of safety for most of her life, but because of that, her perception of the world was skewed. Actions that were odd and wrong in the eyes of society wouldn't always feel that way to her because she trusted those that she surrounded herself with.

Her family. The other men. The people she loved.

A woman with Dahlia's family and wealth could afford to do that, and I was glad for it because I didn't think most women would have taken what had happened the past few days in stride like she had.

Which was good, because that meant there was less chance of her wanting to leave, something that I wasn't positive would ever be allowed to happen, as it was. I don't think she realized how deeply she was embedded in all of this. As much as all of this was a risk and our allies could see her as a liability, it was far better than leaving our relationship with her unknown. It was safer for her that we claimed her under our protection, and it allowed us to keep her close all the time. The only trade-off was that there was no escape from any of this.

Considering the abandonment issues I so clearly had, I wouldn't fucking complain. I nearly shook my head at that as I used my foot to push open the door to my bedroom suite. Twenty something years, and I hadn't worried about anyone leaving me; rather, I preferred it. Now this slice of perfection steps into my life and I'm suddenly terrified that she was going to walk right back out, taking her radiant sunshine with her.

Could you blame me though? To be so close to having Dahlia and having her ripped away would fucking gut me.

I think that was in part why the incident with the Denim Moths enraged me so much. Not only had they taken such direct action to threaten her, but the concept of losing her— especially in such a jarring way, to complete fucking idiots— made me furious. I had dealt with far more dangerous shit than that, and normally I wouldn't have thought twice about the gun in that asshole's hand, but one that close to Dahlia? That had me pausing. That had me panicking, and that panic had put her in danger.

I knew she didn't blame me, but that didn't change that I blamed myself.

"Dermot." Her voice was a soft purr that had a depth of seduction that instantly had my entire body hardening. I knew she didn't realize it. It was why I was hesitant to lay her out on the massive bed that took up the majority of the comfortable room. I didn't think she realized how close I was to giving into this lust that continuously slammed into me in her presence.

Especially after dealing with such bullshit from my father, I wanted to bury myself inside of her and forget about anything but her soft moans.

"Yeah, baby girl?" I set her down gently on my massive bed, her tiny, curvy frame swamped by the large, dark covers. I kicked off my shoes before leaning down and gently pulling off her heels, her red toenail polish somehow managing to turn me on... which should have been fucking weird but wasn't.

"You just seem..." She hesitated and then frowned. "Not upset exactly, just stuck in your own head."

"I am," I admitted. "I don't like that my father's arrival was so soon after we got here. It meant that he was well aware of our plans, which we had kept pretty much a secret until an hour or so before landing. It just feels off to me."

"He lives close to here, right?" she whispered.

"Yeah, but he's a piece of shit and usually busy with his own affairs."

Dahlia gently pulled on my shirt, looking worried and wanting me close, and I easily lifted her by the waist and gently tossed her further back on the bed, a small laugh escaping her lips at the slight jostle. I crawled over her and trapped her between my arms as her long, elegant fingers brushed through my hair, causing me to lean into her hand.

I wanted to find comfort in Dahlia; I wanted to tell her about how much I truly hated my father. About what an abusive bastard he'd been. I wanted to tell her that she grounded me in reality when normally what had happened earlier would have set me off worse than King. I wanted to tell her just how much she meant to me. But none of the words that formed on my lips were the right ones. I was absolute shite when it came to anything like this.

"How long have you been living here instead of with your father?" she asked intuitively, the dark room casting shadows on her face that were only illuminated by the fireplace.

Thunder cracked and I could feel a storm charging the air, making me wish that I was outside so that it could wash over me. Sometimes, after a particularly bad night with my father, I would do exactly that, walking around until the blood washed off my face.

"Since about sixteen," I admitted, brushing my lips over her cheekbones. Since I was old enough and big enough that I could fight back. I didn't include that part, though.

"Sounds lonely," she murmured.

I nodded, tucking my head against her neck as her hands smoothed through my hair, nearly causing me to let my eyes close. *Bloody hell.* Her touch was something else entirely.

"Doesn't feel as lonely right now," I whispered, my voice rough and unsteady.

As if hearing the pain in my voice, Dahlia gently pushed on my chest and rolled us, her skirt riding up as she straddled my much larger frame. A soft affection that I hadn't ever dared hope to see in her eyes for me filled her gaze. It was addictive.

There was something between us that I had never thought I would experience. I shouldn't have felt this strongly about her or with this intensity. It couldn't have been normal.

When her lips brushed against mine, they were gentle and sweet, and despite how goddamn turned on I was, I didn't try to take control of her mouth or pin her to the bed. I let her explore as a deep groan left my throat. My hands ran up her silk-covered thighs before gripping her soft waist, loving the feel of her rocking against me. When she pulled back and looked down at me with a soft smile, her nose brushing against mine, an emotion pounded in my chest and tried to escape my throat.

"I'm really glad you left here, Dermot." She tucked her head against my neck, spreading out on top of me. "I'm glad you came to Wildberry."

My lips brushed the top of her head as I nearly admitted to the emotions I could feel growing for her. The ones that seemed absurd for only knowing her such a short amount of time. The ones that I had never felt before. They seemed to consume me for a minute, knocking the air out of my chest.

When I finally got myself under control, her soft breathing told me she'd fallen asleep, and I locked my arms around her further. I was suddenly thankful for jet lag for saving me from saying something that would probably sound absolutely ridiculous to her. It didn't change the reality of how I felt, but hopefully I could hide it from her a bit longer.

After all, who falls in love with a woman within a week of meeting her?

Someone fucking crazy. Someone like me.

———

It couldn't have been more than a few hours later when my eyes opened, finding my room bathed in darkness and Dahlia's warm body on top of me. I breathed in her familiar scent and slowly moved my gaze towards the fireplace, where I knew King was sitting.

I didn't say anything at first, wondering if he realized I was awake, but I shouldn't have been surprised when he spoke. The bastard always had a creepy ability to tell what people were doing around him.

"We have Ian's brother here," King said quietly. "He says he doesn't know where Ian is either, although I am honestly not positive I believe him."

My brows rose as I shifted Dahlia to the side, pulling the blankets over her as she grabbed one of my large pillows and curled around it. I watched her for a minute, brushing her hair away from her face, before I looked back at my cousin. I silently put my shoes back on before standing and shrugging on my suit jacket, offering King a slightly amused look. Mostly because he was staring at my baby girl.

"Come on, let's see if he really doesn't know where he is," I suggested. "Then I am going back to fucking bed."

King flashed a dangerous smile and got up, crossing the room to kiss Dahlia's forehead before following me out. As we left the room, I made sure to lock it from the outside, knowing that she could unlock it from the inside. I didn't have to ask King where George McCaffrey was being held. It would be unusual if he was anywhere but the basement, considering the circumstance.

"Who is down there right now?" I asked curiously.

"Lincoln and Stratton." He smiled at the second name. "I was surprised by that element, truth be told."

"What about Sterling and Yates?"

"Sterling is knocked out, but I'm not sure about Yates." King shook his head. "Probably doing some stalker shit."

I laughed at that and shook my head. "Right, because you're so much better."

"Never claimed I was." He smiled. "But then again, I don't have an entire surveillance room, so I don't look like the crazy one."

"No, you're right, you just do other crazy shite. Wait until Dahlia tries to leave and realizes the security team you've put on her," I pointed out, causing him to grunt.

"I didn't know how to explain that the security team at the airport wasn't normal, so I just told her it was," he muttered. "I knew she would end up saying it was unnecessary, and trying to convince her otherwise would be nearly impossible considering she doesn't see the value in her safety as much as I do."

"Because you're obsessive over it," I pointed out.

"You think I should pull back?" King offered me a knowing look. "I mean, we could reduce the amount of security—"

"Fuck no," I hissed. "Just making a point."

My cousin shook with silent laughter as I flipped him off and opened up the door that was hidden in the corridor on the opposite side of the building from the bedroom suites and office. The door was heavy, made of wood and iron—something out of medieval times, like this damn castle—but it opened silently. When we let it close, we were bathed in darkness for a moment until we reached a turn in the staircase that I knew by heart. Suddenly, the space was filled with a cold, fluorescent light that highlighted the center of the room where George was tied to a chair.

I felt a bit bad for the guy because not only was he knocked out with a rather nasty bruise covering his face, but I knew he would be terrified when he woke up. I hated Ian, but I pitied George. The kid had absolutely no ability to stand up for himself, and if he wasn't so sleazy, I would have felt guilty about tying him up down here. As it stood, I didn't because I had caught him way too many times trying to prove his manhood to his asshole friends by harassing random women at the events we both attended.

"Drink?" Lincoln offered me a glass.

I nodded my thanks, noticing that Stratton looked particularly tense right now, exhaling on his cigarette, two other butts at his feet. I wondered how long they had been down here. I shot back the pour of whiskey and took out my own cigarette, lighting it and looking back at George.

"Everyone is coming to the compound tomorrow," King noted quietly so only I could hear. "If we get the information we need tonight, we can send people out by tomorrow night."

I nodded and walked to the side of the room, sliding a

bucket under a water spigot, the icy droplets making me know that this would work perfectly. Once it was full, I took it over to the kid and grabbed a wooden chair, dragging it so I could sit in front of him. I wasn't even the one who normally handled stuff like this—King was usually far better at extracting answers—but I had a considerable amount of frustration coursing through me right now, so even if all I did was get to beat him up a little bit, it would make me feel far better.

I dumped the bucket of ice cold water over him and stepped back, inhaling on my cigarette and watching the kid wake up, nearly falling out of his fucking chair as he gasped like he was drowning and tried to... well, honestly, I had no idea what he was trying to do because he looked like an idiot.

"George, good to see you," I offered, taking a sip of my drink. Instantly his eyes were wildly darting around the room, but I knew he couldn't see more than a few feet, the rest of the room bathed in darkness.

"What the fuck is going on?" he growled, his body shaking in fear and probably in reaction to being cold. Mostly fear, though.

"We just wanted to have a little chat," I said as I heard King walk forward. "Figured this was the easiest way to get your attention."

"By kidnapping me from my fucking girlfriend's bed?" he snarled.

"She was a hired prostitute," King amended. "Good try though."

"See, when you lie about shite like that, Georgie, it makes me worried that I can't trust you. That I am going to have to use influence to get the correct answers that I need out of you." I sighed as his skin paled to an almost sickly shade. He knew exactly what I was talking about.

"What do you want?" His voice was shaky as he watched

me carefully, like I was going to pull a knife out and slit his throat or something. Although... The idea didn't sound horrible, considering the day I'd had.

"Just some easy answers." I smiled, causing him to shake even more.

"Where is Ian?" King's voice wasn't nearly as relaxed. I didn't blame him. I think everyone wanted Ian's blood on their hands at this point. The man better hope for his sake that he died before we found him, because there were plenty of ways to prolong torture. You wouldn't believe what your body could withstand before giving out.

"I don't know," he grunted, his eyes unblinking and seemingly honest.

"I don't believe you," I sighed, almost sounding disappointed.

His temper sparked. "Fine, I'm not going to tell you."

I looked at the knife in King's hand as he chuckled and walked around George, curious just how angry he was right now and what that meant in terms of how much time I had to question him. I was hoping George broke fast, because King and probably Lincoln would be perfectly happy to take out their anger on him. I had some frustration to work out as well, but I had to be honest, I would have rather done it in bed with my baby girl.

"Are you positive that's your answer?" King asked, his smile growing as George jumped, the chair almost flipping over because he hadn't realized he was behind him.

"Yes," he snarled. "I'm not giving my brother up to you fucking bas— Fuck!"

I relished in George's cry as King took the thin, small dagger in his hand, a signature line with a gold and emerald grip that we kept down here for this specific reason, and sank it into his hand. I watched as the knife sliced through his flesh and embedded itself into the wood of the chair beneath his palm. Blood began to seep from the wound, dripping down onto the basement floor where there were already plenty of stains.

I blinked, realizing that George was crying and whimpering as King continued to ask him the same question again.

"Fuck you, no." He bit back a cry as another blade sank into his other hand, making me wonder if I had underestimated this kid. We were two knives in and he was still holding out. Although I had a feeling not for long, considering sweat was drenching his body along with blood and the slight scent of piss. Fucking wonderful.

"George," I chided as King walked away to get more knives, his shirt splattered with blood that had spewed from the injuries, "we don't want to hurt you. Your brother is a piece of shite, and you know it. Just tell us when you last saw him. It's a simple question."

His breathing was rough as his jaw clenched, his eyes closed. "Yesterday morning. I saw him fucking yesterday."

"And what was your interaction with him?" I asked curiously, tapping my cigarette against the chair and watching the ashes fall onto the cement floor, acting bored of this conversation.

George's eyes widened as King came back holding several more knives, inspiring him to talk faster. "He appeared at our estate, grabbed some shit and left. Wouldn't tell me where he'd been."

That rang true.

I hummed and nodded. "And where do you think he went?"

A shadow passed over his gaze as his breathing went fast again. "I don't know."

"Liar." King walked forward as George let out a whimper.

"Fine!" he shouted. "Fucking fine. He's going to find Dahlia. I don't know that for sure, but when we first got back here, she was all he would fucking talk about. I had to listen to him talk about the prude bitch for hours—"

King embedded another knife into his thigh. My eyes narrowed on George as he screamed, wondering if I could fucking kill him. I knew he was useful, but him calling Dahlia a bitch in any context made me see fucking red. Luckily, King seemed to have a good solution in mind.

"How many times?" he growled.

"How many times what?" George cried out as King twisted the knife in his hand.

"How many times have you referred to her as that in your life?"

I smiled at his question.

"I have no idea!" His voice went high-pitched as King pushed the knife in his leg down further. "Fuck, fine. Three, maybe? I have no bloody idea!"

"Three it is." King nodded and walked towards the back of the room as I stood.

"Wait, where are you going?" George demanded.

I offered an arched brow. "Unless you have anything else to tell us, I'm done here. Do you?"

"No," he admitted and then tried to wriggle out of his ties as King walked forward with an assortment of tools, Lincoln grabbing my chair from me. I made it to the staircase, Stratton offering me a head nod as George called for me to not leave him with them. I didn't sympathize with him at all.

"What are you going to do to me?!" George cried out as I heard King laugh at something Lincoln said, making me know they would be down here for a bit. Hopefully the piece of shit would survive. Or pass out and save himself from feeling the pain.

As I walked upstairs, I looked down at my shirt and realized it was covered in blood. I couldn't go back to Dahlia like this. Pulling both my jacket and the shirt off, I walked towards the staircase to my left and took it down, leading to a massive underground weapons vault that I had to use my handprint to get into. Once I was inside, I lifted a gun off the rack and went towards our indoor shooting range.

I knew I should go back upstairs and get some sleep.

Go back upstairs and see Dahlia.

Instead, I found myself grabbing a shit ton of bullets and setting up the range for long distance shooting. I needed something to keep my mind focused, mostly because I had only one thought on my mind, and I knew I wouldn't sleep until I got my damn answer.

Where the fuck was Ian McCaffrey?

Chapter Eighteen

DAHLIA ALDRIDGE

When I woke up, I was disappointed to find that Dermot was no longer underneath me.

I blushed, realizing how that sounded but still feeling very much the same about it. Falling asleep on top of his muscular chest had been absolutely amazing. Especially because of how warm he was and the feel of his arms locked around me as I listened to his strong, steady heartbeat.

Sitting up, I looked at the moon that was breaking through the heavy clouds outside, the rain having lightened but still coming down. His room was beautiful, reminding me of something you would see in a medieval castle, with stone walls and floors, a large fireplace, and comfortable, dark, masculine furniture.

I wrapped a blanket around me, tucking myself against the headboard as I wondered where he had gone. I considered going to look for him, but when I yawned, I decided against it. Instead I reached over to the night table and picked up his phone, the screen lighting up as my thumb brushed the center of the bottom. I had meant to just check the time, but when it opened, I frowned.

Did Dermot not have a password? That seemed odd.

Closing the phone, I pressed it again and watched it light up. My brows rose, realizing that it recognized my thumbprint. Had he added it? I yawned and blinked, squinting slightly, wondering if I was imagining shit. After three more times, I realized I was very much *not* imagining shit.

Honestly, I had no idea what to make of the fact that he'd added me. I mean, it was flattering and made me think he trusted me a ton, so I didn't feel as bad when I opened his Instagram. I was curious to see what people were saying about us... but from a distance.

I didn't have the nerve to ask for my own phone back. I had a feeling that would send me spiraling.

As I opened the app, his profile came up, and I realized that I had never looked him up on social media before. Which was probably good, because almost instantly, insecurity hit me hard. Not because of anything he was doing, but because the pictures that he had on his feed—the latest from about two years ago—featured him with a group of people out at a bar. It was a simple photo, and he looked like he was having fun, but what got me were the two women on either side of him.

A wave of jealousy slammed into me as I smoothed a hand down my throat, realizing that I had spent so much time secure in my boys' emotions for me, even if not in a romantic way, that I had grown used to them not dating anyone... so this concept of him being with other women made me uncomfortable. Jealous, even. He wasn't even with them as far as I could tell, but it still made me feel almost dizzy with insecurity. My throat tightened as I closed his phone and tossed it to the side.

God, they had been beautiful though. That alone made

me feel inadequate. Why was he hanging out with models? I mean, that just wasn't necessary, right?

Of course, my stomach rumbled at the exact same time, a wave of anxiety crashing over me. I was both hungry and not wanting to touch any food, ever. A flush broke out on the back of my neck as I found myself standing and searching out the bathroom.

I opened a heavy, dark door I found, the lights flickering on as I found myself in a luxurious black bathroom accented in gold, the tiles seeming to glint with an embedded metallic shine. I washed my face in the sink, wondering when this was going to start to feel more... normal? Not just the boys and I, but everything I'd experienced. Right now, I wasn't completely convinced that this was reality to begin with. I mean, there were just so many reasons why this wouldn't work.

Why did I think I was good enough to keep the attention of six men? Six gorgeous men, nonetheless. A whimper slipped from my lips as I put my face in my hands and tried to massage out the tension, bile beginning to work its way up my throat. I hadn't even eaten anything in the past day or so. Nothing of note. Yet I could feel the need to purge riding hard, knowing it would give me a sense of control over something.

I hadn't weighed myself since we left Wildberry.

I hadn't purged since Tuesday.

My anxiety was nothing new, and I shouldn't have been surprised at its appearance. Just because of my moment with Yates and Stratton didn't mean I was fixed. I was still messed up. Still broken. I'd just been praying I would be distracted enough to not think about it...

But now I was. Now I could feel it heavy on my shoulders as a tremble began to take over. A small, wounded noise broke from my throat as I felt my knees go weak. This was going to be bad. I could feel it. The world around me spun, and I wondered if I was going to pass out. It wouldn't completely surprise me, if we were being honest.

My throat felt dry as I tried to remember when I'd even had water last.

"Angel." Stratton's masculine voice echoed around me as I squeezed my eyes shut further, trying to keep the puke down. I trembled when I felt his hands close around my shoulders as he pulled me into him, my hands grasping his shirt. Tears began to flood my eyes, making my eyelids hot as I squeezed them shut, refusing to bring myself into reality. A reality where I knew I wasn't good enough for any of these men.

"Dahlia!" Stratton shook me slightly, but I couldn't. I knew if I opened my eyes, I would have to face that I was a pathetic imitation of the type of woman they *could* have.

This was all a dream. That was the only explanation. There was no way men like this would want to share someone when they had all the options in the world. With all those choices, why would they want someone like me? Someone who had lived her life so incredibly isolated and in a bubble that she didn't even have the ability to respond right to situations. I was so freakin' messed up in the head—

Stratton's lips slammed into mine as the bile that had been working its way up my throat disappeared, my head spinning as the firm, hard press of his lips worked its way into something more dangerous and deep. I let out a soft moan against his mouth as I pulled him closer, his massive hands lifting me up onto the counter before he pressed against me, his hard length rubbing against my center. I spread my legs further as he pushed the skirt I was wearing up over my hips, causing me to roll my center against him in a needy way.

If this was a dream, it only made sense that this would be part of it. That the pleasure I'd been feeling at the hands of these men was part of it.

When he suddenly lifted me against him and carried me from the room, I clung to him, hoping that he wouldn't let me go. I buried my head against his neck as I felt the cool air of the hallway hit us, making me wonder when he'd come into the room in the first place. I kissed his neck gently, shaking as he murmured something softly against my ear, his words not translating to my fuzzy brain but keeping me more grounded.

When I was dropped in a bed that was large but not Dermot's, I instantly reached for Stratton again. I didn't have to wait long before the man was there, over me as he pinned my hands above my body, his lips devouring mine once again.

"I need you back, Dahlia." His voice was soft and commanding, the feel of his ringed fingers against my body bringing me back. "I need you to pull out of this."

I blinked, realizing tears were still dripping down my face as I tried to breathe in and out, the sound raspy and almost pained.

"I can't," I admitted as I squeezed my eyes shut, feeling like my lungs were being compressed. Crushed. Destroyed by the reality that I wasn't good enough.

Why did I ever think I was?

"Fucking hell, angel, snap the fuck out of it." Stratton shook my shoulders as he grasped the back of my neck in a demanding hold, so much so that I whimpered, my eyes flying open as I found him in my space and filling my vision. I wanted to cling to the reassuring strength he surrounded me with, but I couldn't grasp onto it. I had a tentative hold on everything right now, including reality.

"Stratton," I cried, letting every ounce of pain I was feeling radiate through my voice. His jaw clenched and he leaned down to sear our lips together, his pull on me nearly inhuman, feeling as though he was trying to pull my soul from my body with such a persuasive and deadly kiss.

I had never felt this side of Stratton. I had experienced

the dominance underneath only in small quantities, but this was almost an out of body experience. There was a strength and tone to his entire demeanor that demanded ownership. The man wanted to own me, and I was about to let him.

"I am not letting you do this," he whispered, pulling back slightly to run a hand up my thigh. My legs fell open more to welcome him closer. "I am not letting you go. You need to get through this. You fucking promised me that you would be here with me, Dahlia. You said you loved me at that fight. You don't get to fucking disappear on me."

Something that would have been all too easy.

When his fingers brushed my upper thigh, I let out a small whimper, the spark of desire surging over my desperate and drowning anxiety. His eyes sharpened as he slid his fingers further up, his grip on my jaw with his other hand possessive and demanding as he watched me with an unnerving focus.

"Tell me what you need." His voice was rough. "Tell me how to bring you back from this."

I wanted so badly to tell him what I needed, but I didn't know myself.

But didn't I?

"I need you," I whimpered softly. "I need you, right now, Stratton."

It wouldn't fix the problem or the anxiety that was crushing my chest, but it would ground me. His steady intensity and strength would ground me to the land of the living. Remind me of something I could count on.

Stratton wasn't going anywhere. He wanted me, I knew that. *I knew that.* I just had to keep reminding myself.

But what if he had meant what he'd said in the grocery store?

What if I was a burden to him?

"You will always have all of me," he growled, his fingers

easily pushing my skirt up all the way before he tugged off my panties, slipping them down my legs as I let my body relax into the bed, trusting him to take care of me.

Stratton knew how to fix me, I knew he did. Even if it was a temporary fix.

We had never been together, but I could feel it deep in my soul that he knew how to help me. How to calm me down. I hadn't known exactly what our first time together would be like—or heck, if that would ever happen—but this was something else... This was already extraordinary, and I almost felt as though this wasn't really us. Like there was no way a man like this could want me with this force or intensity.

His name came from my lips on a cry as he slid two fingers inside of me, causing me to seize up as my back arched and pleasure crashed around me, pulling me with a hard tug from the depths I was sinking into. Each pump of his fingers and the sound of him undoing his jeans with his other hand brought me closer and closer to the surface. The water in my lungs was heavy, though, and anguish was trying to drag me back down into the depths.

"Fuck, you are so wet," he groaned, pressing his forehead to mine. I moaned at the loss of his fingers as his hard cock pressed right against my pussy, the feel of his length causing my body to tremble. I was also nearly positive that I could feel a cold, hard piercing on the tip of his length, making me nearly climax right there and then.

Before I could beg him to slide into me, he did so with reckless abandon. I screamed out his name as he groaned, his full length seated inside of me as my body exploded in pain and pleasure. I was sore as heck and he was big, like really big, stretching me out as I tried to not let the tears slip from my eyes. Mostly because they were from a mixture of relief and sadness, joy and anguish, a combination I didn't know how to express. A combination I couldn't explain to him even if I tried.

Clearly I was shit at hiding that though, because Stratton dragged my hands above my head as he began to pound in and out of me, my back arching as my chest pressed against his, his lips tracing the tears that streaked down my cheeks.

My legs were tight around him, and I kept trying to pull him closer and deeper. The low groan that left his throat let me know he could feel how much I wanted him. How much I truly needed him.

His words were soft and dangerous against my ears as something inside of him seemed to snap completely.

"I want all of it, every single ounce of your pain," Stratton demanded as my gaze met his, those blue eyes nearly black and holding me captive. "I want all of you. I want to absolutely wreck you and piece you back together, Dahlia. You're mine, my fucking angel, and you're not allowed to go anywhere. You're not allowed to give into this, do you understand me?"

The words were sharp and so unlike Stratton that they sent an exhilarating thrill through me. They should have been messed up, but instead I found them like a symphony, like everything I'd been wanting to hear, my hips rocking against his and meeting every thrust. This man, this version of Stratton, was demanding everything.

"Tell me you do, Dahlia."

It was a freakin' order if I'd ever heard one, and I wanted to follow it. He wasn't allowing me to give into this darkness. This sickness. His order filled me with a sense of relief. I needed his demand. I needed him to tell me that I couldn't give into it, that it wasn't an option.

"I do!" I gasped as a climax slammed into me, my eyes rolling back as he let out a low moan and railed into me until I was just a puddle of lust and relief. I felt him hit his own release, triggering my own, as my entire body trembled, my thighs shaking and my entire body prickling with heat. When he finally stilled, buried inside of me, I clung to him, unable to survive in the moment without him. I was an absolute mess, and tears leaked down my face as he finally pulled back, his face filled with both concern and something that looked almost like awe.

"Angel," he whispered, cupping my jaw, "tell me you're okay."

"I'm okay," I immediately answered, his eyes tracking my expression as he exhaled, looking down for a moment before seeming to gather himself.

"Holy fuck," he muttered and pulled out, my eyes riveted to his face and the transformation I saw there. Whatever this moment had let loose, I knew it wasn't going away, and I loved that.

"Stratton?" I whispered softly.

His eyes flashed to mine as he pinned me to the bed with an intense stare. My voice was shaky. "Thank you. I know I am sort of a mess, and—"

"Not a mess," he insisted, kissing my face gently. "You're perfect, angel. Absolutely perfect. But don't ever scare me like that again, you understand?"

I nodded.

"Good." He exhaled again as if I had terrified him.

When he picked me up, I didn't even ask where we were going. It didn't matter. I knew he would take care of me.

Chapter Nineteen

STRATTON LEE

The hot water of the bath surrounded the two of us as I leaned back against the clawfoot tub, Dahlia's smaller frame laying against my chest as her hand ran over my pectoral, her eyes closed and breathing far more even than before. There was color back in her face, and her entire frame seemed void of tension, giving me a sense of relief that was completely unparalleled.

Sure, there was the fucking relief that I'd finally been inside the woman I had loved for my entire life... but it was more than that. It was the fact that I had been able to pull her back from something I worried had the ability to push her to the point of no return. It was the fact that she had trusted me to take care of her. That even now she was pliant and relaxed in my arms, allowing me to completely shelter and protect her, even if it was from her own thoughts.

I thought I'd been terrified before. Hell, I knew I had been when I'd seen fucking Julian holding a gun to Dahlia at that stupid fight. But oddly, the most terrified I'd ever been was watching the pure desperation and desolation invade her expression as she stood in the bathroom alone, looking as though her heart was breaking.

It had been enough to snap something inside of me. The part of me that wanted Dahlia's full submission had come out, wanting her to listen to us, wanting her to let me fucking fix her problem... and she'd let me. She had embraced that side of me and completely given into my touch. Given into my demanding orders and words.

I didn't deserve it. I really didn't fucking deserve it, but I wasn't about to deny it, especially as she laid curled up against me like a kitten.

We'd been in the bath for some time now, and I had washed her hair, taking time to give her a scalp massage, before moving to the rest of her body. I had never considered aftercare and what that would be like with Dahlia, but the way she practically purred when I'd kissed her skin after washing it left me feeling like for once I was doing something right. I'd fucked up friendships, failed at fixing the family business, failed at keeping her safe and at a distance... but taking care of Dahlia? I could do that.

I would do that forever, if she let me.

"Stratton?" Dahlia's voice was soft and languid.

"Yeah, angel?"

Her head tilted up as she offered me a small, shy smile. "When did you get so many tattoos?"

Was that what she'd been tracing? My lip twitched as my eyes darted down to the flower to the right of her hand.

"Are you talking about the flower, Dahlia?" I asked knowingly.

Her eyes warmed. "Maybe."

"I got it when we were sixteen."

Those soft lips parted open as a blush invaded her face. "Oh."

I hummed knowingly. "Go ahead and ask."

Her small laugh had me smiling. "So that's a what type of flower?"

"A dahlia."

She flashed a smile. "Any reason you picked that one?"

"Just my favorite flower." I shrugged playfully as she pressed a kiss to it.

Before she could say anything, the door opened and Yates stuck his head in, looking completely unperturbed with interrupting us. "Sorry, love birds, we have a slight issue. Ian was just reported as having been seen in town early today. We have no idea how accurate it is, but King wants help organizing tomorrow, if possible."

I knew he was talking to me and not Dahlia. Her eyes were half closed in sleepiness, but there was also a tension in her body at Ian's name.

I offered him a nod, and he stepped out as I tilted her jaw up.

"I really don't want to see him again," she admitted softly.

"Don't worry." I kissed her lightly. "We've got this, angel."

I frowned when I heard something from the other room, most likely Yates going through shit trying to find her some clothes, as I secured a towel around my waist and motioned for her to stand. I wrapped her in a robe tightly as she practically curled back into me.

I loved sleepy Dahlia. She was fucking adorable, and that was a word I almost never used.

"I'm going to grab you something to wear." I kissed her hard before leaving the room, frowning as I looked around for Yates, wondering where the bastard had gone.

As I rounded the bed, I cursed, finding him knocked unconscious, blood dripping from his nose. Turning around sharply, I felt a pinch in my neck, and something hit my face hard before I was down for the fucking count.

Oh, fuck no.

Rage filled my veins as I struggled to stand up but was hit again, hard, whatever they'd injected into my system causing dizziness to ram into me.

Dahlia's scream echoed through my ears.

It was the last thing I heard before seeing someone dragging her from the bathroom, the darkness casting shadows as everything closed in around me.

Someone took Dahlia.

Someone was going to die for that.

AFTERWORD

Want more from Dahlia and her men? The third book in *The Shadows of Wildberry Lane* trilogy, *Carnage of Misery,* is already available for purchase!

The Shadows of Wildberry Lane
Book 1 - Perfection of Suffering
Book 2 - Execution of Anguish
Book 3 - Carnage of Misery

Interested in exclusive access to teasers, cover reveals, and the most updated information on your favorite M. Sinclair series? Make sure to become a raven today by joining my reading group: Sinclair's Ravens.

M. SINCLAIR

International Best Seller

M. Sinclair is a Chicago native, parent to 3 cats, and can be found writing almost every moment of the day. Despite being new to publishing, M. Sinclair has been writing for nearly 10 years now. Currently in love with the Reverse Harem genre, she plans to publish an array of works that are considered romance, suspense, and horror within the year. M. Sinclair lives by the notion that there is enough room for all types of heroines in this world, and being saved is as important as saving others. If you love fantasy romance, obsessive possessive alpha males, and tough FMCs, then M. Sinclair is for you!

PUBLISHED WORK

M. Sinclair has crafted different universes with unique plotlines, character cameos, and shared universe events. As a reader, this means that you may see your favorite character or characters... appear in multiple books besides their own storyline.

Universe 1

Established in 2019

Vengeance

Book 1 - Savages

Book 2 - Lunatics

Book 3 - Monsters

Book 4 - Psychos

Complete Series

Vengeance : The Complete Series

The Red Masques

Book 1 - Raven Blood

Book 2 - Ashes & Bones

Book 3 - Shadow Glass

Book 4 - Fire & Smoke

Book 5 - Dark King

Complete Series

A Raven Masques Novel - Birth of a Raven

Tears of the Siren

Book 1 - Horror of Your Heart

Book 2 - Broken House

Book 3 - Neon Drops

Descendant

Book 1 - Descendant of Chaos

Book 2 - Descendant of Blood

Book 3 - Descendant of Sin

Book 4 - Descendant of Glory

Reborn

Book 1 - Reborn In Flames

Book 2 - Soaring In Flames

Book 3 - Realm Of Flames

Book 4 - Dying In Flames

The Wronged

Book 1 - Wicked Blaze Correctional

Book 2 - Evading Wicked Blaze

Book 3 - Defeating Wicked Blaze

Lost in Fae

Book 1 - Finding Fae

Book 2 - Exploring Fae

Book 3 - Freeing Fae

Universe 2

Established in 2020

Court of Rella

Book 1 - Fae Fiefdom

————

Paranormal/Fantasy Series

(These series are not currently affiliated with a specific universe)

The Dead and Not So Dead

Book 1 - Queen of the Dead

Book 2 - Team Time with the Dead

Book 3 - Dying for the Dead

Completed Series

Silver Falls University

Book 1 - Lost

Book 2 - Forgotten

I.S.S.

Book 1 - Soothing Nightmares

Book 2 - Defending Nightmares

————

Contemporary Universe

Established in 2021

The Shadows of Wildberry Lane

Book 1 - Perfection of Suffering

Book 2 - Execution of Anguish

Book 3 - Carnage of Misery

Standalones

Peridot (Jewels Cafe Series)

Time for Sensibility (Women of Time)

Willowdale Village Collection

A stand-alone collection about the women of Willowdale Village.

Voiceless

Fearless

Collaborations

Monarchs of Hell

(M. Sinclair & R.L. Caulder)

Book 1 - Insurrection

Rebel Hearts Heists Duet

(M. Sinclair & Melissa Adams)

Book 1 - Steal Me

Book 2 - Keep Me

Completed Duet

Forbidden Fairytales

(The Grim Sisters - M. Sinclair & CY Jones)

Book 1 - Stolen Hood

Book 2 - Knights of Sin

Book 3 - Deadly Games

Printed in Great Britain
by Amazon